KNOTS

CLUB IMPERIAL 3

BY

KATHERINE RHODES

KNOTS

Cover by JRA Stevens

CONTENTS

PROLOGUE

THE MAN KNEELING INSIDE WAS in perfect submissive position.

She was already intrigued by him, just from that alone. Circling the wonderful torso, free of tattoos and scars, her assessment and acceptance hinged on a few simple questions. "Did he come from a house?" she asked quietly.

"No," Franz said, "or none that we know of. He's been paired with a few of the others, but he called and requested you the other day."

"Any particular reason?"

"Shibari," Franz answered. "He called and asked if you had any specialties."

"So he likes being bound." She smiled. "Anything else?"

Franz nodded. "Always the mask. It was a condition of his. He wouldn't agree to the tribute unless you agreed to the mask."

The mask was fascinating. She stepped into the room and circled him. He was wearing a tailored, loose silk, full-hood mask, with the eye mask tied up and back so he could see.

For the moment.

"And what have his other mistresses said about him?"

"Very obedient. Very willing, and a very high

tolerance. No one has heard his safe word yet. Which is surprising, considering who he has been subbed with. Jaida, Amaryllis, Jemma..."

They both saw him shudder at Jemma's name and she smirked. "Perhaps Jemma was near to hearing it."

"Mistress," came a deep, sultry, resonant voice. He was seeking permission to ask a question.

"You may speak," she said.

"Mistress Jemma was not near my limit of what I enjoy, but rather at the limit of my ability to stand dispassionate, disinterested handling."

Franz pursed his lips and shook his head. "Not the first time I've heard that about her. But as for your subject here. Are you interested, Dusty?"

"To use my Shibari?" she asked. "I think so, as long as Mister...John Smith, was it? Realizes that it is not something that is done and undone in the place of an hour. He will be here all night."

"That was made clear. In fact, Mr. Smith was very happy to hear it."

Dusty nodded. "Very good. I agree to the mask, as long as the blindfold is mine to control as well."

"It is, Mistress," John said.

Dusty took the crop in her hand and slapped him hard on the ass. He didn't flinch at the hard sting. "I did not ask you, John. Speak only when you are spoken to."

"Yes, Mistress."

"We have the shibari room set up?" Dusty asked.

"We do," Franz said. "He must remember to tell the room administration when he wants that room booked for this. I know we don't have many who want it, but there are enough it could be a problem. John, am I understood?"

"Yes, sir."

"Good. Dusty?"

"We have an agreement."

"Excellent. I'll leave you to your interview." Franz backed out of the room and closed the door.

Dusty circled the sub on the floor slowly. His eyes were down, and he was unmoving. He was very well trained. "Your real name isn't John Smith."

"No, Mistress," he answered.

"I'm intrigued by this game you want to play, so I'll go along with you. I am going to explain the rules of the Shibari room. Are you listening?"

"Yes, Mistress."

"First, the room must be booked. I will not work on a shibari creation anywhere else. That room was designed to my specifications and I can be the most creative in there," Dusty informed him.

"Second, shibari is an art, Mr. Smith. It will not be rushed. The more complicated designs will take me hours. If you do not think that you can hold submissive for that long, do not bother me with a request for a complicated design.

"Third, do not expect that I will tie you up and let you right back out. You have sat for me for that long and now you are where you want to be. You will remain in the creation for no less than two hours.

"And fourth, if there is anything else you wish for me to entertain while you're in the room, you will write the request down and leave it on the side table. We are not here to discuss your proclivities and desires. We are here to indulge them."

She was standing directly in front of him. "I don't deal with bullshit, Mr. Smith. I don't have the time or desire to do so. I very much enjoy shibari. I can get lost in the intricacies of the ropes just as much as my subjects. It is my delight to bring you the joys of silk ropes. But as any other room in this building, it is necessary for you to choose a safe word. I am assuming that the ropes are not your only desire in this, as you have visited with several other mistresses. Am I correct?"

"Yes, Mistress."

"Since I do not wish to mince words or waste time talking, I will request that you give me a list of your hard limits and your soft limits. A person who cannot write down his desires is not a man I wish to assist. Is that clear?"

"Yes, Mistress."

"Then when I see you have booked the room, I will expect that we have an agreement, Mr. Smith." She walked around him one more time and slapped the crop on his ass, hard. "Now. Shall we play?"

"I would enjoy that, Mistress."

"You have read your contract," she stated. "No intercourse on the premises. No exceptions."

"It's understood, Mistress."

"Do you have a previous safe word?"

"Yes, Mistress." "Tell me."

She was shocked when he hesitated for a moment, but her knees nearly gave out when he spoke the word.

"Applejack."

She'd had a childhood dog named Applejack and named him after the cereal. She looked down at him and approved of the word despite her shock. "Very good. And since I have not had time to read your application, nor you time to write your letter, what is your pleasure this evening?"

"Ropes, Mistress," he said. "And a flogger."

Dusty nodded agreeably, though she knew he couldn't see her. She opened the top-most drawer in the chest of drawers. Her favorite flogger lay coiled on top. Next to it were several lengths of rope, and she pulled out two shorter ones and a carabiner. She neatly arranged them on the top of the dresser and glanced back at the man in the mask. He was deliciously muscular and possessed of himself. He knew what he wanted.

Dusty moved around the room. Every room in Imperial was set up the same: a chest of drawers with a lamp, a Queen Anne chair in leather, a side table. There was a spanking bench moved to a corner, as well as a multipurpose bench that could handle several different positions. The back wall had a St. Andrew's cross on one side and several other wicked looking sets of hooks and chains. There was also a small cot and nightstand opposite the chair and dresser; that was for the client. Sometimes they needed a moment or two to compose themselves. It was also an effective place for aftercare; Dusty never let the subs leave until she had made sure they were tended to.

She grabbed the shorter length of rope and walked up behind him. "Hands up," she said.

He had them up and crossed quickly. She was impressed she didn't even have to tell him to cross them. She wound the rope in a crisscross pattern around his wrists and pulled it tight with each loop. She heard little grunts from him with each pull, and she smirked. He liked the ropes tight.

"Stand," she commanded, once she had finished binding his wrists. He rose gracefully and kept his head down; his erection was visible through his boxers, and she smiled. He even knew that rule already—never fully naked unless told to be. She grabbed the ropes and led him over to the wall, pulling down a hook. She slipped the carabiner through the rope and latched it to the hook. The chain retracted and pulled his arms up over his head. She walked back over to the dresser and grabbed the other two pieces of rope.

She bent down and tied one to his right ankle tightly, then hooked it to the wall. She repeated the process on the other side. He would now only be able to move his legs further apart. She leaned against the wall next to him. "Mr. Smith, do you require more rope?"

"I will wait for the shibari room, Mistress."

"Good." She walked back over to the flogger on the dresser. She swished it a few times and swung at his lower back with a soft hit.

"Mistress." His voice was heavy. "Please, with my ass naked."

Dusty smiled. She tossed out the flogger in a trick she had taken time to learn and perfect—it yanked the boxers down and exposed his firm, pale ass. She could certainly appreciate that. And her little trick elicited a groan from him.

She set her feet and flicked the flogger at him again. He barely flinched with her first hit. She approved; he liked it harder than most. She added more strength to the next hit. He groaned this time and only flinched a little.

Oh, she was going to enjoy this client. With a smirk, she really let the flogger fly.

CHAPTER ONE

Four months later...

"OH, HOW PERFECT. COME ON OUT, *everyone! Come and see the whore Nathaniel has been dating!"*

"You are a psychotic asshole," Tessa growled at him. Cece agreed.

"Come on!" he said, motioning to the people who were hiding with her around the corner. "Come on. She's always willing to take on new clients. Get a taste of the mistress's whip. She's very good at dealing with you if you've been very bad."

Cece wanted to run out and punch him in the balls. How dare he, he of all people, insinuate that Tessa was a whore. She played by the rules, always. She was part of the lifestyle, the right way. People paid her serious cash because she was so good—

"I am not a whore, Lance. I never was and I never will be."

"You're deluding yourself," he said. "But then again, I guess I don't really care since I'm taking you with me." He looked down at Nathaniel. "Take a good look, Natey. Your slutty little delight is mine. And for good measure all of your friends and family now know that she is a Domme who likes to beat and hurt men."

Cece felt her stomach plunging to her feet. Lance was forcing who she was, what she did, on bystanders who did not understand what the lifestyle was about.

"Isn't that why you *want her?"* Nathaniel *asked. "Isn't that the whole reason you're chasing her down and taking her with you? You want her to hurt you. And you know what?" He turned his head from his position on the ground and looked right at her. "Emmy, beat the shit out of him. Whip him. Flog him. Make him feel every ounce of pain you know how to give out. Drive him to the edge of insanity and never let him come back."*

Cece sucked in a breath as Tessa did the same. He knew! *Nathaniel knew and was still in love with her. Lance looked horrified, and snarled. "She's mine! She'll never listen to you! She's going to do exactly what I want her to!"*

"She'll never listen to you." Nathaniel never looked away from Tessa. "She belongs to no one."

The gun twitched in Lance's hand. Cece saw it and Tessa caught it out of the corner of her eye. She knew that twitch. It was the one that happened just before he couldn't and wouldn't stop himself from pulling the trigger. He was staring at Nathaniel on the ground, and it was Tessa's perfect opportunity.

Cece watched as Tessa took it; she clearly knew Lance as well as Cece did. Tessa yanked the whip off her hip, dropped it, and with a quick flick of her wrist, she snapped it out at him. Bullwhip! A full size bullwhip! Thank God; Tessa knew how to use whips and a full size one? Lance didn't stand a chance. She aimed for his wrist, and it was clear she had hit the target when the blood welled on his forearm by the wrist.

He whipped his head around and she snapped the

whip again, wrapping the tip of the whip around the barrel of the gun he was holding. She pulled back hard, but before she could rip it out of his control, he pulled the trigger.

Nathaniel screamed and jerked on the ground.

Cece felt the cold run through her veins and saw Tessa lose control. She pulled the whip back and the gun popped out of Lance's hand. She snapped forward and slashed him across the chest. She took a step forward and snapped again, this time on his upper arm. Another step, another snap across his thigh. She stepped closer and closer and flicked the whip around like it was a part of her.

"You fucking asshole," Tessa screamed.

"What are you doing?" he yelled.

Tessa screamed at him. The words were lost in the wind, but what she did was clearly seen. With every sentence she snapped the whip either across him or just barely missing him. She snapped the whip up over her head and was finally close enough to plant her heal on his neck. And suddenly everyone could hear her again: "How many women have you killed? How many have you raped and killed and fucked after you killed them? You're accusing me of being a pervert. Fine! I like the lifestyle! But at least I don't kill people or fuck dead bodies!"

Cece had both hands over her mouth in shock. She had never imagined that Tessa Saint would lose control like this. She was ready to kill Lance, and while some part of Cece knew it was wrong, there was a much larger part that wished she could grab her whip and help Tessa finish him off.

Tessa leaned down and punched him in the face. "I will not ever be used against my will again! I will never go with you! I would rather die than ever have you lay a finger on me again!"

Franz put a hand on her shoulder, pulling her back away from him. "Enough, Emmy! Enough. You've won." He pointed to Lance.

Lance was terrified of her, the white of his eyes showing like a spooked horse and his lips drawn down in a grimace. There were welts and open cuts all over him; there was blood all over his clothes and he was bright red because her foot was cutting off his air.

Tessa gasped and stepped back, realizing the situation. Nathaniel's brother had Sylvia in his arms, one of the bodyguards had the other woman down, another was waiting for Lance and the third was taking care of Eric. She looked over at Nathaniel.

He wasn't moving.

"Oh, God," she gasped, falling down next to him. "Nathaniel?"

Killian shoved everyone out of the way and tore up the gravel drive, diving for the unmoving Nathaniel. His brother was trying to get over to him, but Bradley Albright had appeared and was holding him back. Killian shoved Tessa out of the way, screaming, "Call an ambulance NOW!"

Tessa fell over to the side as Cece pulled out her phone and leapt out of the crowd, dialing the emergency number. Killian ripped Nathaniel's pants wide open and there was actually blood pulsing from his leg. It would surge and recede.

"Motherfucker, it's the femoral," he said. "He's

bleeding out!"

Chantal came tearing forward and grabbed the whip that was now on the ground. "Tie it off," she said. Cece managed to get all the information to the 911 operator in a single shot. There were apparently already cops on the way; someone from inside had called about the gun shots.

"We need needle and thread, fast!" Killian took the whip and tied it above the leg as best as he could. Albright spoke into a walkie and less than thirty seconds later someone else came tearing to the area with a first aid kit and put it next to Killian. "Knife, water, sponges or cloths. Something. We're going to lose him."

Cece shot straight up in bed. She was going to relive those moments forever, watching Nathaniel nearly die, watching Tessa's world nearly crumble around her. Her nightmare: the whole world finding out that she was a Domme. She would be exorcised from Pittsburgh.

She thumped back on the pillow. She wondered if the nightmare would ever go away.

* * *

"To Emmy and Nathaniel!"

The raucous little group let out quite the whoop and lifted the shots to the sky. Cece watched as Tessa and Nathaniel stared into each other eyes, the unyielding love coming off the two of them in waves. Even she couldn't help but smile, and her eyes landed on Killian as he stood next to them.

"If I may," he called to the audience. "I would like to say something." The group, made up of some of the wealthiest families around Pittsburgh, settled a moment later and turned to Killian. "Emmy and Nathaniel have been through a hell of a lot in the past year and for them to come out this end together and more united than before is nothing short of a miracle." He picked up his beer. "To the miracle couple, may every year find you happier, may each month bind you closer, may each week find you joy, may each day the sun shine upon you, and may each night be filled with unbridled sex in at least three different positions!"

The whole group whooped and laughed again, and Cece saw Tessa/*Emmy* pale and hide a giggle behind her hand. Nathaniel instantly turned bright red and lifted his glass. Cece hid her smirk and saw Morgan, Olivia, Amaryllis/*Chantal* and Tyrone do the same behind their glasses of wine.

But her own smirk fell a moment later.

Diane Hamburg had wrapped her arms around Killian and was smiling a wicked grin. A victor's grin. Cece tossed back the rest of the glass and put it down on the table. She excused herself and walked to the private restroom for the party.

She stared into the mirror. *They don't understand. Killian would never take a second look at me. Diane is perfect and gorgeous.* She swept a tired hand over her face and sighed.

"Are you okay, Dusty?" came Emmy's voice quietly from the door.

Cece turned and looked at the gorgeous woman standing there. "Oh. Hi. Yeah, I guess so."

"I saw you laughing but the instant you saw Diane…"

Damn. "Well, she and I don't really get along. You

haven't been in the circles long enough to catch that. It's a…long standing disagreement."

"In other words," Emmy let the door shut, "you think she's a bitch."

Cece laughed. "Yes, exactly."

"Well, for the record, she *is* a bitch," Emmy said.

Cece laughed again and leaned against the wall, oddly comfortable around Emmy. Perhaps because she knew she didn't have to pretend there wasn't a huge swath of her life that didn't exist. "Diane and I came to different conclusions about life in fifth grade, and we've never been able to resolve our differences. I'm the black sheep of my family, anyway, so it's been pretty easy to steer clear of her."

"A Domme is the black sheep? No. Say it isn't so!" Emmy put a dramatic hand to her forehead and the women shared a laugh. Emmy sobered a moment later. "Dusty, I really—"

Cece held up her hand. "Hang on. We're not in the club and we're probably going to be seeing each other socially more than once in a while. My name is Frances, but everyone calls me Cece. Cece Robbe."

Emmy stuck out her hand. "Emmy Westerly."

Cece laughed and took it. "Not like I haven't known you for three years or anything." She paused. "Are you leaving the club?"

"Sort of?" Emmy questioned herself. "I'm going to be working the office with Franz now. I'm going to help with the books and scheduling. There, you can still call me Tessa. But anywhere else, I'm Emmy."

"It's…nice to talk to you outside the club," Cece said.

"I'm getting used to the vanilla world." Emmy glanced at the door. "Nathaniel helps a lot."

"Oh, does he?" Cece teased.

Emmy laughed. "He has a certain interest in some of the proclivities, yes. But it's more than that."

"You two are disgustingly in love." Cece made a gagging noise to tease her. "I can see it. And, Emmy, you deserve it."

"Thank you," she said. "I have to get back out there, but I just wanted to make sure you were okay. You tossed that wine back!"

She laughed. "I did. Diane does that to me." Cece opened the door for Emmy. "I'll be out in a minute. Just have to actually use the bathroom."

Emmy nodded and smiled. "We'll have to do lunch one day!" Cece agreed and watched her walk back over to the tables, and she let the door close. She stepped into the stall and put her head in her hands. If she wasn't trained...she would have broken down, right there.

It wasn't Diane. It was Diane *all over Killian* like cheap suit. Diane was every man's dream: blonde, busty, a huge family fortune, and every advantage she didn't have. Killian's whole family adored her and it was a foregone conclusion that they were going to get married just as soon as Killian's career started to take off. He was only a year or two from that.

And here she was, mostly in love with him for years. He was a dream, and she was...well. She was the black sheep. She was not only the black sheep of her family for not flaunting her trust fund, but she had a master's degree, worked a 9 to 5, she had never had a boyfriend she could bring home to her parents, she didn't buy into the bullshit of the 'charities' that her mother and sister ran, and she lived her own life.

Killian would never look at her. No one ever noticed Cece.

The door popped open, and Cece heard a few voices walk in and she recognized Diane immediately. And now she was stuck there.

"Who are these women?" Diane's friend Tory asked. "I mean, this woman comes out of nowhere and brings all these odd-balls with her."

"They are so...odd," came another voice Cece identified as Saundra.

"Well, Cece seems to get along with them," Diane said.

"Exactly," Tory said.

They all had a giggle at that one.

"Can you believe that Nathaniel is going to marry her? She doesn't have money, she doesn't have a family except for that odd little sister of hers," Diane said.

"Well, at least he's not marrying that horrible harpy he was dating for so long," Bridget said.

"That harpy is in jail for the foreseeable future," Tory said. "Good riddance."

"Do we have to throw a bachelorette party for her?" Saundra asked, the exasperation clear in her voice. "If I'm going to go to a strip club, I'd rather go with you all. I don't think they would really enjoy it the way you're supposed to enjoy mostly naked men. Like they don't appreciate a hot body."

Cece had a very hard time not snorting out loud at that statement. The girls Emmy kept company with were more appreciative of a hot body than those Botox-enhanced, big-titted bimbos could possibly imagine.

"Well, if no one says anything, I'm not taking the initiative," Saundra said. "Her kooky friends can do that."

"They'll probably go to the Grange." Diane giggled.

Tory laughed. "They can get a kick out of the gunshot scars."

"And all those sexy c-section scars," Saundra offered.

"Bad fake boobs everywhere!" Diane said.

Bridget and Tory laughed hard at that one, and Cece wanted to punch all of them. The guys and girls at the Grange were human, and just because they weren't in at a place like Imperial didn't make them any less deserving of respect.

"They should all pool their tips and get those fixed," Saundra suggested. "At lease mine look good."

"Yes, they do!" Tory said. Cece wanted to laugh *again*. Saundra had one of the worst boob jobs she'd ever seen.

"So then we agree," Diane stated. "We're not going to any lengths to set something up and if someone does, we'll hope we're not invited. Let them enjoy those skanks." The three of them giggled and kept chatting quietly as they walked out.

Down, Cece, she chided herself, trying not to vault out of the stall and beat the shit out of them. These bitches just didn't know any better. They had never been in the real world and didn't know those guys and girls at the Grange. She did.

Cece sighed, finishing up her business and walked out of the stall just as Morgan, Lisa, Nadine, and

Chantal walked in led by Allison. Allison squealed when she saw her. "Yeay! You're here!" She shoved the door closed and leaned against it.

Cece looked at the young girl and smiled. "What are you up to?"

"I heard someone mention a bachelorette party and I realized that as my sister's maid of honor, I was supposed to do that!" Allison's tone was conspiratorial.

The four of them exchanged glances, and Olivia spoke first. "Allison, how much do you know about your sister...?"

Allison rolled her eyes. "Plenty," she said. "She likes it kinky. She used to work the rooms at Club Imperial, and you all still do."

Chantal put a hand over her mouth and Morgan laughed. "We don't all, but I do work there," she said. "Who explained this to you?"

"Victor. He seemed to be more comfortable explaining it to me. He was nice and clinical about it. Anyway, what's that got to do with anything? My sister is getting married and she needs a bachelorette party."

"Ally." Chantal employed her explanation voice. "Most bachelorette parties *go* to places like Imperial for the party. Your sister was the Prima Domme. It's not exactly a party if she worked there."

"Duh, I know that," Ally answered. "I was thinking that we could all go out for a nice plain night out. Just to like a bar or something. Something that comes off as normal for everyone else and exotic for you guys."

"You're fifteen, girl," Olivia stated. "You can't get into a bar."

"Well..." Morgan drawled. "I do know a bar that has

an eighteen-and-over night once a month."

"You missed by three years," Chantal said.

"I also know someone who makes impeccable fake IDs," Morgan continued.

"You're going to be a judge and you're going to get someone a fake ID?" Nadine was clearly appalled.

"I am not contributing to the delinquency of a minor." Lisa folded her arms in mock protest.

"I am," Chantal said.

"Me too," Cece agreed. "I like the idea that instead of going to a strip club, all of us kinky chicks take her out for a nice vanilla night on the town." She looked at Morgan. "What club were you thinking of?"

Morgan blushed. "Downbound."

Chantal laughed. "Judging by how you just pinked up, you've got someone there you're interested in." Morgan smiled and shrugged. "Fine, keep your secrets. Get Ally the ID and we'll get this all together. Should we invite anyone else?"

"No," Cece said. "Just the people in the bridal party, and us. The others won't get it."

"Deal." Chantal put her arm around Ally. "Good call, kiddo." Ally smiled and stood a little straighter. "Now, we all need to get back out there. This is one of the best restaurants in Pittsburgh and I'm not missing this dinner!"

The five of them walked out of the bathroom and back to the tables. Cece saw Diane watching her and delighted in the mortification that slid over her face as she realized Cece had been in the restroom and overheard all the nasty remarks the three of them were making. Cece smiled and wiggled her fingers at her. The mortification turned to disgust, and she wrapped her arm around Killian again.

Cece turned away and sat down. The food smelled fantastic and she decided that it was worth it to see the horror on Diane's face and the love on Emmy's.

* * *

Killian watched as Cece sat down near Morgan and Chantal. They were conspiring with Emmy's little sister about something, but Emmy didn't notice. Diane noticed Cece's sarcastic little wave and let go of his shoulders. She trotted off to go talk to someone or another; he really didn't care.

A body plunked into the chair next to him. He looked over and found Nathaniel sitting there. He stared at him, then followed his line of sight, then came back to stare at him. "Something you like over there, man?"

Killian grunted. Of course there was.

"Why don't you get off your ass and go over there and talk to her?" Nathaniel asked.

Killian slowly turned his head. "With Diane *right* over there?"

"You are not engaged to her." Nathaniel reprimanded him.

"May as well be. "

"Because everyone had me and Jillian married, too." Nathaniel shook his head. "Clearly, I'm not marrying her. Don't let them tell you what to do, Kay."

"I don't know, Nathaniel. Cece Robbe is about the hottest thing on the planet, and she's super intelligent. What on earth would she want with a screw-up like me?"

Nathaniel turned in the chair to face him. "Doctor McInnis, did you just call yourself a screw-up?"

"You know I am." Killian took a sip of his beer.

"How the hell are you a screw-up?"

"Do you know what they call the person who graduated at the bottom of their med school class? Doctor." Killian put his beer down and looked at him. "I almost didn't make it."

"You were in hell those last few months of med school. And you saved my fucking life, asshole. So you are not a screw-up. And Cece Robbe loves a brilliant mind. If you're really afraid that you're a screw-up, why don't you apprentice under someone? Get a little more confidence."

Killian blinked a few times, and then tapped a finger on the table. "You know, that's not a bad idea."

"You are better than you think you are. Go find a doctor who's going to show you that. And then you can go after that sexy vixen."

"Which sexy vixen?" Emmy stuck her head between them. "Is this a private confab?"

"Killian here has been lusting after Cece Robbe for years. At least fifteen, if not more." Emmy choked, and coughed to clear her throat. Clearly that meant something to Nathaniel because he slowly turned his head and looked at her with his eyes wide. "Emmy?"

She held up her hand, a smirk plastered on her face. "I'll tell you later. Look, Killian, if you like her, go after her."

"I wish it were that easy."

"It is," Emmy said.

"Not with Diane around."

"Why are you so worried about her?" Emmy quirked an eyebrow.

"Her father is the head of surgery."

Emmy poked him in the shoulder. "You need to decide if your career or your heart is more important, Kay."

He looked at her. "How can I think about supporting her if my career is in the flusher?"

"So you'd give up something you could love for something that has cheating bitch written all over it?" Emmy asked. "It's not all about the career, Kay."

"Oh, you can say that now, Miss Future Millionaire."

Emmy stood up straight, and her face went blank and angry. "Don't you dare throw that in my face."

Killian cringed and saw Nathaniel do the same. He'd crossed a line: that was not something you said to Emmy Westerly-soon-to-be-Walsh. Because either she was going to beat his ass or Nathaniel would. "Sorry. That was rude. Forgive me. I know you're not like that."

She cuffed him on the back of the head. "You're lucky you're cute."

"Hey now," Nathaniel said.

"You have a whole other set of qualities, especially that ass." She slapped him through the chair and Nathaniel jumped, laughing. She looked back at Killian. "Seriously. You can't base your life on what the head surgeon thinks of you personally. Impress the hell out of him and it won't make a difference if you're fucking his daughter or not."

Killian mentally heaved. Diane in his bed? Well, that's what he was signing up for if that was the case. If he was really choosing career over love. He looked over at Diane and she was talking to one of her friends. He could almost hear the cackling among the hens.

"You should talk to her." Emmy took Nathaniel's hand and pulled him out of the chair. "Cece Robbe is one of the last genuine women left in these circles. If you expect to keep your family happy, which I think is bullshit, you'd better make your choice between her and Diane."

And Nathaniel was gone, pulled down the hall by his fiancée. Probably to have some party sex in the lounge. He looked around to find Cece and didn't see her anywhere. Her friends were still there, but she was gone. He wanted to see if he could find her to at least talk to her.

He walked by Diane and the hens and ignored them, even though Diane was clearly motioning him over. Killian wandered down the hall to see if perhaps Cece had gone to get some fresh air, and heard her arguing with someone.

Curiosity killed the cat. He edged closer to where the voices were.

"...disown you," the male voice said.

"Chas, stop." It was definitely Cece and she was clearly upset. "They aren't going to disown me because I choose to work."

"You have no idea how upset your mother is with this silliness." Her brother's voice was condescending and rude. "Cece, they just want the best for you. Sell that cottage. Come back home. Paul Wainwright has been asking after you for years. Let Mom and Dad set it up."

"Paul Wainwright?" Cece gasped and laughed, and Killian had trouble keeping his same reaction under control. "You are kidding. The boy who pulled my hair and shoved me in the mud, and called me Pee-pee?"

"He's grown up, Cece."

"So have I," she answered. "I'm *really* not interested in Paul, Chas. And frankly, I don't think he's even remotely interested in me."

"What about Monday night dinner? Mom wants to make it a weekly thing."

"I...can't." Cece's voice hitched and stuttered. "I have a standing engagement on Monday nights."

"Engagement?" Chas asked. "Do you have a boyfriend?"

"No...it's...uh. It's complicated. I can't do Mondays or Thursdays."

"You do have a boyfriend!" Chas exclaimed, but there was only accusation in his tone.

"No, Charles, *please*," Cece begged. "I don't have a boyfriend. Please don't spread that rumor. When I have a boyfriend, I'll let you know. I swear. If Mom will agree to dinner on Tuesdays, I'll be there. I just cannot get out of my Monday-Thursday arrangement."

"Cece, Mom just wants to see you happy," he repeated.

"For *fuck's sake*, I am happy!" she snapped. "I am happy working at the library and hanging out with my friends. I don't need Mom and Dad imposing their brand of happy on me. I like my house. I like my whole damn life. So stop it, please. Don't tell Mom I have a boyfriend because I don't. Tell her that I'm happy for dinner on Tuesday. And, Chas, try to understand that what I'm doing makes me happy."

He heard her turn and walk down the hall, slamming her feet on the floor and disappearing.

Chas Robbe turned the corner and ran smack into Killian.

Killian didn't let himself miss a beat. "Hey, Chas. Whoa, slow down! What are you doing here?"

"Nathaniel invited me," he snapped.

"Not what I meant, man. How have you been?"

"Fine." Charles was immediately suspicious.

"I couldn't help but overhear." Killian changed tack. "Paul is asking after Cece?"

"Yes." Killian cringed. Now the slimy bastard was smiling. "His mother and father approached ours and talked about it." Chas perked up and took a hard look at Killian. "Do you think that you could talk to her? She's being irrational and—"

"Chas, Chas." Killian put his hands up. "I don't know her that well. She's not going to sit down and talk to me about marriage. I doubt she'd even have a drink with me."

Chas sighed. "I just don't know what to do with her."

"Why don't you just let her live her life?"

Chas shook his head. "Because she's upsetting my parents. She doesn't go to church anymore. Did you know that? She doesn't come to dinner on Friday nights, she doesn't have a boyfriend. She has some odd, long standing engagement." Chas leaned in conspiratorially. "They're afraid she's a lesbian."

Killian shook his head. "If she is, she is. There's nothing they can do about that."

"Well, you and I know that, but the whole thing oogs out my parents," Chas said. He looked around. "I have to get going. I have a date."

Now Killian was curious. "A date? With who?"

"Saundra Oetler," he said.

Killian stopped. "You mean Saundra Milhouse."

"She's about three months from her final divorce papers," Chas answered. "She's going back to Oetler because she doesn't want to be associated with the freak deviant that her ex-husband is." Chas shook his head. "Did you know he likes to be beaten?"

"I don't need to know this shit, Chas," Killian said. "Keep your pillow talk on the pillow."

Chas laughed. "Exactly. I'll talk to you later, Kay."

Killian watched as Chas walked away. He felt sorry for Cece, having to deal with her family. And for himself—having to deal with Diane and the hens the rest of the night.

* * *

He watched.

He watched everything and everyone around him. He absorbed the feelings and the vibes of the people. There was a levity and joy in the air, surrounding the two people who were at the center of the fete. The ones who were there for the true joy of it were stronger than those who were obligated to show affection. It was easy to see who Emmy and Nathaniel gravitated to.

But most of all he watched two men at this gathering. There were more that he kept his eye on, but these two, here and now, were the victims of his relentless watching.

Killian McInnis—doctor, former playboy. Son of

Angus McInnis, doctor, philanthropist, and one of the biggest players in the upper echelons of Pittsburgh. He had also been a known figure in the bigger circles— Washington DC, New York, Boston. The family was not unknown and that was what ultimately was their undoing.

The elder Doctor McInnis was found dead. One of the ugliest scenes he'd ever witnessed. A shotgun shoved up his rectum and fired. The buckshot had torn through him and killed his mistress, the lovely Miss Patrice Fulbright as well. A double murder with no witnesses and no solid leads. The two random hairs found were inconclusive. Whomever had done it had never been in the system before.

But he never said they hadn't killed before. He had cause to believe there was a serial killer; the DC police had reported a murder like this. So had Chicago. All with their mistresses. All within weeks of a divorce.

He watched Killian carefully. The young doctor, only months from his graduation in the top ten percent of his class, was utterly destroyed—first by the death of his father and his mistress and then by the callous action of his mother.

The parts of the wealthy echelons he hated: most men and women married, had children and let the nannies raise them while they went out and had affairs and dalliances with mistresses. Once the youngest was old enough, usually sixteen or eighteen, the couple divorced and went on their way. Lineage preserved, everyone miserable.

Killian and his sister, the very adorable Bridget, made out better than most. Angus had never hid his dislike for their mother. Angus had actually been very much in love with Vanessa; Vanessa, however, returned only as much affection as was required to marry and have children. She turned on him then, trying to turn the children on him as well.

Most people thought that his murderer was indeed the callous and jealous Vanessa, but the two displaced hairs were blonde, and short. Certainly not belonging to the raven-hair beauty.

So the horrible murder of Dr. Angus McInnis sat unsolved. His son was climbing out of its horrible impact slowly, clawing his way up and out of the depression and destruction. The young doctor McInnis was a brilliant surgeon, but had fallen to eighty-sixth out of eighty-nine students in his class. He had lost his confidence and it was only by the literal pummeling by his sister that he had realized what he was doing to his seven years of school and eighteen months of internship. He was starting to get his confidence back.

And then, Charles Robbe, middle manager at the now enormous Walsh-Tyndale Corporation, was a quiet, church-going man. Far too old to be unmarried in his social circles, he was an overbearing presence in his younger sisters' lives.

The boldly gorgeous Frances, Cece, had a wild, fiery streak in her that led her away from him, led her to rebel. Chas didn't like that at all. Hannah, the sweet pretty younger sister, was a meek and obedient girl who suffered her brother's meddling with restraint. She truly believed that Chas spoke for her parents' interests for her.

What had piqued his interest in one Charles Robbe was his newly formed relationship with the Oetler heiress. Saundra Oetler-Milhouse was an angry soon-to-be divorcee that maligned her husband to anyone who would listen. That had started only a few weeks after the birth of their precious daughter. Apparently the very chivalrous Everett Milhouse did not want to go against the doctor's orders when it came to his wife's health, when she did.

She told people that he liked to be beaten and tied up. He liked whips and paddles, anal play and being dominated. The rumors were vicious and ugly.

And utterly true.

Now that she was done with Everett, Chas seemed more than happy to have her in his arms. Though it was a real question how long that was going to last if Charles didn't agree to take her to bed. That was the harpy's problem—she was insatiable in bed, but didn't want to help her partner keep her happy. Chas didn't know what he was getting into with the vindictive woman.

He would keep an eye on both of these men. He was fascinated by them.

For now, there was nothing more to be seen here. There was work to be done, but that would come later.

He headed down the hall and out to the parking lot where his car was waiting. He drove across the town to the small house he desperately wanted to move into. He pulled out the key and let himself into the living room.

"I was wondering when you would get here," came a voice from the kitchen.

The object of his desires walked out of the kitchen wearing an apron and nothing else. And the apron barely hid what shouldn't be shown.

"Sorry," he said, walking over to the delicious cook standing there. "I was just checking some things before I came over. Party was uneventful. Clearly the after party is where I want to be."

"I'd hope so. Do you like?"

He watched as the mostly naked man turned himself around once. He smiled.

"Hunk, I'll take you any way I can get you."

"Is this ever going to be over?" the Hunk asked.

"Yes, yes," he said, stroking his cheek gently. "Soon. I swear. Everything is going to come to a head soon and I can stop pretending." He leaned in close and could smell the Hunk's aftershave mingling with his desire. "You know I hate pretending. I hate that I can't come out yet; I want nothing more than to spend my life with you, in your arms, building a family together."

"I know," the Hunk answered. "I am here for you, lover. I will wait until this is over."

"I feel so fake," the Watcher said.

"Because you are acting," the Hunk said. "Soon enough. And I know what you are doing is good, and that all of this has a bigger purpose. If you're right..." He let the statement trail off. "You have a big heart, one of the many things I love about you."

The Watcher smirked and untied the apron. He wrapped his hand around the Hunk's engorged cock and pumped slowly. "And this is one of the things I love about you."

"The dinner is going to burn if you don't let go."

"Fuck dinner," he said. "Better still, fuck you. In the bedroom."

The Hunk flipped off the burner.

CHAPTER TWO

"GOOD MORNING, MISS ROBBE," CAME a familiar voice.

Cece looked up and found Everett standing there, and a quick smile passed across her face. "Well, good morning Mister Milhouse. Is it research day already?"

"Yes, ma'am," he said. "I have a list of books I'm going to need today. Do you have time to assist me? I'd like to get down to business as soon as possible."

"I think I can do that." Cece stood. "Vanessa?"

"Yeah, no problem," the undergrad said, half paying attention.

"Vanessa!" she snapped.

Vanessa finally looked up. "Yes, Miss Robbe, I'm fine. I know this is an Every Tuesday thing. You don't have to remind me."

"Thank you." She shook her head. She walked out from behind the counter and headed out to where Everett Milhouse was standing. She looked him up and down, and very much approved of his outfit for the day. His pinstripes were perfectly pressed, and the white shirt was crisp and clean. He had his purple tie on today, so his research list was legit.

He held out the sheet of paper with the names on it. "Thank you, Miss Robbe. As always, I appreciate this."

"Quite welcome, Mister Milhouse," she said, looking at the list. "I'll be at your cubicle in about twenty minutes with the first five of these."

He nodded and peeled off to the right to head to his study cubicle. As a doctoral candidate, he had one of the very rare, very hard to get private cubicles that he could leave things at and lock up. Everett was a brilliant researcher and that he was getting his PhD in medical research was quite impressive.

The books he was looking for would absolutely be found in the stacks. He always checked to make sure that if he legitimately needed them, they were on the shelves and not easily found on the internet or microfiche. She did love her job. Library science fascinated her, and she adored research. She loved working with good researchers. Everett was a good researcher, among other things.

She found the first book and laughed lightly. It was the height of irony that he was researching sexual habits and the pleasure/pain principle in the BDSM community. He was looking for the biological basis of the main drive in the Lifestyle. Cece had read a lot of thesis and his research. He had some of the best theories and information that she had ever seen, in any doctoral research.

Cece headed for his cube. She patted her pocket to make sure she had the key to her office on her, and stepped out into the research area. There were always a half dozen students around, and this afternoon was no exception. The masters students had to share, and that was always a disaster. They were always arguing and accusing and just generally pissing off the doctoral students. Which was what she walked into. Five masters students yelling at each other.

She had tried a dozen different ways to get them to stop arguing and pay attention to her. None of them were nearly as effective as straight violence. Cece grabbed the yardstick she kept in the corner for this reason and whacked it on the desk, cracking it through the air. The five students jumped and turned to see what was going on. Cece was standing and tapping the yard stick on her shoulder.

"This is a library," she said, strictly. "If you feel the need to argue, you will take it outside this room, and outside this building."

Four of the students she knew; it was philosophy's big leaders. The fifth was new to her, but he was standing in front of the Religious studies area. The group of them were rightfully chastised and they nodded. They were still arguing after that, but it was much more quietly. She still wasn't pleased, but they would be quiet for a while now.

She walked over to the doctoral area and put down the books she had gathered for Everett on his desk. He looked up and smiled at her. She put the key down next to the books and smiled at him. "Purple today, Everett."

"Yes, Mistress. I came across several old studies that we have on hand and they should really provide some more direction for where I want to go."

She nodded; he was thrilled about the old journals. "Then shall we say one hour?"

"Yes, Mistress," he answered.

Cece went back to her station at the front desk to wait out the hour helping clueless undergrads trying to figure out the Library of Congress system. She much preferred the Dewey decimal herself, but most colleges now ran on the LoC system. It stank because she couldn't go directly to the fiction section. Now she had to use the computer to find out where it was in the stacks, which meant that if a patron didn't have a name and author in mind, they couldn't just peruse. Unless they were willing to put up with things like "Biodiversity Among Slime Mold in Azerbaijan and the Southern Caucuses."

She wasn't.

She had a gaggle of clueless freshman walk in and they were terribly confused as to how to look things up on their computers for the class. She gathered them all around her at one of the reference computers and gave them a short lesson on the use of the system and the stacks, and sent them off on their way. She preferred when they came in groups; she had the quick lesson down pat. She logged off the computer and was about to head back to her desk.

"Excuse me, miss, but I'd like some help from a sexy librarian."

She turned around to give Everett what for and instead, froze.

Doctor Killian McInnis was standing there in a three-piece suit with a briefcase and the scent of sandalwood wafting off him. His brown eyes sparkled with intelligence and humor and his face was freshly shaved, utterly smooth, alabaster perfection dotted with the remnants of childhood freckles. His dark red hair was cut short, and despite the styling, looked as soft and finger-soothing as a kitten's fur. The suit had to have been tailored because it fit him in the most delicious way, everything falling perfectly, showing his broad shoulders and narrow waist. She wanted to throw him to the ground, unwrap him and have filthy dirty sex right there, damn the rules and onlookers.

"Hi," she finally answered. She shook herself off. "What are you doing here?"

"I'm actually here to do some research," he said. "My mentor is trying to figure out a new procedure for a heart defect and he's sent me to do the old fashioned research on the defect's medical history. I could use a little help since it's been a while."

"Oh," she said. "Sure." She gestured to the chair next to her and motioned for him to pull it over.

"Did you have a nice time at the party on Saturday night?"

"What?" she asked, caught off guard. "Oh, Emmy and Nathaniel? Yes, it was a nice party."

"You knew Emmy before she met Nathaniel?"

Cece was having trouble getting her head back in the game. Killian smelled so good. "I...uh. Yes. We worked together."

"She is such a nice person."

"She is," Cece agreed. "She deserves Nathaniel."

"Nathaniel deserves her," Killian answered.

"So, uh...what are you researching?" Cece shook her head. "No, wait...what are you doing here? Did you graduate from Dusquene?"

"I did. But UPitt has better and more comprehensive research journals." He leaned forward and looked at her. "And sexier librarians."

What? Cece was glad she didn't let that last 'what' out, and instead, she smiled at him and turned back to the computer. "So, what are we looking for?"

Killian swung the briefcase up on the desk and popped the locks. He pulled out a binder and put it on the desk, laying his hand on it. "Cece, I came here because you do have better facilities and access to older journals. But I also came here because this is unpublished and I trust you with this information. I know you're not going copy and distribute this. This is critical research."

Cece was actually surprised. "Killian, I'm not in the habit of coping proprietary research. If you need to leave anything here, it gets locked in a filing cabinet, which only I have a key to, in my office. I wouldn't ever be tempted to photocopy for money either. I," she said, and paused for a dramatic effect, "am a librarian!"

Killian threw his head back and laughed loudly, instantly realizing he was disturbing the whole building. Cece wanted to take him across her knee and spank him good. She also wanted to trail her tongue up that gorgeous white throat. He brought himself under control and put a hand over his mouth. "I am so sorry. That was rule number one broken."

"Yes, it was. I'll have to think of a suitable punishment." She arched her eyebrow. Killian coughed and readjusted himself on the chair. *A girl can dream.* "So, let's get started on the research. I have somewhere to be in about half an hour, but I'll be back to check on you."

"Thank you." He flipped the file folder open.

It turned out that what Killian was looking for was in the very old section of the library. She was going to have to do some serious searching for the journals. Over the years, it had turned into a mess down there and she was going to need at least a day to find some of them. Meanwhile, she pointed Killian in the right direction for some of the other references in the regular stacks.

"You'll be okay? I have something I have to do."

"I'll be fine," he said, focused on the screen.

She stood. "I'll be back in a few hours."

He nodded and she walked away. She felt heady from being so close to him. His sandalwood scent was burned into her mind, and all she wanted to do was fist her hands into his hair. She was going to go straight to her office, but she had to stop at the bathroom to cool herself down.

Killian McInnis knew her. Knew her name. Where she worked.

It was almost as though the angels in heaven were singing, and she wanted to skip down the hallway like a kid with a new toy.

Her logical brain kicked in with the first touch of the cold, damp paper towel. It didn't matter if Killian knew who she was. Even if they got along perfectly, he was vanilla. He might consider letting her tie him up once in a while, but the hard stuff she liked? The whips and floggers and shibari? He would never agree to that. Her subs loved their bruises and she loved giving them; she didn't think that someone as Alpha as he was could deal with her Domme side.

And there was Diane. The perfect wife for the perfect man. She sighed and looked in the mirror. *Just enjoy his company. You might be lucky enough to get a friend out of him.* That would be nice.

Meanwhile. There was Everett. She saw the wicked smile light up her eyes.

She unlocked the door to her office. She glanced at the clock and saw she was still right on time. She loved Mondays for just this reason; the scene started at two in the afternoon, and kept going until she was done or he offered the safe word. She also knew this part of the scene was dangerous. Personal interaction—she snorted at the delicate phrase and tried again. Flat out fucking like she and Everett did in the office were grounds for at least suspension and more likely termination and charges. They were careful, but it was still a danger. The danger played into their scene so well.

There was a knock on the door at exactly two. Cece smiled briefly and called, "Come in!"

Everett let himself in. He locked it behind himself at her nod. "Good afternoon, Mistress." He crossed his hands behind his back and bowed his head.

"Good afternoon, Everett." Cece unlocked the desk drawer. "Purple tie today."

"Yes, Mistress."

Perfect submissive. And she knew the body that hid under that suit. Her blood ran a little hotter.

She motioned him to the couch tucked in the corner. He walked over but remained standing. Cece selected several items from the drawer and stood in front of him. "Then you've cleaned?"

"Always, Mistress. I know the rules."

Oh, he did know the rules. "Good." Cece stepped closer to him—close enough to feel his hard-as-steel erection through his pants. "Always so eager. Did you jerk off this morning, after your cleaning, knowing what you were preparing for?"

"Yes, Mistress," he hissed.

Cece caressed his hard length through the fabric. "Drop your pants."

His hands were quick, and Cece saw that he was commando. She approved, ever so much so; it made everything so much easier and she rather enjoyed the view. Placing a few drops of the lube she had retrieved from the drawer on her finger, and pulling herself even closer, she snaked her hand around to his backside. She grabbed each firm globe in her hands and pulled him apart.

She felt his erection twitch in excited anticipation, and she easily slid her finger into the ring of his anus. He didn't react; again she approved. He loved anal play and it was something they were working on, getting him to control his reactions. She slid her finger in and out slowly, and it was only as she added the second finger that he reacted, and it was more controlled than ever before. His breath was long and low—and he didn't move.

"Very good." Cece withdrew her fingers with the whispered praise. She cleaned off and picked up...*a toy* off the couch, holding it for his inspection. This time, Everett gasped. She had picked the largest of the anal plugs; he was ready for it even if he didn't think so. "If you're uncomfortable with this idea, speak the safe word now. Because once it's in place, it's not coming back out." She cocked her head at him, daring him to say no. "Objections?"

He shuttered, and his cock trembled temptingly with that motion. "No, Mistress."

She leaned in close. "Good. I look forward to removing it later."

He swallowed and nodded. "Me too, Mistress."

"Bend over. Spread your legs, and hold on to the couch."

He complied as a good sub would, and Cece spread the lube on the toy. She pressed the wide head against him, and without any warning pushed in. Her fingers had started to prepare him for this, but this was bigger than even her fingers. He gasped and trembled and she paused. "Relax, let yourself get used to that."

"Mistress, please, just go all the way." She could see his legs shaking, and let the topping from the bottom go.

"All right." Cece eased the massager all the way into its hilt. She pressed it and then let go slowly.

His breath was jagged, sawing desperately in and out. "Mistress, please, may I come?"

Well. She smiled. "No. Not yet."

His legs trembled even more. Cece didn't want to prolong his torture at this stage; he had at least six hours of delightful withholding ahead of him. She picked up the rope she chose and began the convoluted patterns that would hold him for the rest of the day. She cinched it around his waist and twisted the end under. There would be no actual knots, just patterns holding the rope in place. That was the beauty of shibari. Nothing was truly tied.

She crossed the ropes over his lower abdomen and passed them under his legs, on either side of the heavy erection and clenching sac. They wound around his legs, and she made sure they crossed right over the hilt of the plug, pressing it in. Everett groaned quietly, trying to keep a rein on himself. The ropes continued up and around his waist again and then down over the outside of his trim, muscular hips. She brought them back around, under the firm white ass, between his legs again, and then over his sac below his erection. She intertwined the ropes up to the waist, one last time, and tucked in the windings of her most basic shibari creation.

The ropes were tight and would leave their patterns on his skin. They were also tight enough and placed in such a way that no one would notice them under his clothes. Cece couldn't resist the firm ass he presented; she slapped him hard once on each cheek causing him to groan, and making it hard to not let her own lustful moan out. It was time. She was wet and ready for him from all the rope play.

"Stand." He did and once again groaned, losing some of his control. His cock was hard and purple and straining from under the shirt and tie that he still wore. "Now…" Cece smiled at him. "Sit."

She knew exactly what 'sit' was going to do to him. He gasped when the pressure hit the twisted rope over the hilt of the plug, and she watched his face as the shock of lust raced through him. "Hands up and crossed." Everett complied immediately and she took a short length of rope and bound his hands, tossing the rope over a hook on the wall, immobilizing him.

Cece rolled up his shirt and tie to move them out of her way, palming his painfully hard dick in her hand, adoring the feel of his straining desire, knowing that her ropes, their play did that to him. "Do you want to come, Everett?"

He groaned. "Oh, God, yes, Mistress."

"You have permission to come when I say so, and

you will come inside me."

Cece decided to give him a little striptease, turning so he could watch her slip the skirt up her hips, revealing one of Everett's favorite things: black silk thigh-highs, a garter and nothing else. He let out a breath and watched riveted. She smoothed the skirt to her waist and straddled him, her smooth pussy wet with desire right at his eye level. She caressed his engorged cock and held him firmly, then lowered herself onto him, sinking him home.

Cece let out a slow breath, enjoying the feel of him stretching her as she welcomed him. Everett knew everything she had done was as much a turn on to her as it was to him. She loved her ropes and winding them on. She enjoyed every gasp and groan he let out, no matter how controlled.

She seated herself on him, wet and ready. Holding him fast inside her, she made herself wait before she started moving on him—just a little bit more teasing and torture. Everett was so hard he was nearly painful, and she liked it. She rocked a little harder and a little faster, and she felt the silk rope sliding over her clit.

They were silent by necessity, but she was panting hard very quickly. She had wound herself up tying his ropes. Everett had tossed his head back as Cece ground down on him, his cock finding home each time. She braced her hands on the wall and lost herself in the motion on him and the feel of his dick in her. She spiraled up quickly to her peak. This was why she enjoyed Everett. His cock was amazing and his willingness to be bound and submissive to her was what she needed. It pushed her to the top, made her crave the fall. She slammed her hips against him, dragging his cock in and out of her pussy. And then Cece was about to drop off the precipice into a shattering orgasm.

She leaned down to his ear. "Come, Everett," she said.

A quiet low moan escaped him as he thrust his hips up into her once, twice and as she came down hard on his third thrust, he exploded inside her as she hit her climax. She threw her head back and rode his dick, squeezing out every last drop of come into her.

Their motions and moans diminished slowly, and finally they rested, joined by his cock in her pussy. She took a few slow deep breaths and finally moved off him, enjoying the sated sensation and the satisfied wobble in her legs. She cleaned herself up, then took her time cleaning him up. Aftercare was part of the fun, listening to him try not to react to her ministrations. And finally, she grabbed the ties of the rope that held his hands immobile and unbound him.

She knelt next to him on the couch and spoke softly. "No touching, no jerking off. You'll leave everything where it is until I remove it."

"Thank you, Mistress." He was quiet and still calming from the scene.

"Dress." Cece gave him a clear command as she adjusted her skirt to its proper position. She watched Everett redress himself, enjoy the little show. She ran her hand over his clothed ass and could feel the ropes. "Tonight, at eight." She slipped a keycard into his back pocket, tracing her fingers over the edge of the ropes.

"Thank you, Mistress."

"I look forward to tonight, Everett." She backed

away and leaned against the desk, folding her arms.

"I always do, Mistress." He smiled.

"You may go."

Unlocking the door, he let himself out. Cece waited until he was gone to let herself relax a little, letting the wonderful feeling of sex bleed through her muscles. Every orgasm with Everett was amazing and it took her a few minutes to really come down from that. She dropped into the chair and let her head fall back. So. *Damn*. Good.

After giving herself a few moments to recollect, she looked down at her legs and realized the stockings were completely askew. Lifting her right leg, she pulled her skirt up. She unhooked the right garter and rolled the stocking down to straighten it by pulling it back up, and clipped it back up. She hiked the other leg up and just as she rolled the stocking down to adjust it, there was a knock at the door and it pushed open before she could object.

Killian stepped in.

She froze and couldn't react. He froze, his eyes locked on hers. After a moment, his eyes slid down her body and landed on her naked sex. He slid his eyes back up and broke the stare. He stepped back out and closed the door.

Cece stared at the door, stunned and voiceless. She closed her eyes, let her leg fall to the ground, and grimaced. *Shit*.

CHAPTER THREE

KILLIAN FOUND CECE'S OFFICE IN THE BACK of the building. He was having trouble finding some of the journals he needed, but the library system said they were available. He knocked on her door and turned the knob, pushing in when he found it unlocked.

He had the question on his lips but instead of finding her seated properly at her desk, he found her leaned back in the chair, one leg hiked up. He caught her eyes and when his brain caught up, he realized that her skirt was hiked up while she adjusted the thigh highs she was wearing. He couldn't stop his eyes from wandering down.

She was gloriously naked and shaved clean. Her pussy glistened in the light of the room, wet with her own desire. He memorized in those few seconds the contours of her sex, and finally slid his eyes back up to hers. Neither of them knew what to do, so Killian finally just backed up and closed the door.

Holy fuck, she was sitting like that next to me.

He had an instant erection pressing against the inside of the zipper.

She was gorgeous. He had always known she was beautiful, but seeing her bared, naked and clearly excited was something he didn't ever expect to be treated to. She was just adjusting those gorgeous thigh-highs and clipping them back to the garter.

Killian grabbed a magazine, draping it in front of him quickly and casually. He tried not to run from the library. He sped up to the guest researcher lounge, pacing back and forth after tossing the magazine on a table there.

Christ, Cece was so hot. He tried to block the image from his head. He tried to forget what he had just seen. But instead of letting it go, his brain started to come up with images of him bending her over that desk and sliding his dick home in her.

He cut that one off only to have it replaced with an image of her slipping him inside her and riding him. He tried to cut that one off as well, but nothing was stopping him. His hard-on was painful. There was only one thing he'd be able to do to get rid of it.

Killian pushed open the luxurious bathroom stall and locked it. He unzipped himself and pulled his cock out from behind the zipper. He hadn't been hard and unable to get rid of his erection in years. He leaned against the door and fisted himself, pumping hard.

He imagined it was Cece with her lovely long fingers wrapped around his steel hard cock, pumping slowly. He could see her watching him slide up and down in her hands, maybe thinking about licking at the head and cleaning off his pre-cum. He remembered that clean, light perfume she had been wearing mixed with the faintest scent of her sweet, sexual cream.

She was sitting next to me, exposed. I could have reached up and made her come right then and there, and licked her off my fingers when I was done.

He imagined running his finger ever so lightly over those pale pink lips her legs hid so well, and feeling her shiver from his touch. He could imagine slipping a finger inside her and using his thumb to tease and torture her clit. Her breathy voice would whisper his name so only he could hear her. Moving his finger in her wasn't enough; she'd beg for another. And he would slip another finger inside. She would be hot and wet and it would be so good to feel her wrapped around his fingers.

Her hand would wrap a little tighter around his cock and she'd move just a little faster in her excitement. Cece'd breathe heavy in his ear and drop her head on his shoulder. She'd try to push herself down on his hand harder and faster.

And he would stop her, demanding she let him play. He could see taking her free hand and pinning it behind her, holding her in place. He could hear little protests that weren't really protests but sighs of delight as he held her still while he brought her closer and closer to her climax. Killian wanted to see her pert breast thrust forward with her gorgeous nipples peaked and straining the fabric. He could hear her begging him to finish her off. He would hush her; he was in charge. Cece would keep up her strokes on his erection, pumping a little harder to entice him.

He could see her eyes close in pleasure as he moved his hand faster and harder over her clit, and in her wet tunnel. He found the G-spot inside and he pressed until she was panting and ready to come, then backed off. Her hand would tighten around him, but she would take the dewy drops from his head and use them to lubricate her hand, sliding over him with less resistance.

He would tease her up to near climax at least twice more, and finally as he felt his own sac tighten he would plunge a third finger into her sex and find her G-spot one last time. Cece would arch her back and squeeze her legs around him, biting her lip hard to not scream in delight at the orgasm that was coursing through her. And through her orgasm, she would still be pumping his cock harder and faster, and hearing her struggle not to scream her climax to the world as his hand worked her sex, would finally bring him to his release.

Killian cupped his own tight sac and a moment later, his cum exploded out of his dick as he pumped his hand hard and fast over himself. He thumped his head back against the door as he fired his release into the space ahead of him, four, five, six times. He drooped against the door, releasing his sac and feeling the erection finally start to retreat in his other hand.

"Fuck," he whispered aloud. He hadn't even touched her and that was one of the hardest climaxes he'd had in a long time.

Killian looked down and found that he had made a mess on the floor in front of him. He took a deep breath and cleaned himself up, tucking his now relieved cock away in his pants again. He cleaned up the mess his come made as well.

He was going to have to avoid Cece for the rest of the day, which was not what he needed or wanted to do. He needed to do this research. Killian knew he'd wonder every time he was near her if she was panty-less.

How was he going to deal with this now?

The phone in his pocket dinged with a text message, and still trying to recover with a few deep breaths, he pulled it out. *Diane.* He opened the message and it was a picture of her breasts. Her extremely disappointing, disinteresting, badly enhanced breasts.

Well, that did the trick.

He texted her back.

Dr.K: Haven't I told you not to do that?

Diane-pookie: Just a little something to cheer you up.

He looked at the face of the phone. *Diane-pookie?* What the hell?

Dr.K: You went into my phone?

Diane-pookie: Tee hee. Just changed the display names.

Dr.K: I AM A DOCTOR, Diane! You can't go into my phone!

Dr.K: If I had a personal convo with a patient on there, I could be in deep shit.

Dr.K: HIPAA exists for a reason.

Diane-pookie: I didn't read anything.

Dr.K: You damn well better not have.

Dr.K: If I lose my license, you will seriously regret it.

Diane-pookie: Lighten up, Kay. You're not going to lose your license.

Dr.K: Don't you EVER touch my phone again.

He shoved the phone in his pocket. Well, that was a very effective way to kill his libido—risk his licensure. He couldn't believe she had swiped his phone and paged through it and changed the display names. What else had she done in the phone?

He pushed out of the stall and into the lounge just as the door opened to the room to admit someone. For just a moment he was terrified it might be Cece, but when he looked, he let out a breath of relief. It was Everett Milhouse. He nodded at him and Everett nodded back, but Killian hurried out, way too pissed that Diane had tampered with this phone. He paged through it, trying to see what else she had done and had a horrifying thought:

What if she had put a tracker or a keylogger on it?

Jesus shit, what if she had?

He leaned against the wall. *Oh, God.* He'd been good with deleting the messages, but who knew how many times Diane had grabbed the phone and looked at it or played with it. If the tracker had been on there for more than a month, she would know exactly where...

Shit, shit. He tried to remain as calm as possible, but moved back to the desk he had been using as fast as he could. He shut down the computer and packed everything up, and ran back to Cece's office. He knocked and put a hand on the knob. He was going to shove in, but that was what had started the whole mess. He knocked again and this time he heard her call.

"Come in."

He opened the door and Cece was seated at her desk. She saw him and instantly went bright red. "Killian—"

"I need to go." His words were quick, and he cut her off—rude, but there was no time to explain. "Can you lock this stuff up for me?"

"Uh, sure." She opened the cabinet. "Killian, I wanted to—"

"It's fine. Don't worry about it." He dropped the binders and files into the drawer. "I have to get going. This is really critical. Will you be here on Friday afternoon?"

"Yes..." Her voice was quiet and curious.

"Thank you." With a nod, he was out the door before she could ask another question. He was in the car less than five minutes later and shut the phone off. Killian couldn't take the chance that Diane had a tracker on it. He drove across the city, over the Monongahela, past Mt. Washington, and another ten miles out beyond that.

The tree-lined drive he turned down disappeared into thicker woods, then came to a large circular drive. Killian pulled as close to the main house as he could, and shut the car off. He marched up the porch stairs and had to push back all the memories of the first time he had approached this door. He knocked: two sharp, pause, one sharp, pause, and three short quick raps.

It was only a moment before the door swung open and Killian was surprised. Darien himself had answered the door.

"Killian." Darien was all business all the time.

"Darien." He nodded sharply. "We may have a problem. May I come in?"

Darien stepped out of the door. Killian walked in and Darien motioned him to the den.

"You're not here until next week. So this must be serious."

Killian held up the phone. "I think I've been compromised." He took a deep breath. "I think the house might be compromised."

Darien's eyes flared—and at one time, that would have scared the shit out of Killian. Now, he faced Darien as an equal. "What do you mean." There was no question. He demanded an explanation.

"I'll go in order of how this happened. Starting with Diane texting me a picture of her breasts."

Darien leaned against the desk. "And you've told her not to do that."

"Repeatedly, of course," Killian confirmed. "And then I realized that her name in my phone had changed. She had been in the phone to change her label to Diane-pookie."

"Ah," he said. "HIPAA."

Killian paced a little in front of the couch. "I don't know how long it's been there. As I desperately try to not communicate with her. She must've swiped the phone at some point in the past few days. But, I had no idea she was handling my phone. It could have been as long as six months. She may be swiping it whenever we're in the same room. I never realized she was doing this. If she installed a tracker or a keylogger..."

"We come to the heart of the matter." Darien was cool and collected. "You're afraid she's gotten your messages or tracked you here."

"Yes." Killian held out the phone. "That's why this is off."

Darien walked over to the bar and tapped his finger on the counter for a moment. Killian watched him carefully. He could read the other Dom like the back of his hand now. Darien picked up a decanter and two glasses, pulling a set of whiskey stones out of the freezer. He placed three each in a pair of tumblers and poured the twenty-seven-year-old Macallan over the stones until there was just barely an inch in the glasses and handed one to him.

"Leeann," Darien called.

A petite woman scurried in, head bowed, hands clasped behind her back. "Yes, Sir?"

"Fetch Pamela, vite vite."

She scurried off. Darien took a sip of his drink and looked at Killian. "You need to rid yourself of that woman, Killian. She is a demon."

"She is who my mother wants me to marry," Killian answered.

"And since when the fuck have you ever listened to

that rotting whore?" Darien demanded.

Killian wilted, his strength seeping out of him. "Never."

"Listen to me, Doctor McInnis." Darien swirled the golden liquid in his glass. "Your father is dead. Your sister nearly beat you into a coma to make you realize you were throwing away your life. You came back here to regain a sense of balance and control. You have that now. Again." He sipped the whiskey carefully. "And you're going to let a money grubbing twatwaffle like Diane take all that away from you?"

Killian shook his head. "Her father is the head of surgery. What choice do I have?"

Darien put his glass down and stepped up to him, putting a hand on either cheek, framing his face. "That is pathetic and lame. You are far, far more man than stooping down to the level of those money driven, good for nothing shits. Especially that thing who wants to call you son."

Darien pulled him in and kissed him hard. Killian gave into it immediately, relishing the different feel of a man's lips, a man's tongue against his. He wrapped his hand around Darien's neck and pulled him in close, tasting him and feasting on his lips.

It had been nearly ten years since a man had Dom'ed him. While he was far more interested in women, he didn't object to this. He had long ago realized he was heteroflexible, and this kiss, the deep penetrating kiss that Darien had imposed on him, was liberating and a hard reminder that he was much more than just someone who could or should be subjugated by the will of others.

Darien released his face, but snaked a hand around

him, and pulled him closer. Killian could feel the man's arousal pressing against him, but after another moment of the deliciousness of his tongue, Darien pulled back. "You were always one of my favorites, Killian," he whispered against his lips. "You needed to be reminded who you are now."

"Master?" came the question from the door.

They both looked over, Darien still holding Killian close. A buxom brunette stood there, a corset cinching her waist and a thick leather collar at her neck. "Pamela, come in." She walked into the room and dropped in the middle, hands to knees. Darien looked back at Killian and smirked. "Anytime you want to continue this, just ask."

Killian felt his cock twitch as Darien released his waist. The offer was tempting, but it was not what he was here for. And quite suddenly, the image of Cece's hot, wet sex slid into his mind. That was even more tempting.

Darien had walked over to the submissive. "Stand, Pamela." She readily complied and Darien motioned her over to the bar. "Doctor McInnis has a problem with his phone. Someone may have installed a keylogger or a tracking problem. Do you think you can help him?"

She smiled at Darien and Killian knew this was currently Darien's favorite little plaything. Darien was hardcore bisexual, but he delighted in having a favorite plaything. "May I speak freely, Master?"

"Yes, pet, you may." Darien granted permission.

She held out her hand for the phone. "Please, sir?"

Killian handed it to her, and she turned it on. She waited for it to boot up, and Darien explained what was going on. "Pamela is a communications expert. She works in software design for the OS platforms for Android phones. She'll be able to tell you if there's any odd software on the phone very quickly."

"Oh, there is," she said, watching the boot. "Sir, I have to go into your boot sector."

Killian tersely nodded his ascent. "I need to know what she put on and when."

Pamela smirked. "Easy enough, sir." She quickly started typing and swiping across the keyboard and it was only a couple of minutes before she had an answer. "There was a keylogger installed but never activated. It actually looks like it needed a passcode and the person who installed it locked the passcode." She smiled and looked up at him through her lashes. "Whoever installed it didn't have a clue what they were doing, sir."

"Nice," Killian said. "That would be typically idiotic for her. What else?"

"There is a tracker on it, sir, but it's locked to the GPS feature," she answered. "Very amateurish move. It was installed five months ago, and it's only used the GPS four times since then. It also had the data rejected each time."

"Rejected from where?" Darien asked.

"An email address, Master. Diane dot hamberg at AOL dot com."

"That's her name," Killian said. "How is it spelled?"

Pamela spelled it out, and as soon as she hit the second "e" in Hamberg, Killian started laughing. "That's awesome. She spelled her own name wrong." He shook his head. "Can you get both of them off there, Pamela?"

"Of course, sir. If you'd allow me, I could make it so that no one but sir could install anything on his phone. And, I would suggest you put a passcode on the screen. Something this clearly desperate woman would never guess."

"Birthday is out." Darien raised an eyebrow.

"Very nice," Killian smarted.

"Go ahead, pet," Darien said.

"Thank you, Master. This will take me a few minutes, sir." Killian nodded his ascent and the sweet little thing wandered out of the room.

Darien looked at him. "For the love of God, Killian, will you please get rid of Diane? Get her out of your life. Attach yourself obviously to someone else, even if you have no intention of marrying them." He gestured grandly around the parlor they were standing in. "There are a dozen submissives in here who would gladly play the game with you."

"Darien, I'm really not looking to get that deep back into the lifestyle." He could see the other Dom was about to lecture him. "But I agree with you, one hundred percent that I need to lose Diane. I don't know *how*, though, without pissing her off so badly that she goes crying to her father about this and I lose my place in the surgery mentorship program."

"Find another hospital," Darien said.

"I tried that. No one wants number eighty-six."

"This from the man who saved Nathaniel Walsh's life while he lay dying in his driveway."

Killian shook his head. "I wish it were that easy, Darien. I am a good surgeon, and I know that. But it is *very* hard to prove you're more than your graduating number for years. And saving Nathaniel happened before my father—" Killian choked on the words.

Darien folded his arms. "Don't start that 'poor me'

bullshit, Doctor."

Killian narrowed his eyes. "I'm not starting anything, for your information. I'm doing a thousand times better with the fact that—" he hitched and the forced the words out, "that my father was shot in the back and the buckshot killed his girlfriend, too."

Darien nodded. "Good. I'm glad to hear you say it."

"Six months of therapy," he said. "Doctor heal thyself." He took a hard gulp of the scotch and avoided looking at Darien.

Pamela walked back in with the phone nearly ten minutes later and held it out for him. "Here you are, sir. All fixed. No one can install anything on there at all as soon as you choose your password, which can be any combination of letter and numbers."

"Case sensitive?"

"Of course, sir." She smiled.

Killian tapped in the password while Darien pulled Pamela over to him and kissed her deeply. "Go upstairs, pet. I think a reward is in order."

"Thank you, Master." She was gone in an instant.

Killian paged through the phone. Not only had she passcoded the whole thing, but she organized it. "Whatever you're going to reward her with, give her one for me."

Darien nodded. "Now that you don't need a new cell phone, you just have to figure out how the hell to get Diane out of your life."

CHAPTER FOUR

THE KNOTS WERE PERFECT.

She'd had so many chances to practice kinbaku with John Smith that her good knots were now perfect. And her perfect knots were delightfully tight.

She brought the flogger down on Everett's ass again with precision and strength. He groaned loudly, and she knew he was going to have stripes of bruising to remind him of tonight. Just the way he wanted it. Just the way she liked to give it.

Cece drew back and whipped the flogger forward again. He yelped but the sound was muffled through the ball gag. She massaged him and brought the flogger down again. She raised an eyebrow he couldn't see; he was getting loud and she didn't like that. She leaned into his ear. "I put the gag in for a reason, Everett. Keep quiet...or I'll withhold."

He whined a little, but quieted down. She knew he was aching from the near constant stimulation he'd been experiencing the whole day. He didn't want her to withhold his climax any longer. Really, neither did she. She enjoyed this just as much as he did.

She raised the flogger and brought it down over his exposed ass and created another set of red welts. He groaned quietly from delight in the pain, and tried not to move. She moved and caressed him again. She did that four more times, reaching twenty and she knew he was at his limit. She dropped the flogger on the floor and took her hand, smacking his ass very hard on both cheeks. He gasped behind the gag and she was ready to bring this scene to an end.

She rolled him over onto his back from his submissive position on his knees. His cock stood straight and angry red, and the slick pre-cum slid down the shaft. She leaned over and unhooked the ball gag he was breathing around and panting. She took it out of his mouth and leaned down.

"You have been very good, Everett," she said. "You may come when you're ready, but you will not be finished until I have come. Understood?"

"Of course, Mistress."

She slid her hand down his sweat-slicked chest and climbed onto the bed with him. His eyes were lit with expectation. He didn't know what she was going to do, how they were going to finish the scene. She always played the element of surprise with him.

Cece threw a leg over his chest, facing his hard dick. She wrapped a hand around him and pumped slowly; he was painfully hot. She slid her legs back up so that her sex was over his mouth, and he knew exactly what she was expecting when she did that.

A moment later, she felt his tongue on her clit, teasing lightly. This was something Everett enjoyed doing and was an expert at. He flicked softly at first, and once in a while would dip back to tease her entrance, rimming her and then moving back to her clit for a lick or two.

He moved back again and found her bridge and

scraped his teeth on her. She gasped and ground down on him. That was a new trick and she liked it a lot. He started moving around her sex faster: a lick of her clit, rim her entrance, a flat brush of his tongue over her lips, and a nip at her bridge.

Cece kept one hand on his shaft and moved up and down. The other hand she moved to her breast, pulling herself out of the bra and roughly tugged on her own nipples. They were already erect, but she pulled them until they were hard. The rough pinches and tugs helped her speed toward her climax; she was just as hot and ready for that as he was. She was spiraling up fast and hard on his expert tongue.

Cece leaned down and took his hard length deep in her mouth, sucking lightly at first. She was able to lean her arms on his pelvis and use both hands on her nipples, and even with his whole cock in her mouth, she could concentrate on the feelings his expert tongue was creating on her sex.

He moved back again, but instead of stopping at her taint, he went all the way back and lightly rimmed her anus. Cece wasn't expecting it; the sensations caught her by surprise and threw her nearly all the way to her orgasm. He moved back to her clit and started his feasting again there.

She started moving Everett in and out of her mouth more quickly, sucking harder, and adding her teeth in. She swirled her tongue around his hot, swollen head and she could hear and feel him groaning. The faster she went, the faster he went, and she was caught up in the frenzy of his lips and tongue dancing across her sex.

His tongue found her tight bud again, licking, and

she was panting hard. Without any further preamble, he dropped back down to her clit and bit her lightly. She came hard, reminding herself to keep moving over his hard shaft with her mouth. As he heard her orgasm, she felt his cock throb and twitch, and he was near. She let go of her breast, reached down between his legs and pulled out the plug.

He screamed his orgasm and released his flood of cum into her mouth. He'd been holding onto it all day; it filled Cece's mouth and she swallowed each mouthful as he pumped it out. He released mouthful after mouthful, and finally started to calm after that. She sucked him lightly until he started to lose the erection. She leaned down and let herself recover for a moment, feeling Everett's hot panting on her own sex.

She reached down and started carefully unwinding the rope from around his body, tracing the silk with her hands, letting her body unwind with it. She crawled down his body, sliding the ropes over her hands, and slipping them free of the intricate weavings and patterns she used to bind him. This was the part that was just as erotic to her as the binding and sex was to him. This was where she truly took her pleasure.

There was something about the twisted silk, this very special rope she bought for Everett and John Smith alone, that set her senses afire. The rough yet gentle slide of the material, which she wound around her own arm as she disentangled him. The smell of the silk that she kept immaculately clean. The evidence of the binding revealed as she untied him.

She crawled over him, losing herself in the unbinding. Somewhere in the back of her mind she could hear Everett letting out little whimpers of pleasure as she released his bonds and ran her hands over his entire body. It took her nearly half an hour to unwind the ropes; this was her Domme space. She felt herself floating on the endorphins from the high of their scene and when she finally started to come out of her meditative state, she saw that Everett was erect again, and she was wanting. She left only the original bindings on him and ran her hands over them.

He lay still, and without a word from her, he grabbed the headboard behind him. She slid herself over him once again and lowered her sex onto his waiting cock. She was ready for him, and he filled her all the way to her base. She moved over him, sliding him in and out, dragging him over her clit. She grabbed the ball gag and slipped it back in his mouth, clipping it in place.

The friction she created wound them both up again, and Cece grabbed the crop that was nearby. She slapped his sides with it, and then dragged it over his nipples. She leaned down to create a new sensation between them. "Play with my breasts," she directed, quietly. "Don't be gentle."

He brought his hands down and away from the headboard. He grabbed her slightly distended nipples and pulled on them. Cece heard herself gasp, and she thrust herself down on him and he held onto them, pinching and teasing. She saw him biting down hard on the gag, and while he was pulling on her breast, his eyes were shut and his back arched. Again the ropes were just the right feel against her, and she was winding up quickly.

She grabbed the ropes around his waist and pulled.

She knew the knot in the back pressed against his sensitive anus and felt him buck up against it. Everett would have cried out if not for the gag, and she felt him bottom out inside, his erection swelling even more.

She changed her direction, and he pulled her nipples. Cece hissed and slammed down on him harder, pulling the rope again. He bucked as she wanted him to and she felt her precipice just there. "Come, Everett! Come!" she gasped and pulled again. He crushed her breasts and the pain of his rough grab sent her into a mind-bending orgasm.

"*Fuck*," she gasped, riding the orgasm hard. Everett pushed hard into her and she felt him explode, pressing up and arching his back to hold his cock inside her pulsing sex. Cece coaxed his cum out, bringing them both back down slowly.

She leaned forward, sated and exhausted. She unsnapped the ball gag again, and this time removed it for good. She slipped off of Everett, feeling slightly empty from the loss of him, and finished the last of the unbinding, dropping the rope off the side of the bed.

She smiled at him. "Good boy. Roll over, Everett. Let me take care of the welts."

"Thank you, Mistress," he said, rolling over on his stomach.

Cece carefully applied the cream to his backside, back and legs as he lay there. This was also part of her winding down; the aftercare soothed his hot, bruised skin and soothed her mind, which still sometimes revolted against the results of their scenes. She didn't know why her mind got bent about the very thing he enjoyed, but this was a balm.

"Do you need anything else?" she asked after applying the cream to the last of the welts.

"No, Mistress. Just for you to get a good night's sleep." Everett pulled the sheets back on the bed, and motioned her between the sheets.

Cece leaned over and gave him a quick peck on the cheek as she crawled in. He knew she needed the weight of blankets and sheets to sleep; she knew he wouldn't sleep under them because they would injure the welts. "Good boy, Everett."

"Thank you, Cece. Good night."

She didn't even remember putting her head down on the pillow when she cracked her eyes open again the next morning. Her alarm was going off on the nightstand, but she didn't remember putting her phone there.

Cece rolled over and looked at the other side of the empty bed. She yawned and stretched, and knew that she had to be at her desk about ten in the morning; she had plenty of time. She trotted into the hotel room bathroom, and opted to just go ahead and take a shower. She didn't really feel like swinging back to her place, since it would be out of the way.

Half an hour later she walked out into the suite's main room in her robe and hair only partially dry to find Everett fully dressed at the stove. She smiled and sat down at the table.

"Good morning, Ev."

"Good morning, Cece." He grabbed a mug off the counter next to him. He put it on the table in front of her. "Extra light, extra sweet, a shot of hazelnut."

"Perfection." Cece wrapped her hands around it. He

kissed the top of her head and walked back to the stove. Cece sniffed the air. "What's breakfast?"

"Eggs, hashbrowns and linguica," he said.

"Fancy." She laughed. "Something wrong with Bob Evans?"

"Yes, actually," he said. "Reminds me of *her.*"

"Oh." Cece grimaced.

"She loves cheap breakfast sausage. About the only cheap thing she actually likes."

Cece didn't press the issue. "How's Imogene?"

"She's doing well." His tone was only briefly light. "For as often as I see her."

Cece put the mug down hard. "You're kidding."

"She keeps her away from me."

Cece shook her head. "Ev, that's court mandated. You have every right under the law to see your daughter on your appointed days. Don't let her do that to you and Genie."

"I know when we get the final custody settlement it's going to be fair. Everyone has said so. She's showing her bitch to the world, so I know that's right. But in the meanwhile, the temp order says I get every other weekend and at her discretion."

"She has no discretion."

Everett snorted. "Isn't that the truth!" He laughed and scrambled the eggs a little more. "I wonder what I ever saw in her."

Cece turned the mug in her hand once, twice. "You saw exactly what she wanted you to see. You know that. All of these women are taught to hide who they really are until they catch a man. It's part and parcel of the upper echelons."

"Doesn't seem to apply to you."

She shrugged and took a sip of coffee. "I don't play their crappy games. I don't have the desire to get caught up in what is displaced court intrigue. I'll stick to my books and my whips, thank you."

He laughed, but there was a sigh in the laughter as well. "Damn, Cece, there are days when I wish there was more between us."

Cece smiled and shook her head. "We tried that, remember? We would be a terrible couple. The spark just isn't there. We're just incredibly sexually compatible and you know as well as I do, we can't base a relationship like that on sex." She took a sip of coffee and smirked. "But a relationship like this one, yes."

Everett laughed. "Yes, definitely this one." He scooped the eggs onto a plate. "I cleaned up just about everything. Do you need me to do anything else?"

"You know you don't have to clean up. That's my part. I'm supposed to take care of you in the morning."

"Eh." He shrugged. "I wanted linguica. You wanted to sleep. It all works."

"Do you need any more Arnica?"

"I'm fine. I was surprised I made it all day with the plug."

She raised an eyebrow. "Did you like it?"

"Of course I did." Everett sat down with the two plates.

"I knew you were ready for that, even if you didn't think so."

"We're still on for Thursday night?"

"Of course," she said. "I'll book the room when I check out. Just the evening, right?"

He nodded. "I have a lot of research to do

and...well. I didn't get a lot done yesterday. I was, ah, distracted."

"Happily so, I'd guess."

"You know me better than I know myself, sometimes, Mistress." He smiled.

"You never answered my question. Do you need me to put on more cream?"

"I'm fine."

"You're sure?"

"You are such an enigma, Frances." He laughed. "I'm fine. You really do forget that I want this. I ask for it. If it hurts a little bit the next day, well...I just get to remember what went on." He cut a piece of the sausage off and chewed thoughtfully. "I sought this for a long time, and you're so good at it. I think that even if I found someone else, I would want this to continue. With her permission of course. And yours."

"We can cross that bridge when we come to it," Cece said. "I would be sad if we had to part ways, but I will not interfere if you find someone who can take my place." She looked up at him. "You really are a good friend, Ev. It's more than just these scenes and the sex, which don't get me wrong, is fantastic. I feel like you're the only person I grew up with who gets me."

"But now you have all these Imperial friends showing up." He smiled.

Cece laughed. "True, but my statement still stands."

"I feel the same way, Cece." He cleared his throat. "Now don't go getting all mushy on me, Mistress. I like the hard side of the paddle."

* * *

Cece shut her computer down and sighed. Six

o'clock, and she wished it wasn't. She shut the light off on the desk and just sat for a moment. She wasn't in the mood for this evening's plans, but this was the better of the plans: have dinner with the parents at their house, or have to deal with them in her cottage when they invaded, trying to find out where she was.

Worse, risk Chas showing up. Chas in her personal space. *Dear God.*

Cece steeled herself and stood, grabbing her purse. This had to happen, and it was best to get it over and done. She finished tidying up the few stray papers and locked the desk, grabbing her coat. It was getting cold in Pittsburgh and she hated being cold.

She walked out of the library and to her car—one of the few extravagance she let herself have—an Audi A8 L W12. It was a gorgeous, over the top vehicle with a pearlescent blue color, and soft black leather interior. Cece had walked into the dealer to buy something far more understated, but once she had the W12 on the road, she was completely enchanted. She wanted it; she so rarely wanted something as ridiculously priced as something like this, and just decided to tap the bank account this once. She never regretted the purchase.

Cece drove the car through the oddly light traffic out to the Indianola estate that she had been raised on. She pulled the car around the rotary drive and aimed it back down the drive so she could get the hell out once they were done.

She looked up at the semi-imposing faux-Center Hall Colonial entrance. She hated this place. Formal rooms, and formal dinners and fancy guests—never anything genuine. Everything was breakable and nothing was real. If someone touched something it would shatter.

As soon as she received her acceptance letter from UPitt, she was out and gone. She moved into an apartment, and then as soon as she could, she'd bought the cottage. All with the money she made at Club Imperial.

Cece walked to the front door and rang once. She had the key, but she never let herself in. This wasn't her home; it had never been a home. It had always been a house where she lived. The cottage was home. Cozy, small with all kinds of *her* in it.

Her heart dropped to her feet when the door swung open. Cece stared at the face there for a long, hard minute before either of them spoke.

"Frances." She heard the fear in his voice.

"Gordon." Her own voice shook. He stepped out of the way, and Cece glanced around, walking in. "I thought you weren't working for my parents anymore?"

"I left," he said. "But they asked me back last year. I guess…we just haven't crossed paths."

"Entirely possible since I avoid the place." He closed the door as Cece looked through the hall to see if anyone was around, or waiting for her.

Gordon considered her a moment. "Understandable."

She gave up. Cece stepped in to him, pulling him into a hug. "It's good to see you, Sir."

"It's good to see you too, Dusty," he whispered in her ear. They quickly pulled away from each other, knowing that Chas and her parents would have a fit about a member of the house hugging the help. Never mind that Gordon had inducted her into the lifestyle, just that she hugged the help.

"I would like to have coffee with you, Sir. It's been

so long."

"I would like that very much, Dusty." He smiled. "But you must stop calling me 'sir'. Or I'll be forced to start calling you mistress."

Cece laughed—they'd always had an easy rapport. "Of course. Donny."

"Thank you, Cece." He motioned her into the house. "I believe that your family is waiting in the den for you, and Mister Robbe is pouring."

"He's going to be pouring a big one for me." Gordon choked back a laugh as she walked down the hall to the den.

She couldn't believe that Gordon was back at her parents' house. He had been her saving grace when she lived there. He was her confidant—nearly a parent— right up until the day she came home, hysterical, because she'd made the mistake of losing her virginity to Miller Harrington. He became far more than a confidant at that moment.

Cece stopped dead. *Oh no.*

She turned around and ran back to where Gordon had been. He was gone. Cece looked around desperately, then stilled herself. There was no reason to panic right this instant; if there was something wrong she was sure that Gordon would find her and tell her. They were slated for coffee anyway. She could give Sir—Donny the third degree then.

She nodded to herself and turned back to face her family. She walked into the den where her father was indeed leaning against the bar with a scotch in his hand. Charles was sitting in the Queen Anne chair, looking very much like he was holding court, with their mother and Hannah on the couch across from him.

"Frances, darling!" her mother popped off the couch and rushed over. "Oh, I'm so happy to see you!" She offered air kisses lest she smudge her makeup, which Cece noted was more akin to spackle now than Cover Girl. "You are such a rarity around here now, my dear! Whatever keeps you away?"

Oh, the list. Cece just smiled indulgently. "Work, Mom. I have a bit of swing schedule and it's hard to just get up and leave. And there are always things to do around the house."

"Frances, won't you at least hire a maid?" Her father tossed the question at her from the bar. She looked over and could see that it was not his first scotch of the evening. "For God's sake, girl, you're a Robbe. You shouldn't be cleaning the fucking toilets."

"Roger!" her mother chastised him. "You need to watch your mouth."

"Oh, for God's sake, Marjorie." He swished his scotch in the air. "She's been to college. She knows the word."

"You need to stop encouraging that college talk, Dad," Chas said from his throne—chair. "Cece really needs to come back and take her place in society."

"In high society," Cece corrected. "I already am in society, brother dear. I have a very respectable place in it, in fact, as a researcher, student, homeowner, librarian. I'm sorry you can't deal with the fact that your sister has ambitions beyond being a bauble on a man's arm."

"You will still make an excellent wife, you know." Chas stared at her, boring into her. "Your school work will certainly give you the ability to understand your more intelligent husband."

Cece stared at Chas. Of all the people in the world,

she didn't know that a person could hate their brother most of all. She imagined tying him up in one of the rope creations, naked, and leaving him somewhere nice in public so everyone could see him. A little humiliation went a long way, and she wasn't even thinking in terms of her lifestyle. Just in terms of getting the asshole to leave her alone. She was ready to give him what for when there was a hand on her arm.

She looked over and Hannah had walked over and was facing away from their brother. "Please don't," she whispered. "Please, Ce. Just let it go. You don't have to deal with him when you're gone. I do."

Cece looked over at Hannah and had a burning desire to go get Gordon and squeeze the truth out of him about what was going on in the house. For the moment, though, she smiled at her sister, sending her a look of understanding. She really hoped Hannah was all right.

The cook, Mrs. Perkins, popped her head into the room. "Dinner's served, Mister Robbe."

Roger lifted his glass in acknowledgement and Charles rose from his chair. They led the way into the dining room and Cece had to check herself. It was just dinner, she'd be able to leave very soon after, and she wouldn't have to come back for a week.

Roger took his place at the head of the table, and Charles sat to his right. Hannah sat next to him, Marjorie at the other end of the table, and Cece alone on the remaining side. Figured. The black sheep. She just wished that Hannah had sat on her side.

Mrs. Perkins and two of the other staff members brought dinner out, already plated. Cece wanted to roll her eyes. Even when she had gone to Nathaniel and Emmy's, Joanne had severed everyone family style.

Nathaniel Walsh had more money than the Robbes and four other families; he wasn't too good to pass the potatoes. She looked down at the plate in front of her. Her mother's portions: about half of a cup of potatoes, three ounces of the Chicken Marsala, half a cup of green beans, five baby carrots and one half of a candied pear. The last of which she hated.

She looked over at Hannah's plate and saw basically the same thing. Her mother's plate had even less of everything. But glancing at her father's and brother, the food was heaped on the plate. Looked as though she'd be stopping on the way home for a snack. And perhaps she should take Hannah with her. Wendy's was open late.

Once Mrs. Perkins and the two other staff retreated, Cece reached for her knife and fork.

"Frances." Charles' one word carried the contempt of a thousand parents. She looked up at him and saw that he had his hands folded in front of him in prayer. Hannah, Roger, and Marjorie had as well. Her parents weren't looking at her, Hannah had pleading in her eyes. Chas was just pissed.

"You are kidding me." Cece put down her silverware and dropped her hands into her lap.

"We say grace." Chas stared at her hard.

"You say grace. I'll wait."

"We all say grace."

"So? Say grace. I'm not digging in, I'm waiting for you."

"Why aren't your hands on the table in prayer?"

"Because—" Cece cut herself off. Her comment about fingering herself under the table was way beyond the pale. "Because I say my own prayers in my own time."

Marjorie gasped. "Oh, no. You haven't joined one of those store front religions?"

"Did you know there are two things that you should never talk about in polite company?" Cece bore her gaze into Chas. "Politics and religion. Say your prayers, Charles, before we all waste away." She left her hands in her lap, desperately biting her tongue from any further comments.

Charles stared right back her for another minute, then bowed his head. He said the short prayer that fell completely inauthentically from his lips. "Dear Lord, please bless the meal before us. We are grateful for your bounty and for your generosity. Continue to heap your grace upon us. Amen."

Cece waited until her brother picked up the utensils. She picked up her own and carefully cut into her delicate portions.

"So, Frannie." Roger's voice boomed through the large space fueled by his scotch. "Why can't you make it on Mondays?"

"I have a standing meeting at the library and I can't miss it." True, not a lie. They just didn't need to know what that meeting was. "I have the chance to move up here and I need to be at that meeting every week."

"You know your husband won't approve of your working," Marjorie said and smiled at her husband. Roger didn't even see it. He was busy cutting up his overly large portion of dinner. "You should really think about your future, Cece."

"I'm not getting married right now, Mom." Cece stabbed a carrot. "I need to pay the bills for the house."

"Your father and I think it's high time you quit that

job and moved back home." Marjorie was ignoring her again and listening to herself talk. "You'll never get a husband if you're so...so...independent."

"You say that as if it were a bad thing."

"Darling, independence never won a husband."

Cece closed her eyes for a moment. "It's not contest, Mom. I'll find a husband when I find one."

"You're twenty-six! When I was your age—"

"You were already pregnant with me, yes, I know." Cece tried not to react, just cutting into her chicken carefully. "Things are different now, Mom. I don't have to race down the aisle and have kids before I'm thirty. It's okay. I mean, Chas isn't married."

Out of the corner of her eye, she saw her brother bristle for just an instant. *Well, that's curious.* Her mother, however, didn't see a thing and plowed on. "Frances, sweetheart, the older you get, the more likely you are to have a retard."

Cece dropped her fork on the plate with a bang. "What did you just say?"

"It's true." Marjorie plowed on. "Once you hit thirty, you are in dangers of having one of those retarded children. We don't want to burden anyone with one of those."

"Do you have even the slightest clue what an asshole you sound like right now, Mother?"

"Language!" Roger snapped.

"No! I will not watch my language!" Cece stated loudly. "Mom just indicated that she wouldn't be interested in having a *retard* for grandchild because I'm not having children young enough for her liking. It does not matter what age I am! A child with a birth defect can be born at any age! And for the goddamn record, the word 'retard' is horrible insult and you need to cull that from your vocabulary immediately."

"It's a—"

"*Immediately.*" Cece was boiling mad. She ran a few of the Learning Disabled programs at the library for the college students, and to hear her mother call them the 'R' word made her want to punch things. "You will not use that word around me."

"It's just a word."

"It's not just a word. It's an insult. Do you know how many brilliant LD kids we have at the college? They are at a disadvantage, but they are brilliant and sweet and no less deserving of your respect than anyone else on this whole frickin' planet. So lose the word."

"Someone needs to curb you," Charles snapped. "Your mouth and attitude are repellent."

Cece grabbed her napkin off her lap and tossed it next to the plate of barely touched food. "I'm leaving. I came here because I thought that maybe, just maybe we could be civil to each other. Instead, I'm insulted, demeaned, and told that I'm repellent."

"You're not leaving." Marjorie pointed at her. "Stay where you are."

"I am leaving." Cece stood from the table.

Chas was around the table and pushing her chair back in under her a moment later. "You will stay, and you will listen, little sister. Keep your mouth shut, your hands folded, and stay. Right. There."

"Charles!" She yelped, stumbling back into the chair. "Let me out."

"No!" he snapped at her. "Mother, tell her."

Cece felt the pit of her stomach plunge to the floor. She was even more frightened when she saw the helplessness and tears in Hannah's eyes. She switched her glance over to Marjorie, who had delicately put her knife and fork down, and folded her hands. "Mother? What is going on?"

"We've decided that it is time for you to marry."

Cece wanted to puke. She whipped her head back to her father. "Dad! You can't let them do this!" But Roger was engrossed in his scotch again.

Oh God.

Marjorie retrieved a very expensive leather portfolio from the sideboard. She moved Cece's plate to the side and put the portfolio down in front of her. "This is a pre-nuptial and marriage contract for you. Your brother and I spent a lot of time getting this set up, and it's a binding document already signed by three of the four parties involved."

Cece looked at her mother. "Are you fucking kidding me?"

"I am not joking when it comes to your marital status, Frances."

"I'm not getting married! I'm not signing this!"

Chas looked at their mother, giving her a slight nod. Marjorie walked away from them and Chas leaned down to her ear. "Listen carefully to me, Frances Michele. Very carefully. It has already been arranged that if you should refuse this contract, your house is going to go into foreclosure. Your car will be repossessed. Your pretty little job at the library will disappear."

"Why are you doing this, Charles?" Cece felt sick, helpless.

He turned so Marjorie couldn't see his words. "Mother thinks this is because you need to be married. But your mother owes an enormous gambling debt to the Wainwrights. They have already threatened Father, and they will take all of the Robbe family fortune unless you agree to marry their son. You...or Hannah." He turned and looked at Hannah sitting there. "It doesn't matter to them who their son marries. But we both know that you love Hannah a little too much to let that happen."

Cece snapped her head to look at her brother. "Paul? Paul Wainwright?"

"That's correct. And they will take everything if it's not you or Hannah. That means your father, mother, and sister will all end up homeless, penniless, and destitute. And we're not going to let that happen, are we?"

"But Paul…Paul is…"

"Is what, my dear sister?"

"He's…"

"Known for his proclivities? His wandering hands? Wandering eyes? Cruelty in bed to those who join him there?" Chas nodded. "All of the above, my dear sister."

"You would put Hannah in that position? You would let Paul handle someone as small and frail as our little sister?"

He turned and looked right in the eye. "No. You would."

"You fucking asshole." Cece felt the walls of a prison slide into place around her. Paul was known to be merciless, sometimes out and out abusive to his bedroom partners. She could handle it; she doubted there would ever be a night in bed for them after the honeymoon—

Shit. She let out a breath. She'd already made up her mind. Hannah couldn't survive his purported cruelty. She wouldn't be able to—she had always been the weak, fragile, quiet girl that Chas had made her, and the illness had caused her to be. "What about Marjorie's gambling?"

"She will not incur any further debts, once you sign this." Chas smiled at her.

"You're going to let her keep gambling?" Cece was furious. "How about an intervention on that?"

"There's no harm in it now." He tapped the portfolio. "She's safe from further threat. And you know the Robbe family doesn't believe in psychiatric help, sis. There's nothing wrong with us."

Cece stared at him. Marjorie would never get help for her gambling. Christ, Cece thought that it had been the occasional OTB wager on a horse or a baseball game. She had no idea it was this bad; her mother had never shown her any signs of gambling addiction. And now she had saddled her daughters with the burden of getting her out of her mess, keeping her sister in a house. Keeping her father in the booze.

Chas held out a pen.

"You are the lowest form of scum that has ever existed, Charles."

By the time the ink was dry, she was already drawing up divorce proceedings in her head.

CHAPTER FIVE

HE WATCHED.

There was a lot to watch right now and it was difficult to keep up sometimes. But this time, there were major stirrings, and they weren't all good.

Frances Michele Robbe, middle child to Roger and Marjorie Robbe. Precocious, spitfire, blindingly intelligent, frighteningly independent and one of the most tender hearts a man could ever hope to hold. Masters in Library Science, minor in Education, self-possessed and determined.

Roger Robbe was so far into alcoholism that he didn't have a say in the family anymore. Charles was now the man of the house. He and Marjorie were horrified at Cece's acceptance to UPitt and her desire to go. They were even more horrified when she moved out of the house and into the dorm. They were losing control of her, which was something that didn't sit well with her mother and Charles.

Marjorie actually passed out when Cece bought her own house with her own money. No one questioned how she had enough money to buy the darling little cottage she lived in—they were just mortified that she had done so. And lived alone without a man to help and protect her.

And pay for her. Unheard of in Marjorie Turing Robbe's world.

Quelle horreur.

Who knew what their reaction would be if they found where Cece had gotten her money for the house.

It was his opinion that they didn't care; they probably just assumed that she had used her trusts to buy it. That was completely against what Cece was trying to prove. But then, her family wore blinders to the rest of the world.

Cece was Prima Domme at Club Imperial.

Not many people outside her weekend job knew that Dusty Rose Milan and the bookish Cece Robbe were the same person. During the week, she wore wool skirts below her knee with impeccably coordinated shirts and blazers. She loved Burberry and loved to pop the color red with it. She even managed to wear their perfume. Cece always had sensible shoes, and a solid sense of time. She was late or early as the occasion demanded. Her weekday life was neat. Organized.

Her club presence was a force to be reckoned with. Her ability to be present in a moment was surpassed only by the former Prima Domme of Club Imperial, Tessa Saint. However, Tessa had moved to management, and engagement, and moved Dusty Rose as the Prima.

Now Cece was fighting against everything her parents deemed proper. Well, everything Charles and Marjorie deemed such. They wanted her in their house, where they could protect the legacy of the Robbe family—because she was the only hope for a grandchild, a legacy. Chas had taken up with the Oetler heiress, who was not interested in having another child. Nothing Charles could do would change her mind. And Hannah...sweet, fragile Hannah. Her chance of ever having a child was small; she was too weak, and too sick. All the doctors she would ever talk to would tell her that if she could conceive, she shouldn't. She just wasn't a woman who could carry a pregnancy. Which meant adoption.

Which to Marjorie meant don't bother. An heir to her and her husband's money could and should only be blood. He knew they had to get Hannah away from the beast that was her mother soon. Things were going to go very wrong with that girl if her father wasn't there to protect her.

Much as he wasn't for Cece.

Thank God for Gordon Macdonald. He trusted that Gordon would do the same for Hannah if it came down to it. Not exactly the same, but help her nonetheless.

He had seen the contract. He didn't know how they got Cece to sign it; she wasn't the kind of woman who would surrender her freedom to the will of her mother. And especially not to her brother.

Whatever leverage they had, it had to be big. Cece knew Paul Wainwright.

He watched and wondered. What had made Cece sign that contract...Paul was not an easy person to get along with.

Paul Henry Wainwright, doctor of forensic sciences and a coroner for Allegheny county. Mostly quiet, withdrawn. While generally the same intellectual level as Cece, there had been occasions where he was embarrassed by his inability to communicate effectively. He was awkward and ungainly as a child and seemed to never quite fit into his body.

Paul was the victim of serious bullying in high school and he quickly became an outcast. So much so that he chose to go to college in California to escape the past. Without the bullying and cruelty he shot to the top of his class and sailed through his education to finish with a doctoral degree in Forensic Science.

He moved back home to Pittsburgh, easily got a job as an assistant coroner with Allegheny County, and forged a solid relationship with Thurmon Chemicals. He worked with one particular chemist, Dr. Nicholas Dovadsky, on a regular basis and had a terrible habit of relying on him to translate his reports into something readable.

The black cloud of his childhood hadn't dissipated, though. Instead of being bullied, he was blacklisted. Rumors started springing up everywhere about things that had never happened in Southern California. Exploitation, under-age drinking and drug parties, statutory rape, abuse. The abuse was the one that everyone seemed to latch on to—abuse of a beautiful girlfriend that no one had ever seen or met.

Several had gone far enough to try and find the girl and the police reports for the alleged abuse. They were never able to find anything—because it didn't actually exist—but the rumors still persisted. It didn't even affect his ability to get the position in Allegheny at all. Rumors persisted.

They grew so numerous that he found himself essentially ostracized from the whole of Pittsburgh society. Which made his family very nervous, only for the fact that they were worrying about their legacy. As an only child, they suffered his expulsion as though they could really understand it. They fretted and worried and finally...

Realizing that Marjorie Robbe owed their gambling businesses more than the Robbe family was worth, they threatened her with the destruction of her family, her money and their way of life. And the simplest way to solve that problem was to offer up one of their daughters for marriage to Paul.

They immediately offered up the black sheep, Cece. They couldn't control her, so they thought that getting her married off—to a known abuser who was never proved to be an abuser was just fine with them—

would get her more under their control again. And thereby forcing the hand that could give them their heir.

And so, they got what they had wanted. Cece had signed the marriage contract. Paul would visit her over the weekend and propose with the ring that her mother had picked out for Cece. Paul was less than thrilled. Cece's reaction would be interesting the next weekend.

The Watcher undressed quickly and slipped into the bed behind his Hunk, all of the day's events weighing on his mind. The Hunk turned in his arms and pulled him close.

"Didn't think you were coming tonight."

"I need to be here," he answered.

"She signed?"

The Watcher nodded. "She did."

"Isn't that part of the plan, though?"

"I don't think that anyone realized what it would take to get that to happen." He sighed. "She's so independent and self-possessed."

"That's what a good Domme is."

"I think that's why it's so hard to watch." He pulled the Hunk closer. "It's breaking her. Breaking her spirit, who she has strived to become."

The Hunk put a hand on his cheek. "It's not going to break her. This is *necessary*. She's stronger than you're allowing yourself to believe. Trust me, love. As much as I hate the whole thing, this is the right thing to do. For everyone. On the other end, we will *all* come out stronger."

The Watcher stared into his Hunk's eyes. "God, I fucking love you."

"I love you, too." The answer was natural. "Let me hold you. You need it."

"I do." He relished the feel of the arms around him, and let them give him strength.

The hard part was still to come.

* * *

Killian closed the book he was paging through and looked on the screen at the microfiche. There was too much research to be done on this, and he didn't know how he was going to be able to get through all of it. The paper deadline was in four weeks, and he needed two of those so he and Dr. Najahan could get the revisions done.

Najahan. His savior, in a sense. The man was a quietly brilliant doctor who eagerly agreed to having Killian as his student and research assistant just two weeks before. Of course, he was also a hard ass that wanted this paper out, but that was something Killian could do. The amazing work the man did on cardiac diseases floored Killian, and he was thrilled to be working with the doctor. He would learn more with him than he could observing a thousand other doctors for ten or fifteen minutes per operation. It was a terrible way to put it, but he'd gotten his hands dirty more times in the past week than in the past year of his internship.

Dr. Hamburg had been keeping him away. Killian had the odd impression that the man wanted him in private practice, not at the hospital. If he was in private practice, at the end of the day, he would be able to go home to his wife and family and tend the fortunes and the legacy that were the Hamburgs and the McInnis. Neither of which he really had any interest in.

The operation room, the hands on, the interaction with the patients was what Killian craved. It was what had suffered when his father was killed. And now with

Najahan, he had a chance.

Selfishly, he added to himself that this was also his chance to get away from the influence that Dr. Hamburg had on his career and life and, maybe, get away from Diane for good.

Two books slipped onto the desk next to him, and the distinct scent of Burberry wafted across him.

His cock instantly started to react. *Damn it.*

Two very long, very sexy legs appeared in his vision, and they were followed by the rest of the gorgeous woman they belonged to as she sat down next to him. He still couldn't believe Cece was helping him with this. Trying to keep his mind on his work was even harder than his dick when all that kept sliding into his mind was sliding into her.

"Here you are, Doctor." Cece tapped the books. She had a wet paper towel in her hands. "I had to nearly spelunk for those in the back room. They were buried and covered in dust. Someone really has to clean that up back there. All those journals are being ruined."

"You know if you say something, it's going to be you."

"Oh, don't I know it." She sighed. "It's going to be me anyway. I have to start really cataloging what we have and organizing it. I think there's a lot more back there than people believe there to be." Cece smiled at him. "A librarian's job is never done."

Killian made a noncommittal noise. "Look, Cece. I'm sorry I busted into your office the other day. I have better manners than that most of the time. I—"

"Stop." It was a powerful word coming from Cece. "I'm not concerned about it, Killian. There's too much going on in my life right now to care if you saw my pu—privates."

He glanced at her and caught the ghost of a shadow passing over her face. He blinked a few times and then pushed the journals away from her. "What's wrong?"

"Don't worry about it."

There wasn't really room for argument in her statement, but Killian decided it was worth it. "I do. I've known you for years, Cece. Nothing gets under your skin, and this did."

She sighed. Cece wasn't going to talk.

"Do you have plans?"

She gaped at him. "What?"

"Right now. Do you have plans? Can you take some time and have dinner with me? Away from the academic environment?"

"Uh..." She was confused, and speechless.

"Come on." Killian snapped the microfiche reader off and grabbed the few books he had. "Let's put these in the drawer and go get dinner."

"You're serious." Cece seemed glued to the chair.

"Yup."

Killian watched a dozen emotions cross her face again. She looked at him and finally stood up. "Well, no one is going to take exception to me leaving early. There's plenty of coverage." She looked at him. "But I have to be somewhere tonight at nine and need time to get ready."

"Not a problem."

They walked up to her office and locked away the research. Killian couldn't help but think about her standing in that room with her skirt hiked up. He tamped down his reaction to her and quickly walked back out of the office, holding the door for her. Killian walked her out of the building, directing them to his car, and ten minutes later found themselves at the Grand Station.

"Kind of over the top for a quickie dinner," Cece said, sitting down.

Killian shrugged. "Good food. Don't matter to me where it is." He looked at the menu. "Do you want to talk about what's going on? You were quiet the whole way here."

"I'm not a talkative person to begin with." Her statement seemed designed to head him off.

"Cece. You can't pull that 'I don't talk' bullshit with me. Not to mention the look on your face is utterly horrified about something that happened this week. So please. Let's talk."

Killian wanted this to work. He wanted to get to know Cece better; he'd pined for her for too long and now that there was a chance he could get away from the assumed marriage with Diane, he wanted to take that chance with this woman.

Cece studied the menu intently. Killian started to doubt that she was going to talk. But he realized that she wasn't really reading it, just glossing over it. He raised the glass to take a sip of water.

"I'm marrying Paul Wainwright."

He choked, dropped the glass, and started coughing. The water drenched the table and part of his pant leg as Cece deftly pushed back and managed to avoid most of it. The waiter and busboy ran over and managed to sop up the table, clean it off and reset it all before Killian could really process what Cece had just said to him.

He had to have heard that wrong. There was no way this was happening.

"I'm, uh." Killian cleared his throat. "I'm sorry. You startled me with that answer. Did you say you were marrying Paul Wainwright?"

Cece gave him a curt nod. "I am."

He shook his head. "I didn't...I didn't even know you were seeing anyone."

"I haven't seen Paul since high school."

"What? Then how are you marrying him?"

"I signed a contractual prenuptial and nuptial on Tuesday night."

"Holy fucking Jesus on a raft with crackers." Killian put a hand to his forehead. "What the hell is going on, Cece? You just told me you haven't seen him since high school and you signed a contract with him? That's not you."

Cece leaned forward on her arms. "What do you really know about me, Kay?"

"You're smart, you're a good person—"

"What if this is exactly what I want? What if I don't want to play the dating game and this is exactly what I wanted?"

Killian felt his hopes falling. "You...want this?"

Cece slumped in the chair a bit, and the defeat on her face ran him through. "I don't know what I want anymore." She picked at the corner of the menu. "They Shanghaied me. Bushwacked. Ambushed. Whatever. I didn't have a prayer and I should have known that *Tuesday Dinner* was a trap. Mom and Dad always try to stay away from me. They can't stand that I'm so independent and..." Cece rolled her eyes, "intellectual.

They can't get past the fact that I don't have a husband and a kid for The Legacy at twenty-six. I don't know why Dad let Chas take over." She laughed, not believing her own words. "Of course I know why Dad gave up. He just wants to be drunk and rich." She pulled the menu back up.

Killian was fascinated. She didn't want this, so why was she going along with it? What had made her sign the contract with someone who was notoriously abusive? He tripped over his own thoughts. "Cece, are you marrying him *because* he's abusive? Are you allowing yourself to fall into the cycle?"

"Fuck no." Cece shook her head. "No."

The way she cut herself off, Killian knew she had a very specific reason for signing it. "You know, Cece, if you tell me what's going on and why you're doing this, maybe we can find a way out of it. A marriage contract is not you. An arranged marriage is not you either."

"Why the hell do you think you know anything about me, Killian?" She snapped the menu closed.

"Because we both suffer from our families. You don't really want this. You don't want your family to have any kind of influence on you and your life. Your brother is a dick. Your mother is a wealthy prig. Your father is a rich drunk. The only person you give a damn about, just like me, is your little sister." Killian blinked. "That's it, isn't it? Hannah. Someone threatened Hannah?"

Cece fiddle with her napkin this time. "I don't even know why I agreed to come here. You live in a very different world than I do, Killian. Even if we did go to school together. You're sweet, you're smart, but you don't know what my family is like. You don't know what my life is like."

"Tell me then." He tapped on the table. "Tell me about it. Tell me what it was that made you sign that contract. And I will help you figure a way out of it."

"And what do you want in return?" Cece asked.

"Nothing." He was earnest. "I want to see you get out of situation that you clearly hate."

Cece shook her head. "I don't know how I feel about this yet."

"You don't like it," Killian supplied. "I know you don't."

She sighed. "I don't. But there's no choice." Cece looked up at him. "You're right. This is all about Hannah, and only Hannah. My father is a drunk, my mother is self-centered, and my brother is an asshole. Hannah is all I have in that family. And I have to do this, for her."

The waiter appeared and, really without thinking, Killian quickly ordered for both of them. He bundled the server away, then saw the look of anger on Cece's face. She leaned forward. "Who gave you the right to order for me?"

"I didn't...know you'd have a problem with it." Killian swallowed.

She picked at the table cloth. "Let me explain this to you, Kay. If you want to help, and you want to be my friend, as it seems you want to be, you don't ever, ever order for me. You don't assume you speak for me for any reason. You don't put words in my mouth, you don't try to put thoughts in my head. That is what my family has done my whole life, and that's what they are doing with this marriage contract. They are trying to think for me." Cece leaned back in her chair. "And I am more than capable of my own thoughts and decisions."

Goddamn it. Killian wanted to slam his hand down on the table, but instead settled for a clenched fist underneath. He had just been friendzoned without so much as a whole meal between them. "Cece, I'm sorry. That was presumptuous of me."

"So you see you really don't know me."

"I'm sorry," he repeated. "I'll call him back and you change your order."

Cece sighed. "Your intentions were noble. And you did order something I'd eat."

"Well, at least I got that right." He smiled at her. A moment later, she gave him a weak half smile back and he was relieved to see it. "I just wanted him gone," Killian admitted. "I didn't want to be distracted, and I didn't want him to overhear our conversation."

"Discretion is the better part of valor," Cece said.

"Also known as 'nonya bidness'?" Killian offered.

Cece smiled and shook her head. "Okay, all right, I get it. You didn't mean anything by it."

"See, that's the smile I'm afraid is going to disappear."

"I have to protect Hannah from..." She sighed. "They tricked me into this by threatening Hannah. There were three choices. One, the whole family was going to lose the house, the fortune, everything we have and be destitute, two Hannah could marry Paul Wainwright and they'd keep everything, or I could marry Paul Wainwright and save the family, which frankly I don't give a shit about, and save Hannah, which is what I do give a crap about."

"Why on earth would you be saving the family from destitution?" Killian asked. "The Robbe family is one of the oldest families in the county and there's no doubt about your status."

Cece picked at the table cloth. "My mother has a gambling problem. I thought it was a horse here or there, maybe a quick trip to a casino." She wiped a finger down the water glass, clearing off a line of condensation. "It's not. She's gambled away most, if not all, of the Robbe family money. And all of it to the Wainwrights."

"Wow," Killian said. This was news. Marjorie Robbe had always been a bastion of grace and gentility when he'd met her a few times. But then again, he didn't live in the house and had the feeling that, just like his house, the Robbes were totally different at home than at a party. "How long has she been gambling?"

"Who the hell knows?" Cece snapped. "She's bankrupted the family and I can only be glad that I have my own income."

"Why couldn't you take in Hannah and let the rest of them out to rot?"

Cece looked at him and cocked her head. Her eyes lit with a smile. "That is utterly devious, Killian. And I wish I could. But they would literally be in a cardboard box in weeks. They threatened me with foreclosure on my house. Mom and Dad have no marketable skills. Chas can't carry them; he's a part time broker who sucks at his job. He loses more in the markets than the little piggy who went wee-wee-wee all the way home."

Killian snorted. "He's that bad?"

"He's terrible." She nodded. "Just awful. He went into finance because he just once turned a profit on a sale of stocks. Someone told him he was good and he ran with it. Do you know what his formal training is in financial market? He read a single Warren Buffett book."

"He'd've been better off eating a Jimmy Buffett burger." Cece laughed; the genuine sound of her humor rang through him. It sounded wonderful. "So winter is coming to House Robbe?"

"Stop!" Cece laughed again. "You're making this funny."

"Just trying to lighten the mood."

"It worked." Cece was calming down. "I've spent the last few days trying to figure out how to get out of this, and the truth is that unless I want all of us to be homeless, I don't have a choice. At least I have a chance of getting out of a marriage to Paul Wainwright in one piece. I hope."

"You hope?"

"I think? He's an alleged abuser. People have done research on it." Cece wiped more condensation off her glass. "It's documented. He was in a few altercations, and the biggest rumor is that they can't locate the girlfriend."

"You would listen to that kind of gossip?" Killian was quiet. He didn't want to raise her ire.

"It's not gossip..."

"Cece, I will do the right kind of research if you like and—"

"Are you saying I can't do research?"

"I'm saying that you don't have access to medical

records the way I do. And I want to prove to you that Paul Wainwright is not an abusive dick," Killian said. "Not that I want you to marry him, because you don't want to, but there's no reason to fear him. I'm sure he's about as thrilled about this as you are, honestly."

"We'll find out when we have our first date on Saturday, won't we?"

Killian shook his head. "I cannot believe you've said yes to this."

"I didn't have a choice, Kay. Not even remotely. Chas backed me into a corner. The fucker knew exactly what to say and do to get me to sign that paper." Cece leaned back as the waiter came over and put the appetizers in front of them.

"Chas isn't the good son he tries to play, is he?" Killian asked.

"I don't know what he is. He danced all over the fact that I would do anything to keep our little sister safe."

"What do your parents think about him dating Saundra?"

She stared at him. "What? Who? Chas isn't dating anyone. He's too busy pretending he's tending the family fortune."

Killian stopped and chewed on his lip. "He hasn't said anything?"

Cece's face fell. "What are you talking about?"

"I thought everyone knew..." Killian folded his hands on his lap, staring at the food in front of him. He looked up at Cece's expectant face. "Chas has been seeing Saundra Milhouse for about two months."

Pure, unadulterated anger sprang into Cece's eyes.

She could have started a fire with the rage that she was harboring. She really couldn't control the anger that his statement ignited in her; she grabbed the steak knife and brought it down point first into the table, driving it a full half inch into the wood of the table. Killian pulled back, shocked. She looked at him, her breathing suddenly hard and her face completely flushed.

She stood abruptly, flinging the chair backward. Without a word she turned and marched for the door of the restaurant. Killian leapt out of the chair and ran after her. "Cece, wait! Wait, please." She ignored him and kept up her relentless walk for the door. He finally caught up to her, just inside the exit, and grabbed her elbow. "Stop." He snapped the command. He was in no mood to play around.

Cece whirled around and yanked her arm out of his grip. "Don't you *ever* grab me!"

"Then you need to stop when I tell you to." The words were growled at her.

She stepped into him. "I am not someone you want to fuck with, Killian McInnis."

"Nor am I, Frances Robbe." The words were hissed at her angrily. "I thought you knew that your shit of a brother had taken up with Oetler. I would have broken that news more carefully if I had known you weren't aware of it."

The host appeared in the hallway with a phone in his hand. "Sir, shall I call the police?"

"No." Killian didn't hesitate. "Ms. Robbe is having a very bad day. We'll be leaving now."

"I'll be leaving now."

Killian gave her a withering look. "*We* will be

leaving now." He looked over at the host. "Please bill me for the table, knife and the meal. And accept my apologies for the scene."

"Of course, Doctor." The host nodded and the relief was visible on his face. "Shall I fetch the lady's belongings?"

"Yes, please." The host walked away and Killian took Cece's elbow again. She tried to wrestle it away, but he held on tight. "Stop. Right now. You stabbed a knife into a table top. You're lucky I told him not to call the cops because that was a terroristic threat, even if it wasn't directed at anyone."

"Let go of me, Killian." She was still struggling.

The host came scurrying back with Cece's purse and jacket. Cece tried to pull free to grab the objects from him, but Killian calmly held her back as he retrieved the jacket and purse. He held onto the purse while Cece grabbed the jacket and shoved it back on. The host scurried away and Cece snatched her purse. She banged through the door out into the cool fall air, and Killian kept up with her.

"What are you doing?"

"Leaving," she said. "I'm going to find my brother and drive a steak knife through his heart instead of the table."

"*Frances*. Stop. Now." He didn't want to pull out his Dom voice, not with her. But Cece was acting completely irrationally, and he needed her to calm down. She halted, then turned on her heel and looked at him. "You need to stop and relax. I understand you're furious, and you have every right to be, but you can't act like this. You stabbed a knife into a table."

She stared at him for a very long moment, and he saw some of her anger leave her face. What left her face was not the anger about her brother, but the anger toward him. She still seethed about Chas, but seemed to realize she was misdirecting. "I…apologize, Kay. That was completely out of character for me and shouldn't have happened."

"You have every fucking right on the planet to be pissed about what your brother is doing here, every single thing. But you can't let it get to you like that." Killian sighed. "Well, we can't go back in there and I'm still hungry and you still need to talk. So. Dinner. Legends?"

"Where?"

"Legends at the North Shore. Oh, you've never been, so we're going." Killian smiled and motioned her down the street to where his car was waiting.

They walked toward the car. "Really, I'm sorry, Kay."

"Don't sweat it." He waved it off. "I really thought you knew. I mean, he's only your brother. Why would he tell you something as important as he was seeing someone who was in the middle of the most contentious divorce I've ever seen."

Cece blinked a few times, and he saw a new emotion darken her face. It was somewhere between confusion and embarrassment, and Killian was as at loss to name it. They walked quietly next to each other for a few minutes to the car, and he had to shove his hands in his pockets to keep from taking hers. They reached the car, and he leaned over to open the door for her. When he righted to hold it open, he found himself just inches from her lips.

Killian stared into her eyes, bright and wonderfully blue. They sparkled, partly with left-over anger, and now with a low, raw desire. He could hardly believe—could Cece actually be interested in him? Or was this just circumstance? He wasn't sure he cared. He wanted to taste her pale pink lips that promised apples and cinnamon and bites of bitter spice.

"Killian." Cece's voice was soft, quiet—husky. "Don't."

"Why not?" He couldn't stop the words.

"You don't know me."

"I want to."

"Oh. Don't do this."

Killian didn't want to walk away from this, from whatever was happening. "You want to know what I feel like pressed against your lips. Against your body."

"Fuck." Her swear was a quiet, weak protest.

"Cece. Let me kiss you."

"You shouldn't." She shook her head lightly.

"You haven't said no."

"I don't think I can."

He closed the space between them and caught her lips ever so gently with his, pressing in with a careful demand. At first, she didn't answer him; she just let him kiss her. But after just a moment, she gave into him and her lips melted into him. He wrapped an arm around her waist and he pulled her in closer, pressing her breasts, her whole body against him.

Cece was warm, and soft, everything he'd dreamed in every fantasy of her. He moved a hand behind her head and slid his fingers into her velvet soft, pitch black hair. He devoured her lips, the apple, cinnamon and bitter spice overwhelming him, as he always thought it would. She parted her lips in welcome.

And Killian knew he was lost. He took her offering and slipped his tongue between her lips, stealing a taste that wasn't enough. He angled his lips across hers and delved deeper, possessing her, memorizing her. He committed every curve of her body, each flavor she sparked, each movement of her across his mouth. And none of it was enough.

Cece pulled back just enough to speak against his lips. "Killian, we shouldn't do this."

"One good reason why not," he breathed against her. "Just one."

"I..." She slipped her hands tighter around his waist. "I can't."

"We'll figure out how to get you out of this contract," he said.

"Killian, just take me home and fuck me."

CHAPTER SIX

KILLIAN OPENED THE DOOR ON CECE'S SIDE of the car and offered his hand. Cece took it and he helped her out of the car. His hand was soft, warm, and steady as he guided her out of the car and over to the elevator to his apartment. Killian lived in one of the prettiest buildings in downtown and when he opened the door on the fifteenth floor, she was delighted—the Allegheny River was right there, and she could see the Warhol Museum across the way.

What the fuck am I doing? Cece wrapped her arms around herself and walked into the living room gingerly. Just because the man she'd pined after for years had kissed her and showed an interest, she went home with him? *Shit. John.* John Smith was due at Imperial at 9.

"Wine?" Killian's soft voice came from behind her, brushing her ear.

"You don't have to seduce me."

"I want to."

Shit, shit. He's too good to be true. "Yes, I'd like a glass."

He disappeared into the kitchen and Cece whipped out her phone, firing off a text to Franz.

Dusty: I have to cancel tonight.

FD: Is everything OK?

Dusty: I had something come up. I can't come in.

FD: That's fine. You never call out.

FD: Smith called at noon and cancelled anyway. I'll find out why you didn't get the msg.

Dusty: Thank you.

FD: As long as you're OK.

Not even remotely.

Dusty: I will be. Someday.

FD: Call when you have a minute. I heard about it.

Dusty: Fab. I'll call tomorrow.

Cece put the phone back in her purse as Killian walked over, offering her the glass of white wine. She accepted gratefully. She really wanted to pound it back, but instead settled for a sip. He smiled at her, and Cece felt her heart start racing. She'd been so infatuated with this man for so long, standing in his gorgeous apartment, having just given him carte blanche to her body…she found herself trembling, almost frightened.

"Cece…"

She held up her hand. "Don't. We're here. This is still a terrible idea."

He blinked a few times. "Maybe it is. You're right that we don't know each other. I've stared at you and pined over you for so long, maybe my rational brain has no control."

Cece blinked back at him. "You've…pined for me."

He laughed, mocking himself. "Stupid word. Best one I can find for this."

She shook her head. "This isn't just a damsel in distress reaction."

He took a sip of his own wine, very much as though he were fortifying himself. Cece wanted to cry at the same time she couldn't believe she had lost this much control of her situation, her whole life. His warm hazel-brown eyes stared at her, looked over her face and almost as though he saw tears in her eyes—which she was careful to keep tear free—he stepped into her and wrapped a stray strand of hair around his finger. "You wore pigtails the first day of kindergarten. You ripped your tights on picture day in first grade, because you played Red Rover like your mom told you not to. You lost your front tooth because you got hit with a baseball in second grade. You made your mother furious when you did your makeup for the Christmas pageant." He smiled. "I thought you looked so grown up, and when I found the picture in my dad's stuff a few months ago, I almost wet myself laughing. So silly, Cece. You looked adorable with the giant blue eye shadow."

Cece couldn't stop the laugh—from relief and from his story. "Your father had that picture?"

"I asked him to take as many of you as he could."

"In second grade?" She was astonished.

"I thought all girls were yucky, except you." He took a hearty sip of wine. "It sucked that even though we were in the same social circles we weren't really. My mother…"

"My mother *still* hates yours. She blames her for my parents' marriage."

"Marjorie wanted Angus in the worst way," Killian agreed.

"Don't you…" Cece paused, and Killian waited for her. "Aren't you and Diane together?"

"Fuck that bitch," he growled. The words, the tone, the very delivery of the statement surprised Cece. "Mom would love it if I married her. But she's pushed her limits too many times with me. She went into my phone. She scrolled through a doctor's phone without permission, and who the fuck knows what she saw in there. I don't like her, I never have. Mom's idea to cultivate a 'relationship' between us, which of course Diane took to like a—" He stopped, then shook his head. "I'm not with her. I don't ever want to be with her."

Killian turned and leveled his gaze on her. "And you don't want Paul. Maybe we can both get out of this."

"I have to think of Hannah." Cece shivered, but not because of Hannah. Killian's gaze was piercing, and for the first time in years, the urge to submit, to offer her utter and entire self to a man overwhelmed her. She wanted Killian to make everything right, and to trust him completely and just to allow her to stop thinking. And at the same time, the incredible desire to dominate him rose up and she wanted nothing more than to see him bound in rope, at her mercy completely.

But she couldn't. Not now, probably not ever.

Was that what she really wanted? To give up her entire lifestyle?

"You're thinking about more than Hannah," Killian guessed.

"There's just so many things..."

Killian put his glass down and stepped into her space. "Cece, I'm confessing this now, to you, alone in my apartment. I want to get to know you. I always have. I don't care what our parents want. I don't care if you have a marriage contract. I don't care if everyone thinks Diane and I are going to get married. I want to know you." She could feel the warmth of his body so close. "I want to know every part of you." He laid his hand on her cheek. "I want you."

Cece closed her eyes, drinking in the warmth of his palm. It was soft, smooth. This wasn't sex—this was intimacy. This was something she had never been privy too. She laid her hand over his, nestling into the feeling of security and tenderness. "I have no defense against you, Killian. I melt when I see you. My walls are crumbling around me as you stand there and tell me I can have the only thing I've ever wanted."

His hand slipped behind her head and she found his lips crushing hers. His taste rushed into her mouth, flooding her with his warmth, and he pulled her into him. "Don't think tonight, Cece," he breathed against her. "Just be with me. Tonight, just you and me. We'll face reality tomorrow and we'll do what we can to make every night tonight. But not now. Not—"

She pressed into him. "I'm yours."

To her shock, Killian dipped down and, quite literally, swept her off her feet. She gasped and he wrapped her tightly in his arms, afraid he was going to drop her. "Oh, Jesus, Killian! What are you doing!"

He placed a kiss on her lips. "The hell with seduction. You want me, I want you, and I want to enjoy every last naked minute with you."

He swooped them into the bedroom, and Cece had just an instant to notice his very male bedroom. Big furniture, big décor, and big bed. A very nice big bed. She smirked and turned to him. "California king?"

"I'm six foot four," he answered. "Anything smaller and I'll fall off." His hands caressed her shoulders and stood her next to the bed. Stepping back, she watched him as he admired her shape, the way the skirt clung to her. After a moment of consideration, he rubbed his hands together. "It's like Christmas! I get to unwrap the gifts!"

Cece threw her head back and laughed, long and clear. She startled herself; how long had it been since she'd laughed with such abandon? Her eyes glided over his body and landed on his growing erection. "Well, I see you got me something as well."

He cracked his knuckles and stepped up to her, plucking the first button open. "I can't wait for you to open that gift." In quick succession, he popped the rest of them open and exposed her lace covered breasts. Like a kid in a candy shop, he reached for the zipper on her skirt.

Cece caught his hand and brought it back around. "Now, now. Let's let the others open some of their gifts too." She hiked his shirt out of his pants and deftly unbuttoned him with one hand and pulled the tie off with the other.

Killian's eyebrows shot up. "That's talent!"

Cece considered the tie for a moment, wondering if she could lash his hands together and have her way with him. Before she could take the thought further, he slid the silk out of her hands and leaned in, his wonderful, sculpted chest pressing against her hard nipples. "Someone looks like they are getting ideas. We're unwrapping, darling."

"Mmm, yes, we are," Cece answered, sliding her hands around his back. He had skin like satin and she imagined what it would be like to have her knots leave their marks in such a flawless canvas.

Killian dipped his head to her neck and nibbled lightly there, and an instant later, her skirt pooled around her feet. Cece was impressed; she hadn't even felt his hands at the zipper. "I think someone is good at unwrapping their presents."

"Only when I can't wait to see what's inside." Brushing the shirt off her shoulders, Killian stepped back as the cloth dropped to the floor. He looked her up and down, and she knew what he was seeing: black pumps, black stockings, the tiniest wisp of panties, garter belt to match, and black lace cup bra. The expression on his face was smoldering, and Killian managed to stop himself from rubbing his hard-on through his pants. But only just.

"That gift looks like it's too big for the wrapping." Cece swung her hips as she walked to close the distance between them. She reached for the button on his pants and in a flash they were down his hips and on the floor. Cece hummed her approval at his choice of boxer briefs. Her fingers trailed along his waist as she circled him, inspecting the whole package.

There was no resisting his backside. She gave it a hard slap, and to her surprise the yelp she expected dropped into a groan. *Oh, really?*

While she wanted a chance to explore that option, Killian grabbed her hand and pulled around to face him, and pulled her in hard. "Sweetie, I have a raging hard-on. There's no time to play like that, not when you're standing here in that lingerie." He wrapped a hand around her breast and plumped. "Christ, Cece, do you always dress like this under your work clothes?"

"Almost," she breathed. "Unless I don't feel like wearing the panties."

"Holy sh—" His breath drained out of his lungs

slowly. "Naughty librarian."

"Do you think about me sitting next to you like this?" Her hands snaked around to his ass and she grabbed each globe firmly.

"I might have," he answered, slipping the cup of her bra down, exposing her nipple. "When I saw that glorious pussy of yours shimmering in your office the other day." Two fingers pinched and pulled the beaded peak.

Cece exhaled slowly. "You liked what you saw."

Scraping the other cup of the bra down, Killian moved behind her and palmed both of her naked breasts. "You want to know how much I liked it?" The length of his shaft pressed into her back, and he whispered in her ear, "Feel how hard you get me? That day, I had to jerk myself off because it wouldn't go away, and I couldn't stop thinking about that pretty pussy." His warm hand trailed down her stomach and he cupped her mound gently.

Cece leaned her head back on his chest, turning to look at him. He was there, waiting and caught her lips, while one hand teased her nipple and the other was busy between her legs, pressing and pushing the flimsy material over her clit. "I want to finish unwrapping my gift." The words danced across his lips.

"Me too." She felt him smile against her, and then he wrapped his arms around her middle. "I go first!"

The laughter spilled out, and she tried to free herself from his embrace. Killian wasn't having it, he pulled her back and she tried to wrestle away again, this time managing just enough room to slip her hand between them and grab his hard length through the boxers. "I go first, you've already gotten to play!"

"That's hardly enough time to be called a tease!" Killian twisted, trying to free himself from her grasp, but that only made Cece start moving her hand up and down his length. "Cheater!"

Cece spun in his arms and threw her weight against him, and they tumbled backward onto the bed. "I don't cheat," she said, laughing at him. "I just make things happen the way I want them to."

"Oh, and how do you want this to happen?" A slow thrust up with his hard cock into her sex made lascivious suggestions.

"Slow. Fast. A lot." It was a short distance to his mouth, and she took control with a sweep of her tongue across his. "Any position you can imagine."

"I might be open to that suggestion." Cool, long fingers traced up her spine to the hooks on the back of her bra and in the next instant it was gone, thrown onto the floor. A warm, soft tongue, in counterpoint to his cool fingers, traced delicately over her hard nipples. The careful bite was a surprise, but not unwelcome, and Cece yelped.

"Let's get on the bed the right way," Cece cooed as he lost himself teasing the excited peaks she offered him willingly.

"And which way would that be?" Killian moved his lips away for only a moment.

Glancing down, she saw his eyes were closed and he was totally focused on her breast. "How good are you at the Kama Sutra?"

His lips curled into a smile. "Oh, sweetie, I have the feeling we're going to have a lot of fun."

"Not if you don't get those goddamn boxers off."

Without warning, she found herself being tossed forward on the bed. Slightly disoriented, she landed on her hands and knees and felt Killian's fingers running under the band of the panties she was wearing. They slipped to the side and his tongue caressed her sex, up one side and down the other mind-blowingly slow.

"Oh shit!" she gasped, almost losing her balance at his intrusion. His tongue found her clit and danced over it, pressing and then pulling back. "Killian!"

"Let me play with my gift," he growled against her. "I'm still unwrapping. There are pretty ribbons to be untied." He slipped a finger under the garter and went back to the task of tasting her.

Cece surrendered and leaned down on her elbows. The tremors were already racing up her body while his tongue tickled and licked her clit. Half a moment later, she realized he had distracted her while he unclipped her garter. The panties slipped down her hips, and Killian lifted his head just enough to drop them to her knees. Putting his head back down on them, Cece realized he had trapped her in that position while he lapped at her wet folds.

"Killian, let me up," she breathed.

"I want to play," he answered and nibbled on her clit.

"Oh, damn it, Kay." The tremulous orgasm he was building was approaching fast and she both wanted it and didn't want it. It was too soon; she wanted to draw this out, spend time winding each other up and finally bringing them both to a peak. But she also couldn't deny he had her wanting the climax. There was far more talent to his tongue than he had led her to believe, and took pleasure in showing her that. It would be far too unkind to not fully enjoy what he was offering her. Never mind that it had been years since she'd laughed and just enjoyed herself. "Make me come, Killian."

"All night, babe," he said. One of his long, cool fingers traced its way down the seam of her ass, past the tight pucker of her back entrance and to the hyper-sensitive bridge between there and the soaked tunnel of her sex. Pausing there for a moment, his finger teased all around her entrance. That same finger slowly snaked into her, giving her a low feeling of being filled, and easily found the inner bundle of nerves. Killian stroked it with care, as he sucked her clit into his mouth and lapped at it much the same as he had done with her nipples.

Cece felt the orgasm just out of reach and even more she felt Killian keeping at bay. He was certainly playing with her, and she whimpered at the realization that he was drawing her out. "Killian, please, please. Just make me come."

There was a tender and taunting 'hmm' against her sex. "I like it here. I think I'll stay awhile."

"Kay!" she cried. She was teetering on the edge and just couldn't get over it. "Stop teasing, oh Christ, stop teasing!"

"You want this?"

"Yes, yes! Please, make me come. Let me come!"

A second finger joined the first in her sex, and Killian swirled his tongue around her sensitive bud while his fingers found her other bundle of nerves. His tongue flicked over her again, and it was her undoing.

Cece gasped and tensed so hard she couldn't make a sound, couldn't move. She dropped her head to the bedcover, gasping and trying to catch her breath as she was swept along. Killian was relentless, teasing more of the orgasm out of her.

She hadn't come that hard in a very long time, and he suddenly crossed the threshold between pleasure and pain. "Oh, stop, stop," Cece gasped. "Stop."

His tongue was gone in the next instant. "What's wrong?"

"Nothing," she breathed. "Just too long, too much. It started to hurt."

Surprising her, he lifted his head and pressed a careful kiss to her mons. "I'm sorry, my pretty kitty. I hope you'll let me play some more."

Looking back at him between her spread legs, Cece laughed at him. "I'm sure it will."

He carefully ran his hands up her sides and rolled the two of them on the bed, and for once, Cece was very grateful to be on her back. She stared at Kay, who was kneeling between her legs. "You're still wearing the goddamn boxers."

"I still need to finish unwrapping you."

"This seduction shit is over." She smirked. "Take your damn boxers off. I want to see that magnificent cock of yours."

A smooth slide forward found Killian's lips pressed against hers. Her own cream was on his lips and she liked the way it tasted on him. His kiss was slow and deep, and ended with a smirk on his face. "You know how to make a man feel good."

"You're not too shabby either," she answered.

He quirked his lip up. "Condom?"

"Well, yes, if you ever show me what you've got."

He slowly slid down her body, pulling the garter off with him, and it and the panties wound up on the floor with everything else. She watched him walk over to the nightstand, and cursorily noticed he put a box of condoms in reach of the bed. His perfect ass was entirely too distracting; even worse was when he turned back to her and she could see the boxers still tented with his erection.

"Please stop teasing me, Kay." Cece's voice was quiet. "I want to see you naked."

He didn't answer her. At least, not verbally. Instead, he gave his answer by slipping his hands under the waistband of the boxers, and pulled them down and off, to the pile on the floor. He straightened and Cece sighed, reclining back. "God, yes," she breathed. He was big, as she thought he was—not much longer than average but thicker than she'd hoped. He looked delicious standing there, naked, cock standing straight and proud.

His eyes wandered over her body, naked except for the stockings. The slow gaze was smoldering, and she could feel it on her skin. She wanted the gorgeous body in front of her; he was even better than she'd imagined and her pulse quickened again knowing she was going to have him. A smirk appeared on his face and his eyebrow rose. "Someone likes what they see."

The soft, satiny cover let her slide back further on the bed. Once she was safely back on the bed, she pushed her legs apart and gave him a seductive, knowing smile. "I think someone else does too. Do you want to keep unwrapping?"

"Take those off for me, babe." He was breathing deeply, clearly trying to stay in control himself. "I want to see you peel them off those gorgeous legs of yours."

It was an easy request for her to grant; she wanted to feel every last inch of his skin sliding against her, touching all of her. As she ran her hand under the lace to slide the stocking down, she paused and looked up at him. "Show me how this makes you feel, Kay. Show me what you did the last time you saw me with just stockings on."

A guttural grunt stuck in his throat, and without hesitation he fisted himself, and ran up and down his length with that same tight fist. "Is that what you want to see? You want to see how hard I was when I saw you sitting on the edge of the desk?"

"Yes," Cece answered without hesitation. Her hands trailed under the lace again, capturing it, slipping it down her leg. She hardly paid attention to what she was doing. She was completely mesmerized by his hand pumping up and down on his thick shaft. The stocking joined everything else on the floor and Cece moved back to the top of the other one. Her eyes were transfixed on him as she slipped the other stocking down. "You are so delicious standing there."

"I cannot wait to bury this in you," he hissed, his teeth clenched.

Her breath came out ragged, and she delicately dropped the other stocking to the floor. "Get over here and fuck me, Killian."

In two strides he was at the bed and a heartbeat later, looming over her on the bed, pressing her legs apart. Cece let herself fall back on the bed, taking him with her as he caught her lips in a scorching kiss. She wrapped her hand around the shaft she had wanted to touch since he first pressed it against her, and groaned at the feeling of him, hard and hot, in her hand.

Killian slid his hands under her and turned them on the bed, sliding Cece up so that her head was on one of the pillows. He didn't let her lips go until he had moved her to his liking, and she was shocked that the Domme in her let this happen so easily. "What are you doing?" she asked, only partly caring about the answer.

"I've waited so many years to get you in my bed," he panted, "I'm going to make sure the neighbors hear it and the walls remember it." The heat in the kiss that followed was enough to set the room on fire; Cece couldn't believe there was this much passion, this much desire between them and she had never, ever seen it before.

She managed to grab one of the condoms on the nightstand—she wasn't really sure how—and sheath him carefully, enjoying the sensation of his heavy cock in her hand. She guided him to her sex, resting him against her entrance. "I want this, Kay."

His lips brushed against her neck. "You're okay with the size?" There was an easy, lusty smirk on his face when she turned her head to look at him. "Need any help?" Cece squinted at him, and his husky laugh danced on her skin. "Lube, babe. Just lube."

"You already took care of that." Cece smirked right back at him.

"You are one dirty little librarian." Killian nibbled on her ear and pressed against her waiting sex. Cece wrapped her legs around him, digging her heels into his ass. She knew he understood the signal, and a moment later entered her slowly, spreading her around him as he moved in. Cece quickly became aware of the fact that Killian knew what he was doing. He was in control of himself and he was slowly taking control of her.

"Holy shit," she breathed as he moved even deeper.

"All right?" Kay paused for just a moment.

"Keep going," she hissed. "Don't stop. Don't you dare fucking stop. Oh, *God.* " She felt so full, and he pushed that feeling of full as he pushed further inside her. She prized her legs off him and spread them wider, welcoming him even deeper.

Deeper he went, and her willing sex spread for him. "Damn, Cece."

With a last little push, he seated himself fully in her, nudging the top of her. She gasped from the tingle the touch spread through her and wrapped her arms around him. "Oh, yes," she hissed, holding him there, not allowing him to move yet. A little lift of her hips nudged him deeper and the feeling raced through her, chasing down a small, quaking orgasm that caught her by surprise. She rippled around his intrusive cock and he groaned against her skin where he had pressed his forehead.

"Let me move, Cece," he begged. "Or I'll come right now and I'm not ready to."

She let out a long breath, closing her eyes. "I want to feel you moving in me." Her grip released a bit, letting Killian know he could move now. But his movements were consuming: she stretched over him, and shrank behind him. He was unlike any other man she'd welcomed to her bed, rough-and-tumble and yet completely gentle and abiding. There was no doubt that Killian knew his body. He had to, with his wonderful, penetrating girth.

Cece's eyes popped open as he started moving more quickly. Instantly, she caught his bright hazel eyes, and the wonder and lust there was overwhelming. It almost frightened her—could they really have been crossing paths all this time without a single hint that this, his firm, desire-infused body looming over her, lording over her burning senses, was what they had both wanted?

More than that, Cece realized, unable to glance away from his adoring gaze. He wanted far more than just a quick fuck, or even a single hot night they would never forget. Killian's desire was manifested in his drive, his relentless thrusts into her slick sex and in the gorgeous wide eyes that bore into hers—memorizing each detail as she moved and moaned and ground into him. Every sound she made, he remembered her voice; every flutter of her eyes, he memorized her face; every move she made against him, he memorized her touch.

Jesus Christ, Killian was in love with her.

She couldn't say she didn't want his heart.

She couldn't even pretend that she wasn't giving her heart to him.

An understanding flickered in his eyes. An unspoken *I love you* danced across his face, and the shared knowledge they couldn't say the words to each other without breaking the world around them. She knew, as he did, that right at that moment, this giving and taking of each other was all they could have.

But she wanted more. She wanted everything with him.

And it hit her: this was not a quick romp for her either. This was not a meaningless fling. This was a brand, a bond to hold their souls together while the people around them conspired to keep them apart. Cece would not have that. She and Killian knew in that instant that they would fight the whole damn world to be together, or die trying.

"Killian," she breathed. The rest of the words were unspoken.

"Cece," he answered, and she heard his unformed thoughts.

"More, give me more of you," Cece whispered.

He couldn't answer her the way she knew he wanted to. Instead, he moved inside her in a gorgeous rhythm she never wanted to end. He filled and withdrew, and it didn't take but a few more of his thrusts to drop her into another, far more consuming climax. And as he had promised, neighbors wouldn't forget this soon. "Killian!" she screamed and his name echoed in the room.

His growl trembled across her skin. His erection throbbed, but he didn't come. It was a look of triumph on his face as he took her through a second orgasm and didn't end the coupling yet. Her body trembled in expectation at his plans.

"That's right, babe, I'm not done with you yet." Killian's eyes were suddenly wicked.

It was a cruel feeling of emptiness as he withdrew from her, but somehow she knew it was only a temporary situation. Cece knew she was right when he laid his hand on her hip and rolled her over. His other hand took its place on the opposite hip and she found herself face down, ass up in a flash. Killian's wonderfully oversized cock pushed its way back into her willing, wet sex, and Cece didn't stop the grunt of delight as he seated himself all the way inside.

"Oh, shit, babe, look at this gorgeous ass." His

words were reverently filthy as he passed a tender hand over her smooth bottom. Killian grasped her hips and pulled her back on him. Her body reeled, still recovering from the orgasm and now being pushed back into the insanity of pleasure again. "You like feeling me deep inside you."

"Fuck yes," she hissed. "Your cock is incredible."

He moved back, then in again. One of his wonderful hands skimmed up her back, tracing up her spine, and around to her breast as his other hand held fast to her hip. Palming her breast, caressing it, he moved himself smoothly in and out of her wet, willing sex. Killian's hand pinched and pulled at her nipple, then released and caressed, and repeated. His thrusts were deep and slow at first, but it was only a moment before he started moving faster. He switched hands, moving to torture her other breast.

Cece was panting at his sudden punishing rhythm, and enjoyed every instant of it. His heavy sac slammed against her clit in the same rhythm. It had been years since she let someone rule her like this, and at the same time she somehow knew that if she wanted to control, Killian would let her. She smirked, knowing he couldn't see it, and tightened the muscles that were gripping his shaft.

"Oh, shit…" he gasped. "Do that again and I'm going to come."

"That's the idea," Cece panted and squeezed him again.

His grunt turned into a groan and his thrusting became desperate. Cece tried to keep up her rhythm of press and release, but Killian was too overwhelming. His hands had slipped back to her hips to help him drive hard into her. "Coming," he grunted. "Cece, I'm coming. Oh, fuck! *Fuck.*"

Cece lowered herself to one elbow, reached back between them and palmed his sac, rolling him in her fingers. It was his undoing—he shouted incoherently as he pushed in again and again to her tunnel. Cece wished the barrier wasn't there; she wanted to feel his come inside her. Killian's surging cock distracted her enough, though. She pushed against him as he came forward, emptying himself into her.

Killian slowed, coming back to himself. "You dirty little minx," he breathed, a smile in his voice. "You have one very talented pussy."

Cece made a sad little mewling sound as his erection retreated. "Are you all done playing?" Cece asked, glancing at him over her shoulder.

He eased himself out of her and discarded the rubber. "Oh, not even close." He leaned over to the drawer and pulled out a small silver object. Cece instantly recognized it as a bullet as he slipped it on to his finger. "It's your turn, babe." Wrapping an arm around her waist and slipping his hand up to her breast again, he righted them to a sitting position and pulled her close. His finger with the toy snaked between her legs.

The vibration shot through her sensitive clit, ripping through her body, tearing the scream of pleasure from her throat. Cece wanted to jerk away, but it was so clear that Killian knew exactly what he was doing with her body, and pulled her tight to him without a word. The buzz teased her sensitive bundle of nerves, making her shiver and quake against him and she felt like she was going to pitch forward. She reached behind her, where she could feel Killian's hot skin against her and wrapped her arms around him. She felt his thick length against the small of her back, resting from its recent assault on her.

Of course, that was the source of the problem—she had been so ramped up by his cock that she was at the tipping point of another climax. With the silver vibrator humming and tickling her, it only took a small pinch at her nipple by his hand and she screamed with the fourth orgasm of the hour. Cece arched back, gasping and squirming; she chanted his name as he passed the bullet over her a few more times, coaxing more and more of the climax out of her.

Cece laid a hand on this arm. "Stop, stop," she breathed. "You have to stop."

The buzz dropped away, while Killian whispered in her ear, "You okay, babe?"

She desperately tried to catch her breath. "Yes, I'm fine. More than, really. I just needed you to stop...my body was just done."

"Happy to oblige." He laughed lightly. "More to come?"

She turned in his arms and looked at the playful smile there. "Oh, I plan on lots to come. For both of us." Cece glanced at the clock, then back at him and pouted. "It's only six p.m. I'm kind of hungry."

Killian nibbled on her neck. "Good. I plan to do some eating out."

CHAPTER SEVEN

KILLIAN HEARD CECE PADDING ACROSS the room to the kitchen. He glanced up and found the gorgeous creature who had spent the night in his bed standing there, leaning against the wall. She gave him a sweet smile while he inspected her clothing choice.

She'd grabbed the shirt he'd been wearing the day before, and because she was so tall, it barely covered the panties she had slipped back on. His cock throbbed hard for a moment, but he gained control of himself; they'd spent six hours the night before bringing each other to ecstatic heights, with barely a stop for some Chinese delivery.

Killian would have never guessed the wonderful sexual things that could be done with mu-shu.

"Good morning, babe," he said, turning back to the stove. "Breakfast."

"Please," she answered. "I'm famished."

"I wonder why," he teased. The laugh that answered was high and full of life; he relished the sound. He tucked it away with the memories of the night before. "Eggs are okay? Canadian bacon?"

"Perfect."

He flipped over one of the pieces of ham in the skillet. "How do you feel?"

"Sore." Killian looked back at her sitting on one of

the bar stools in his kitchen, a little worried. "And it's amazing," Cece finished, catching his eye with a predatory glint.

He laughed and turned back to the stove again. "Use that look on me again, babe, and you're not going to be able to walk."

"That also sounds promising."

He coughed, choking back his desire again. Killian wasn't sure if the night before was a good idea or a bad idea, aside from the fact that it was the best sex he'd ever had. She'd shown her mettle—and kept up with him all night long. He kept thinking about how much he wanted to bring this wonderful woman to Wanderer's End, and tell her everything about him. To see her blindfolded and tethered, his name tripping off her lips as he brought her to another amazing climax. To have her completely at his mercy at the other end of a flogger.

Slow your roll there, McInnis. He pushed the eggs around in the skillet. Neither of them were in a state where learning about *that* would be a good idea. There were a thousand things between them and a night at Wanderer's End. "You look good in my clothes." He smiled.

"I like the way they feel," she answered. "And smell."

Killian turned to where Cece had seated herself at the table. "I want this, Cece. I want a relationship with you."

"I can't, Killian." The tone of defeat in her voice was painful to hear.

"I want to help you get out of this."

"I want nothing more," she admitted. "But you

absolutely have to understand: Hannah is the only part of my family I give a damn about at all. I love her, and I need to make sure she's safe. If they take my house, I can't be sure of that."

"She's nineteen." Killian was confused.

"She's frail, Kay," Cece said, playing with the cuff of his shirt. "She doesn't like to let on, but she's not a healthy, strong person. If my parents lost the house and she was on the street, she'd be dead in days. Because they couldn't get her medicines, they wouldn't keep her warm and dry..." Killian was shocked to hear the tremor in Cece's normally unwavering voice. "I will be happy when she finds someone to care for her the way she needs, and deserves, but until then I have to make sure she's safe."

"What's wrong with her?"

Cece chewed her lip for a moment. "She has myasthenia gravis."

Killian cringed. He knew that disease. Lambert-Eaton Syndrome had been one of his papers in med school. It meant that Hannah's body attacked and destroyed the receptor sites at the muscle. The critical control chemical never got to her muscles to help her use them—both voluntary and involuntary. It explained a lot—about her pallor, her fatigue, her seemingly delicate state. She really was medically frail, and Killian understood why Cece worried about her.

"So we have to get you out of this contract and make sure that Hannah's free and clear of it as well," he said.

"Killian, this can't happen again." Cece's voice barely carried over the sound of the cooking food.

"What?"

"This." She pointed to the shirt she was wearing. "You and I, naked and having sex. It can't happen again. Not until we have some idea what's going on."

"Frances." He dared to use her full name. "This isn't fly by night for me."

Her hand hit the table so hard he thought she cracked the top. "I have no interest in this being a one-night stand either, Killian. At all. But I don't need this to be more complicated than it already is. I have to worry about Hannah. No one else does. If that means going through with this wedding, then so fucking be it." Cece massaged her hand where she hit it on the table. "I don't see as it's a problem anyway. Once I have a kid with Paul, that's it. We can have an affair and no one will—"

"Fuck you, Cece," he growled. "I am not going to be an affair. I'm not going to be your illicit lover who can't spend every waking minute with you. It's all or nothing for me."

Cece jerked back at his reaction. Killian was pissed. He wasn't going to play that fucking game. Everyone he had grown up with had married and had children and then fucked around on their spouse, and he wasn't going to be part of that bullshit. Not with someone who meant as much to him as the gorgeous creature sitting at the table. Shaking his head, he realized he had frightened her too much.

"Cece, do you realize that there are so few people we know who are actually dedicated and happy with their spouses?" And in that instant he took a leap of faith that brought her into his closest circle of trust. "My father was killed because he took part in that bullshit."

Her mouth fell open as she reeled from the admission. "What do you mean?"

"My father and his mistress were killed in her apartment."

"I thought he was killed in a hotel room?"

"Patricia's apartment," he corrected. "And the words 'cheater' and 'adulterer' were sprawled in their blood on the mirrors. He was shot through the rectum, Cece. Someone shoved the shot gun up my father's ass and pulled the trigger, killing him and Patricia."

Her hand flew to her mouth, covering the gape. "They did *what*?"

"You heard me," he said, without reproach. He didn't want to repeat it. "It's never been put out into the public because they are sure that's going to be something they can use to prosecute with. If they could ever find the bastard."

"You shouldn't be telling me," she whispered.

"I'm telling you because I am not going to let either of us get to that level." Killian finally turned back to the stove and pushed the eggs around again. "I won't risk either of us being hurt that way. I loved my father, and even more, I loved Patricia. He would have been happy with her, if only my mother agreed to the divorce."

"Did your mother kill him?"

He paused. "No. She was really and truly with me the whole weekend. She wouldn't have bothered with a hit either; she was too cheap and when my father sued for divorce she would get everything she wanted anyway." The ham snapped in the pan in the momentary silence. "I won't risk our lives. We don't know who killed him. We don't know anything about what happened. And I will not have you die lying next to me."

He heard the barstool scrap across the floor. He thought Cece was leaving the room, but was caught a bit by surprise when she pressed herself again his back and pulled him into her, her cheek against his back. "I'm so sorry, Kay. I had no idea. I know that's the idea, but shit. Shit."

"Do you understand why this is all or nothing for me? That if you marry Paul I can't and won't touch you again unless or until you divorce him?"

"Yes," she breathed, her words dancing on his skin. "Yes, I do, Killian."

Turning, he pulled her against his chest. "I want this, with you. But I understand you as well. We have to make this a one-time thing until we make it a full time thing. And I'm okay with that."

He felt a heavy sigh and shake, and looked down to find tears in Cece's eyes. "Why did we wait so long? Now we have to walk away from this before we know what it can be."

"Cece, we'll figure this out. I promise."

She gave him a half smile. "I hope so." The tears rolled down her face, but the smile spread. "Because frankly, I want a few more nights like last night with you."

Killian quirked an eyebrow. "Just a few?"

"A whole shit ton." Cece laughed.

"And just think," he whispered in her ear, "that was only the beginning."

Cece's eyes grew wide and wicked with his promise.

* * *

The dull, angry thud of leather on leather was the only thing Killian could hear. His knuckle stung, and he was coated in sweat. It dripped and rolled down his face, falling onto his shirt and to the floor beyond, and still he didn't stop.

"This is new for you," came the voice from the door.

Killian let two more punches fall before stepping back from the bag. He pulled off the thin leather gloves and examined his knuckles. They were raw, and it felt good. "What do you mean?"

Darien walked into the room, looking around. "You're not usually into getting the pain. You're usually the one giving it."

"Believe me," Killian said, grabbing a towel and wiping the sweat off, "that bag is hurtin'."

"You are too," Darien said. "What's going on?"

Killian pulled the sparing glove back on and whacked at the bag again, in quick succession with both fists. "I slept with her."

Darien stepped into his line of sight. "Jesus Christ, you slept with *who*? For the love of God, Killian, if you fucked Diane I will kick your—"

Killian's next punch came within millimeters of Darien's jaw. And it was only at the last second that he managed to stop it. "Don't you ever accuse me of sleeping with that rotten piece of meat. I know better than that."

Darien wrapped his hand around Killian's fist. "You need to relax." He lowered the fist out of his face. "Relax. You announce that you slept with someone, and the last time you were here, you were bitching about that rotten piece of meat. So it was my logical conclusion that you had slept with her. Take it down a notch and tell me who you slept with."

Killian pulled his fists back and slammed the bag again. "Cece."

Darien walked back into his line of view again. "Excuse me?"

Killian dropped his fists. "Cece."

"Robbe? Frances Robbe? You slept with Frances Robbe?"

"Yes."

Darien pinched the bridge of his nose. "Holy fucking hell, Kay." He snapped his eyes open. "Does she know?"

"No." Killian shook his head, taking two more shots at the bag. "No, she has no idea."

"And it worked?"

This time, Killian took six punches to answer. "I had to repair the wall before I came over."

"The wall?"

"There were a few holes behind the bed."

Darien laughed. "You fucked her so hard the walls had holes."

"Ripped the sheets at one point, too." Two more shots at the bag. "Damn shame, they were my favorite satins. If my neighbors didn't know my name before—"

"You know she's getting engaged."

Killian hit the bag so hard it swayed and he had to grab it before it swung back at him. "I am well fucking aware of that, thank you very fucking much."

Darien held up his hands. "Just making sure."

"Know any good lawyers?"

Darien stared at him hard. "You are also aware she's marrying Paul Wainwright, right? The coroner? You're not going to find any lawyer who is going to want to go up against the county coroner for any reason. They need his reports, and they are not going to cross him."

"Who said anything about crossing him?" Killian punctuated each word with another hit to the punching bag. "I'm going to talk to him. I want her free and clear."

"Hold the phone." Darien stepped closer. "You want her? Free and clear? What the hell is going on here, Killian?"

"Oh, come on," he answered, hitting the bag even harder. Darien grabbed the bag to hold it for him. "You know I've always been hot for her. I've always wanted to get to know her and date her and see if there was something between us. And now I know there is."

"You're in love, aren't you?"

Killian stopped his assault on the equipment. "You're a fucking genius."

Darien punched him right in the gut. Killian doubled over, sputtering and coughing. "You mind your fucking manners in my house, McInnis. The only reason I'm not hauling you out by your balls is because I like you, and I know what you've been through." He took a few steps back.

Killian took a moment to hold his stomach. And let his pride resurface. He deserved the hit; he was walking on thin ice with one of the most powerful Doms in the 'Burgh. Slowly, Killian let himself stand up straight and take a deep breath, looking Darien in the eye. "I apologize. Your house, Sir. Not mine."

"Answer the question, Killian," Darien said.

Killian eyed the punching bag but didn't swing. "I want to be."

"What the hell does that mean?"

"It means that I've always been in love with her. But now—I see we can try a relationship and the feeling went from a vague infatuation to the reality of: I'm falling in love with this woman."

"You just can't seem to keep your life simple, can you?"

"Simple is boring." Killian sighed. He walked away from the bag and leaned against the sawhorse that was standing nearby. "She's amazing, Darien. Amazing. In bed. In life. Do you know why she agreed to marry Paul? For her sister. She loves that girl. Her passion for everything blows me away. She electrifies my life far more than anything since Dad died." He folded his arms over his chest. "That was one day, Darien. One. From early dinner to a kiss I didn't want to break with her out the door at noon. A kiss I knew, and know, I can't have again. It's driving into my gut that the kiss was only two hours ago and all I want is to find her again and hold her, kiss her senseless. She's meant to be mine, and I want to be able to let the whole world know. And I can't have her."

Darien stared at him for a moment. "This is why I don't believe in love. You are fucked, my friend. Fucked and screwed."

"I know." He let out a sigh. "The one thing I know right now is if I can't have her, I want no one."

Darien poked a finger through the air at him. "Diane

is your first concern."

"I have lunch with her tomorrow already set to tell her whatever she thinks is going on, isn't and we're not an item and she should lose my number. Forever."

"Good." He nodded. "My next concern. You're scheduled tonight for the Training Routine."

"I'm aware."

"Can you handle it?"

Killian raised an eyebrow. "It would be a poor reflection on my Mistress and House if I couldn't, don't you think?"

"I'm serious, Kay," Darien said. "I can't have you slipping."

"I'm fine, Darien," he answered. "You know me better than that. Of course I would tell you if this is going to be a problem. But it's not. The TR is simple for me at this point."

Darien sighed. "If you need to back down, I can still fill in."

"I'm fine."

"Love does stupid things to yins," Darien stated.

Killian smirked at him. "Just wait."

Darien turned and started to leave the room. "For what? Forty-one years, and I haven't had a nibble. I like my life. I like my little pets. I have no use for love."

"You just wait, Darien. Cupid is going to get you hard."

Darien turned at the door and gave him a half smile. "I don't need Cupid to get me hard."

CHAPTER EIGHT

THE DRESS WAS LOVELY, CECE HAD TO ADMIT. The fact that her mother had bought it made it hard to wear. The woman had bankrupted the family, and Marjorie was buying ridiculous clothes. Being the underhanded sneaky bitch that she was, Hannah had arrived with the dress. Which was better all around because first, Cece didn't want her mother in her house, and second, Marjorie knew that if Hannah brought the dress, she'd be less likely to refuse it.

"It took me a while to talk Mom out of the high necked long sleeved disaster she wanted to send. I finally told her that I should really pick it out, otherwise you were going as an 80s reject." Hannah smiled.

"You know I should make her take it back." Cece twirled around in it once.

"Yes, I do." Hannah laughed. "But I know you love it."

"Yeah, I do," Cece answered. She loved the light flair to the skirt and the way it was a demure neckline without covering her up to her chin and down to the floor. That's what Marjorie would have put her in every day if she'd had a say. One of the many small reasons that Cece had her own place.

"Are you going to wear it?"

"Because you picked it out." Cece smiled.

They caught each other's glance in the mirror, and Hannah's smile slid off her face. "Cece, you don't have to do this."

"Do what?" Cece snapped.

"Marry Paul because of me."

"Who told you?"

Hannah threw her hands in the air. "I'm not a child anymore, and you'd all do well to remember that! I know what's going on. There's a contract, and for some reason you have to marry Paul because of me." She turned back to Cece. "You don't have to do this. There's nothing so bad that you'd have to marry someone you don't love."

Cece considered her sister a moment, then said, "I *am* marrying for love."

Immediately, Hannah's face clouded in confusion. "Wait, what?"

"I agreed to this because I love you."

"I don't—"

Cece motioned her sister over to the couch and sat down. "Did you see the contract? Did Chas talk to you about it at all?"

"Chas is the worst of all," Hannah answered. "I'll never be older than ten in his eyes. He'd never talk to me about anything serious."

That was typical of the asshole. Cece nodded. "Of course he didn't. Hannah, I'm marrying Paul because if I didn't, you would have to."

"Why on earth would that happen?"

"Because if one of us didn't marry Paul, the entire Robbe family would be destitute." Cece sighed and explained what Marjorie had done to them all. "The ultimate issue here for me, though, is you. Your health."

"If you don't love Paul, let me marry him."

"Holy shit, no," Cece gasped. "No. Hannah, Paul is a very rough character. You can't marry him. You're not strong enough."

"Strong enough how?" Hannah jerked up from the couch and whirled on Cece. "You all need to stop treating me like I'm going to fall apart! I'm not dying. The disease has been in remission for three goddamn years! Let me marry Paul. There's no reason you have to. I'm never going to get another offer, so let me marry him."

"What do you mean you're not going to get another offer?" Cece was confused.

"Chas has my life scheduled to the last damn minute. I can't do anything without his input and opinion. I have never been on a date. If Paul is my only chance to get away from Chas, please let me take it." She dropped back to her sister's side. "Please. I want to go to college. I want to get away from Chas and Mother and Father. Don't you see that Paul is that chance?"

Cece was dumbstruck. She'd never thought about how staying in that house was destroying her sister, and hearing the words halted her in her tracks. "I never…Hannah, I understand you want out. Believe me I understand that. But this isn't the way to do it."

"Please." Hannah rolled her eyes. "I marry him, I drop a kid, I get the hell out."

"I can't even begin to tell you what was wrong with that statement. But let's start with, one doesn't 'drop' a kid. That's exactly the kind of attitude that got us into this mess. Mom and Dad, the Wainwrights, the

McInnises…God, the only family I can think of that was happy were the Walshes. You don't want to keep the cycle going. I don't either. I want us to have happy lives."

"You're totally contradicting yourself."

"Ugh," Cece said, standing up. "I am doing this to keep you safe, Hannah. I can handle Paul."

Hannah waved her finger at her sister, threateningly. "Just because you have all those big strong friends at the——" She halted her words.

A roiling panic spread through Cece's gut. "What?"

Shaking her head, Hannah tried to dismiss what she'd just said. "Never mind."

"No." Cece was not about to drop it. "Just because I have those big strong friends at the what, Hannah?"

The guilt that Cece caught in her sister's eyes forced her to look down at her shoes. "Really, it's nothing," Hannah tried.

"It's not nothing," Cece growled.

Hannah shook her head and picked at her skirt. "Just because you have all those big strong friends at the club doesn't mean you're a wit better off than I am marrying Paul."

The chair was there to catch Cece as she stumbled back. "The Club?"

"Club Imperial. You never even knew I followed you there." She stared at her sister, and Cece wanted to answer her. But Hannah was pissed and plowed on. "And there's half the damn problem. You're sitting there telling me you're going to marry Paul because you're worried about me. You're concerned about my health. You think I can't handle myself. Chas is being cruel to me to keep me from college—but where the hell do you get off thinking that you know me at all, Frances?"

She stood from the couch and started pacing the room. "You leave me at the house. You never come to visit. You don't know me enough to know who I really am! Are you really doing this because you're worried about *me*, or are you doing this out of some sense of familial obligation?" Hannah stopped in front of her. "You don't know me. And you know who else doesn't know me? Chas. Do you know who else claims to do things for me? Chas. Do you know who else keeps throwing my disease in my face? Chas. See a pattern here?"

Cece felt the dismay from her sister knowing about the club crash into the utter horror of the truth that Hannah had just pitched at her, and came very close to throwing up. She put a hand to her mouth as a sharp pain crossed her heart.

Hannah was right. Her intensions were noble, but her methods were…well, not just flawed, but downright wrong. She couldn't claim to care about her sister when they barely saw each other. She wasn't even sure of her sister's favorite color, never mind what she thought of things like her own health and wellbeing.

Her hands shot out and grabbed her sister's. "I'm sorry, Hannah, I'm sorry. I didn't realize I was doing that. I really do honestly care about you, and your health, and I want to be your sister. I'm sorry I haven't been around more."

"When you say that, I believe you." Hannah smiled, squeezing her hand. "When Chas says it, I want to run away. Far away. Never let him have anything to do with me again." Hannah pulled Cece off the chair and on to the couch with her. "I'll tell you a secret if you tell me yours."

"My…secret?" Cece felt the nervous butterflies slamming around in her stomach.

"Oh, Cece, it's so easy to see you're freaked out by the fact that I know you go to Imperial. I want to know what you're doing in such a high class kink club. But if you want, I'll go first…"

Cece was ready to choke, but Hannah was so earnest and excited to share her secret, she knew she couldn't say no to her without crushing her and the hope for a sisterly bond with her.

And she realized, right in that moment, there were only two things that she wanted in her life: Killian and Hannah. Everything else could fall away and never be seen again, as long as she had those two things. Strangely enough, the thought seemed to unshackle her. Oh, she still wanted to play at Imperial, and she'd never give up her ropes, not as long as she had a choice, but if she had to—she could. To keep Killian and Hannah.

Cece gripped her sister's hand and patted it with the other one. "You go first."

Hannah's face burst into a grin. "I'm going to college."

"What? Where?" Genuine excitement leapt into her voice.

"I've been going." The devilish smile on Hannah was a delight. "I started two weeks before high school graduation. The trip I took to Florida this summer had nothing to do with getting a tan. I had two lab classes I could only take on site. I made it look like I was going down with a group of friends, and I totally didn't. The labs were incredible. I had to be there for eight hours a day for three weeks. I learned so much I think my brain is still working on processing all of it even four months later."

"Where are you going? Oh, my God, Hannah, I have a thousand questions!" Cece let herself laugh.

"Okay, so I'm going to the University of Florida through their online program. It's in forensic studies, and it's a five year master's program."

Her brain stuttered. "Forensics!"

"Yes." Hannah smiled. "At first I only wanted to go to piss off Chas, but now that I know what it's all about, and that I happen to love biology, I adore the program. It's amazing. Oh, Cece, I can't even put into words how cool this all is. It's all online classes, but I've made some real friends online and while I was down there. Well, all online except for the yearly labs in Florida."

"Online?" Cece knew that the U of Florida had online programs, but that her sister was taking them and pursing one of the toughest degrees that she knew off? "You're sure this is the right program for you?"

"Yes, yes!" Hannah was practically jumping on the couch. "Yes. And I have to start doing research soon. Please, Cece, let me come to the library! I want to see where you work, and I want your help writing all these papers up. I wish I could just be out and out honest about this with Mom and Dad, but I can't. Chas will pull everything. Oh!" The hand she slapped over mouth made a popping sound. "If Mom's bankrupted the family—"

"You're fine," Cece answered. "I had a friend

whose wife is a financial guru check into the financial impact of this whole thing and our trusts are safe. Yours and mine; they can't touch them because they aren't actually part of the estate."

"Whew!" Hannah slumped a little. "I thought that I might have to give up the whole charade."

Cece turned on the couch. "Hannah, even if we were so broke we didn't have a bucket to piss in, I would never tell you to stop going to school. I would lie, beg, and steal to make sure that you could go all the way through."

"Ugh! Why haven't you been around more! I need girly encouragement like this every day!"

"You don't need a lick of my encouragement, Hannah." Cece smiled. "You've made it so far without anyone's help. Put a wicked evil disease on top of that, and you're the strongest out of all of us."

"Horse shit." Hannah laughed.

"Not horse shit! True shit!"

"Ha!" Hannah stood and did a little twirl, letting out a string of swear words. "I can't do that at home, you know. A certain prick brother of ours has decided my mouth should be washed with soap if I say a swear word within his delicate hearing."

"Bullshit, he does not!"

"He does."

"Why do you let him do that?"

Hannah paused from her gleeful romp around the cottage's living room. "You don't know? You might think I'm strong, Cece, but you have to remember that forever and always I have to deal with the myasthenia. Even if the flairs and the worst of it are under control and in remission, I simply don't have a lot of strength. Weak as newborn foal. I think Dad accused me of being that one time. I have no muscle mass. I never will. Physically resisting Charles would be about as effective as pitched tent in a hurricane."

Cece grabbed her sister's hand again. "I'm sorry, Hannah, I forgot. And forgetting is a good thing. Since I now have the upper hand, I'm going to make sure he never does anything like that ever, ever again."

"Thank you." The smile was big and infectious. "You have no idea how bad soap tastes."

"Only by accident. I'm not really one to chew on bars."

"Free snack in the shower?"

Cece burst out laughing and pulled her gleeful sister back to the couch. "I wouldn't recommend that."

"But your toilet would be clean all the time."

Cece laughed even harder. "Stop!" But she couldn't because Hannah started giggling with her and before they knew it, they were both gasping for air on the couch, trying to stop laughing. When Hannah had the first hiccup, it started all over.

"Get me—" *hic* "—a drink!" Hannah managed.

Cece laughed all the way to the kitchen and back, returning with a glass of water. Hannah accepted it gratefully and chugged it. Once she let out the most unladylike belch, and pitched them into a fit of giggles again, they managed to settle on the couch again.

"That was the first time in my life I've ever had hiccups." Hannah smiled.

"What?"

"I don't, well—I didn't have the muscle strength to

ever have them. Apparently, the drugs I'm on are working well."

Cece put a hand on her shoulder. "I'm so glad I could be there for your first hiccup and belch session. You do me proud."

"It was a rather rousing belch." Hannah took another sip. "So you're up next. What on earth are you doing in a high-end kink club?"

Cece hesitated only a moment. "This is beyond secret, do you understand? It's not like your college where other people outside the family can find out. This is something I'm entrusting to you to keep utterly secret."

"Of course." Hannah's answer was off-handed.

Cece shook her head. "No."

"What do you mean? Share, share."

"I'm not being flippant." Cece folded her arms. "This isn't something I'm just going share with you sitting there seal-clapping because you get to find out a secret about me. I'm deadly serious. I need you to swear, on whatever you hold dear, that you will not share this with anyone. It has nothing to do with you liking or not liking what I tell you; it has to do with everyone else in the world. It has to do with me keeping my job, my house. Do you understand?"

Hannah settled down on the couch and she studied Cece. "You're very serious about this."

"Think about it for just a moment, Hannah. What is the place we're talking about?"

"A high-end kinky club that is really expensive and hard to get into." Cece waited for Hannah to process what she had just said. Her sister considered a moment, and nodded. "Okay. I get it. I really can't tell anyone ever."

"Well, I won't say no one ever, but for now, let's play the cards close to the chest?"

"I can do that."

"Tell me what you know about the club." Cece smirked, leaning back. "Since I'm guessing you've somehow gotten inside even though it's a twenty-one plus entrance."

"I have a really good fake ID," Hannah admitted, shrugging. "And since I have my own credit card, it was easy to get in. I've been in a few times, looking for you. I just wanted to know what you were doing there, but I've never been able to find you. It's an interesting place, with lots of things that shouldn't be going on."

"That's an interesting way to put it."

Hannah laughed. "It's fascinating. Doms and dominatrixes, whips and chains, and floggers. There are people who come in and push the limits every time I'm in there. They always get called out and told to separate and or they have to leave." She leaned forward. "Sometimes, there are people there who are…more. They don't seem like they are there to get drunk and behave badly. They are self-possessed and serious. I don't see them very often, but when one of them shows up it's…well, magnetic. People just move for them, and move around them. Most everyone turns to look when one of those people walks through the room."

"Do you know about the different levels?"

"I was asked what I wanted when I got the membership, general, VIP, or exclusive," Hannah answered. "I went for general so that I could figure the place out. I thought it would be easy to find you there with that one."

"I work there. You're not going to see me unless I want you to." Cece smiled at her.

"You work there where?" Hannah cocked her head. "I've been looking for you everywhere. I've even thought about asking for you."

"You'd still never find me," Cece said. "Do you remember my trip to Japan about four years ago?"

"Well, yes…"

"I was thrilled I got to go. It was fascinating to be able to study another culture's books and systems of learning. I adored the six months I was there. But it wasn't the only reason I went." Cece stood, motioning for Hannah to stay seated, and walked to the bedroom. She opened the closet, grabbing a gorgeous camphorwood box from the top shelf.

Trembling a little, she paused to consider the box. Most of the time she forgot the box was there, but when Cece pulled it out of its hiding place, she was always struck by its simple, natural beauty and fervently wished she could display it, at least in the bedroom if not in the public areas. The dovetail details on the corners alone were art unlike any she could find in the US. Her name, carved in *romanji* and *katakana,* scrolled across the top, along with a beautifully carved bow in a rope design.

Someone had to know, Cece reasoned. If anything ever went terribly wrong, it was important that this was either destroyed or saved. She had to learn to treat her sister as a confidant. Hannah watched her as she set the box down on the coffee table after heading back to the living room.

"Sweet Jesus," Hannah breathed. "That's gorgeous." She ran her fingers over the *katakana* letters. "Is that your name?"

"Yes," Cece said. "This was a gift from my sensei."

"Why didn't you ever show us this before?"

"Open it." The offer made Cece's stomach clench.

Hannah put a hand on either side of the lid and lifted it slowly. The hidden hinges inside guided the top up and back and held it there. Cece watched as her sister reverently ran a hand over the indescribably satin feel of the wood to the silken velvet that lined the inside.

Her sister moved her hands over the objects inside. Hannah's breath slid out quietly in appreciation. "Silk? Hand-braided rope?" Cece nodded. "A lot of it, too. A blindfold, and satin streamers." She plucked out one of the bright metal objects there. "This is an elaborate S hook. I've never seen anything as gorgeous as this." She traced the filigree set in on the ends with a tentative finger. "Steel."

"Steel," Cece confirmed.

Hannah looked over at her, twisting the hook in her hands. "This is a box of kink, isn't it?"

"Yes." Cece's heart was racing.

Slowly, Hannah's fingers wandered over the rope. "This is all usable, but you're not supposed to. This is to show your mastery of…"

"Kinbaku." Cece spoke the word quietly. "It's bondage art. My kinbakushi gave this to me when he determined that I was a master of shibari."

"Shibari?"

"Kinbaku is the correct term for the Japanese art of rope bondage, and it usually implies that there is a strong emotional tie between the nawashi—the rope artist—and the subject." Cece couldn't look at her sister. "Shibari describes the art of tying or binding, and its sexual connotation exists only in BDSM circles, even in the US. My bakushi, master, gave this box to me when I..." She paused and gathered herself to continue on. "When I mastered all the different types of bindings, and I could prove that I could cross into *semenawa*—rope torture—if I had to. But because of the kinbaku aspect of the art, I can't. Or won't. I can't torture something I have an emotional bond with."

Cece finally looked up at her sister, who was staring into the box. Reverentially, she put the hook back in its place and shook her head slowly. "Shit," Hannah breathed. Cece's heart froze until her sister spoke again. "That has got to be...unfuckingbelievably erotic to see."

Her air rushed out of her lungs. "It is. It's amazing."

"So what do you do at Imperial? I mean...I get the ropes..."

"There are people who work upstairs, with private clients, and I'm one of those." Cece finally managed to get up the guts to look at her sister, who was staring back at her enthralled. "I'm actually a Domme...uh, common parlance would call me a dominatrix. But people in the lifestyle prefer Domme."

"Lifestyle? You mean people who like kink?"

"It's called BDSM," Cece corrected her.

"Okay, fair enough, but I still don't get what this has to do with ropes."

"Some people like to be tied up. You said yourself, it's erotic. And some people really enjoy it. I enjoy it, and I enjoy doing it. When I'm at the club, I am only a *nawashi*, just a rope artist who works with others who like to feel the bindings. I don't have an emotional connection with them, but I enjoy practicing the art. So they benefit and I benefit. But I'm also the Prima Domme of the club. I'm the most expensive Mistress you can visit there."

"Expensive?"

"You snuck in, you have the policies." Cece raised an eyebrow. "I am not a working girl."

"No, no, I know, I didn't think that you were. I'm just trying to cipher this out." Hannah ran a hand over the box again. "You're expensive to…work with because you're so good at what you do. You have a special talent that is sought after. That's why you're upstairs and out of the view of everyone. That's also why you're the…Prima?"

"Yes," she answered simply. "People come to me for things that they or their spouses can't do for themselves."

"Spouses?" Hannah gasped.

Cece nodded. "That part is a little hard to get over at first, but you have to remember that some people don't want anything to do with BDSM and rope play. In a good relationship, this is discussed and the spouse who wishes to have a part in the lifestyle will seek out a way to satisfy that without breaking their marriage or relationship down. Polyamory works sometimes, other times, it's easier to come to the club and find what you need and go home." Cece smiled. "I have a client who loves his wife dearly, but she's tiny and not interested in doing the ropes. She drops him off, and after a session with me, picks him up. I caught them having sex in the car just outside the private entrance after his first time in the shibari room. He told me, the next time, that it was the first time he and his wife had sex in months. Most times now, he comes alone because he's dropped her off at a hotel room to wait for him."

"So it's a turn-on." Hannah said.

"Yes, very much so."

"And you don't get turned on?"

Cece pursed her lips. "All the time."

"But there's no sex on the premises."

"None."

Hannah looked at her. "Then what the hell do you do? I know this can't be a short and simple task to tie someone up and take them down. You've got to get frustrated."

Cece put her head in hands. "I never thought I would be talking about my sex habits with my little sister."

"What better way to get to know you, you kinky bitch?" Hannah gave her a friendly punch in the arm.

Cece laughed and considered her a moment. "Have you slept with someone?"

"Hey, my questions first," Hannah demanded. "How do you deal with the frustration?"

"I never said I got frustrated."

"Ha ha, you didn't have to. You just said that one of your clients fucked his wife in the car outside the door." Hannah laughed. "You think I don't know that runs both ways? And you can figure out my answer to your question with that question."

Cece shook her head with a smile. "Okay, fine. You've been deflowered."

"And you're still not answering my question." Hannah stuck her tongue out.

Cece rolled her eyes. "Okay, fine. In one of the intense session like that, yes. I get very frustrated. He gets to leave and screw his wife, and I don't begrudge him that. I'm left hanging." Cece raised an eyebrow. "In a matter of speaking. But I have an arrangement that the people in the club call an 'offsite'."

"With him? With the rope guy you just sent back to his wife?" Hannah was trying not to be shocked or disgusted.

"No, never. Never with a committed spouse. I don't roll that way. I don't want to give a wife or husband a chance to retaliate against me."

"Husband? Are you…bi?"

"Shibari doesn't discriminate," Cece explained. "I can appreciate a gorgeous woman in a rope art creation, but that doesn't do it for me."

"So how the hell do you take care of this problem?"

"I have someone I meet offsite. He likes ropes, I like tying him up, and untying him. And we have great sex. Like really amazing."

"So he's your boyfriend."

"No." Cece heard the regret in her own voice. "We aren't like that. We tried that arrangement for about a month before we realized there was never going to be more between us than sex and friendship. He's amazing in bed, and we really do care for each other deeply, but…it's not love…"

She was saving that part for Killian.

Jesus Christ, how was she going to handle this now? This was why she had avoided falling in love all these years.

"So you just tie him up," Hannah cut through Cece's thoughts, "schtup him and have dinner?"

"Breakfast, usually," Cece answered without thinking, and then laughed when she realized she had said it. "But yes, that's basically it. We both get what we want and need out of it. It's a good arrangement for now."

Hannah nodded and traced the swirls of the grain on the box in front of her. "Well, that kind of sucks." She looked up at Cece. "Your secret blows mine out of the water."

Cece put an arm around her sister. "Not a contest, Hannah. I feel really good about finally sharing that with someone. All my crazy club friends know all of it, but I've never told anyone who wasn't part of the club or the lifestyle."

Hannah smirked. "So I guess this means we get to be really good sisters now? Can I sleep over?"

"Do you really want to do that in the house of a kinbakushi mistress?"

She looked around and shrugged. "I could probably pick up some tips."

Chapter Nine

"**Mom would kill you** if she found you waiting on the porch for your date," Hannah said, as Cece closed and locked the door.

"This little cottage is my sanctuary." Cece pulled on the door to make sure it was locked. "I am not letting just anyone in. Including a fiancé."

"That's harsh." Hannah walked down the steps with Cece following. Hannah's peppy little Audi TT sat in the driveway, waiting for her.

"Meh," Cece answered as Hannah turned over the engine after climbing in. "I don't know him from Adam, and I won't let him into the place until I do."

Hannah rolled down the window. "Who's Adam? Your fuck buddy?"

The swat Cece gave her sister was utterly harmless. "Stop prying. Didn't you get enough info? And speaking of pissing Mom off, nice mouth."

"I have the vocabulary of a well educated sailor, sis. So fuck off kindly."

"So polite."

"Call me when this is over? I want to know how it all went." The engine revved and Cece didn't even bother to try and answer the question. With a playfully annoyed shake of the head, she stepped back from the car and watched her sister pull out of the driveway and disappear down the block.

She had really let her sister in, in a big way—and it felt good.

She wandered back up to the front porch of the house and sat on the swing. She rocked slowly as the sun started to set. Talking to Hannah had been cathartic and terrifying, with a touch of 'oh shit'-ness tossed in for good measure.

Mostly concerning what the hell she was going to do about Killian and Everett.

Killian was…what she wanted. Everything she wanted. But Everett was what she needed right now. Sex, damn good fucking sex, without a figurative strings attached. Killian knew almost nothing about her, but wanted to—clearly. Everett knew everything about her and held nothing against her.

And then there was Paul.

The car eased into the driveway, and Cece got her first glimpse of Paul Wainwright in eight years.

Holy shit.

The car was a gorgeous, perfectly restored 1965 Cherry Red Mustang, and the engine purred like a kitten. She was no car expert, but she was sure the engine had been tweaked to run quiet. The glass, the chrome, the paint was all immaculate. The wheels shined, the tires were clean and bright, and the cream leather interior looked flawless.

Paul folded himself out of the car; it was the only way to describe the motion and when he stood, she realized why. Paul was ridiculously tall, six foot five or better and built like a fucking Greek God. Broad, square shoulders clad in a casual button down shirt tucked neatly into a black pair of perfectly pressed pants that hugged a narrow waist. He had a strong, aquiline nose that shouldn't have been such a compliment to his nearly-square-jaw, but was. His eyes were big, and nearly black, and his pitch black hair was short, but so easy to see that its natural state was a loose curl.

He walked around the car, revealing plain loafers and a swaggering stride that put Jeff Goldblum to shame. Paul shoved his hands into his pockets casually and strode over slowly. He stopped at the bottom of the stairs and looked over at her.

"Hi, Cece."

His voice completed the whole package: he had a deep, smoky voice. And the whole package just reminded her of Benedict Cumberbatch.

"Hi, Paul," she answered. "You grew up since high school."

"So have you."

He cocked his head with an apologetic smile. "I'm here to woo you, apparently."

Cece couldn't stop the little laugh that escaped her, and they could both feel the tension release between them. "Woo me, eh?"

"Well, I guess technically, there's no wooing that needs done, but if this thing has to happen, why should it suck and we hate each other forever?"

Those were not the words of an abuser. Cece was instantly confused, but kept the look off her face. "I would prefer not to hate you. That would definitely be a bonus."

"So, should I come the rest of the way up, or should we head out to dinner?"

"I'm rather quite hungry." She wondered if he could

sense that she wasn't interested in asking him into her space yet. "Let's do dinner." She stood and walked over to the two steps leading off the porch and he immediately offered his hand for her to take.

She hesitated. There was no way around that, and Paul saw it. He inclined his head, politely, and dropped his hand. "Sorry. That's a little forward of me. It's habit. My momma taught me to always be chivalrous."

"I appreciate it." Cece recovered and held her hand out, palm down, in a peace offering. Paul smiled and accepted, taking her hand and helping her down the two steps.

Nothing.

Cece almost let out a blast of relieved air when nothing happened. No magic, no spark, no tingles. Nothing. Just a warm hand helping her down the steps in treacherous heels. As absolutely fucking drop dead gorgeous as this man was, she didn't feel even the remotest tingle of lust or love or desire.

"You were worried."

Cece's head snapped over to face him, and his dark eyes sparkled with humor. He was teasing and wasn't offended in the least. Nor was he surprised there was nothing in the touch. "I was, for a moment."

"We have a lot to talk about. Let's go to dinner."

He let her hand go and gestured to the car. She nodded and walked over, admiring the car a little more. He opened the door, and she sat down. He leaned on the roof and looked at her through the window. "Fully restored exterior, new leather interior, and I upgraded the entire engine. Any noise you hear is intentional. It has a brand new retrofit super efficient engine, along with

Bluetooth and navigation."

She looked up at him with a smile. "Really. I like it."

"Purrs like a kitten and sips gas like a fine wine."

"You rehearsed that."

"Over and over and over." He laughed and walked to the driver's side.

Paul Wainwright was completely unexpected.

* * *

"So, you like working in the library?"

Cece nodded and swallowed the gulp of wine. "Yes, very much so. I adore books and information and there really is a science to keeping it all organized."

"Such a librarian's answer," he teased.

"Well, I can try and give you a mechanic's answer, but I'm not very good at that."

His chuckle was delightful. Cece sipped the wine and smiled in the glass. Dinner was ending up to be a drawn out affair at a tiny little bistro she'd never even noticed before. Everything so far had been delicious, and she discovered she rather enjoyed Paul's company. He was witty, disarming, intelligent, with a dose of charm thrown in to keep her on her toes. She was really having trouble reconciling all the horror stories she'd heard about his past, the abuse, the torment, the combativeness, with the nearly perfect gentleman sitting across from her.

"What made you come back to the 'Burgh from Southern California?" Cece asked.

"I hated it there." The grimace told her a lot more than just the words could. "Everything there was plastic and pretend, and the weather was hot and dry all the time, which got terribly boring for someone who grew up loving the seasons. They didn't need another medical examiner and...well, I missed...my mother. She and I were close when I was growing up."

"You didn't exactly have the easiest childhood here, so I'm just kind of shocked you came back after you escaped."

"This city is more like Hotel California than California," he said. "You can never leave. Even when you leave on purpose in a hurry to get the hell out, you still dream about coming back and show everyone how good you're doing. But it's not about showing off or showing up. I learned what I could out there, and one day I realized I was just done. I didn't want to be there anymore. There was an opening at the coroner's office, I applied, and I got the job."

Cece played with the rim of the glass for a moment. Paul startled her by leaning forward. "Go ahead. I know you've been dying to ask me all night."

Momentarily shocked, Cece shook her head. "I don't understand?"

"The abuse charges."

"Oh." Her answer was quiet. "I guess I ought to ask if..."

"There are none," he said, cleanly interjecting himself into the pause. "There never were. There never will be. I never hit a woman. I didn't then, I won't now. Perhaps my father doesn't get that, but my mother made sure I understood. You don't lay a hand on a woman. Ever." He looked down at the beer glass he was clenching in his fists. "She wanted to break the cycle with me."

That was a revelation. Bill Wainwright abused his first wife? Did he abuse number two? "For some reason, I don't doubt you at all, Paul."

He stared at the beer, and suddenly slammed it back and finished it. He had his eyes closed as he swallowed it, and took a moment before looking back at her. "Well. Since we're here and the whole point of this is that we're in this contract together, let's discuss it, shall we?"

The bitter notes of anger were as easy to detect as the sun in the sky. He felt the same contempt for this contract as she did. In fact, she would put money down that he was even more coerced into signing onto it than she was. And her own disdain for this whole mess was definitely palpable in the room. She looked at him and nodded. "Then let's."

"What is your motivation in all of this?" It was an interesting way of starting the question.

"Motivation," Cece repeated. "My sister. Did you notice that the contract had a blank space for the first name of the Robbe girl?"

"I didn't…"

"I was given a simple choice: me or Hannah."

"Hannah?" The astonishment on his face was a shock. "Why would they ever get Hannah involved in this?"

"Hannah was the pawn," Cece explained. "You know she's medically fragile. And it was either send her to you as reputed abuser, or risk sending her out into the streets without a penny to her name and penny to her medications. I wouldn't have been able to keep her safe if I had refused to sign, and the people in my family are far less scrupulous and kind. If it hadn't been me, then it would have been Hannah sitting here. And if we had both refused, we would be sitting in a cardboard box."

Paul leaned forward and rested his head on his fist. "Interesting. I was also told I would be ruined, personally. Someone would drum up actual paperwork charges to prove I was not only an abuser but on parole, and my job would have been trashed."

Cece cocked her head. "That's a good point, really. Why has no one realized that? You couldn't possibly work where you do if you had any kind of record. Why didn't *I* realize that?"

"Most people don't stop and think about the qualifications it takes to hold a job in the coroner's office. I have a clean record, and yet people insist I have domestic abuse charges."

"And that's how they made you sign."

"Well, it's important to rein in the wild children, you know. Legacies must be continued at all costs."

"Can't lose the house, and why correct the behavior that risks it when you can just sign your wild child into indentured servitude and not have to worry about them not fulfilling obligations. Like spitting out children for the legacy."

"Lose the house?" Paul was clearly intrigued.

"That's where this end of the contract came from," Cece said. "It appears that Marjorie Robbe has a serious gambling problem and is severely underwater with the Wainwrights' OTB."

"Off-track betting," Paul corrected.

"What?" Cece stared at him hard.

"Oh, Dad has some...not quite above the table

dealings that allow people to run tabs," Paul explained. "The OTB is legit, above the board and makes millions. The other things are not on the board, or anywhere near it and he's got mob connections that help him with that."

Cece closed her eyes and put her head in her hand. "Oh, Christ. She couldn't even legally get in debt? She had to go and do this illegally?"

"So we're both in this for reasons beyond just getting a convenient marriage." Paul sat back and steepled his fingers. "I like you, Cece. I think you're a great woman, smart, sweet, and witty. But I don't think we could have a marriage that wasn't based on lies."

"Lies." Cece considered what he was saying. "There are so many already."

"Exactly." He raised an eyebrow. "So, how about we go through with this, and in the meanwhile we can try to figure out a way out that makes everyone happy? We can work on a pre-nup that gets us out no matter what."

Cece blinked a few times, thinking quietly, and realized if she was going to have Paul on her side, she was better off thinking out loud. "There's no clear way out of this right now, and I don't think there's a way we can avoid an engagement announcement because the half of the Pittsburgh that thinks it matters already knows we're in a contract. If we go through with it, we're really going to have either play enemies or trepidatious lovers."

"What if we just played jaded socialites?" he suggested.

"Jaded socialites?" Cece laughed. "That's not even playing."

Paul nodded with a smile. "That's true."

"I guess that's the easiest way to go, really," Cece said. She looked up at him sitting there and sighed. "I hate this, you know. All this fake pageantry and false relationships. It's why I'm out of my parents' house. It's why I haven't publicly dated anyone in years. I don't want it, I want to go to my library and enjoy my books and clean my little cottage and have everyone leave me alone."

"I tried to get away from all of it, but I moved to another plastic world." Paul sighed. He looked at her. "You're not going to be offended if I say I don't want to marry you."

"Not at all." She shook her head. "I am not really in a place in my life to get married either."

"I will have a friend get on the pre-nup that guarantees our freedom in two years, and we both walk away with equal assets," he offered.

"Two years." She arched a brow. "Separate bedrooms?"

He laughed. "Is there any other way?" After a pause, he narrowed his eyes. "Do you have someone?"

Cece looked at her wine glass. "In mind, yes."

Paul quirked an eyebrow. "Just mind?"

"Do you really want me to answer that? Isn't this whole thing going to be uncomfortable enough as it is? I won't make a mockery of marriage by cheating on you even if this is sham marriage. It's disregarded and rendered moot enough as it is. What I want with someone someday is better served by not acting the ass the first time around."

The expression on his face was astonished;

apparently he'd been of a mind to fuck around with whomever they saw fit. She wasn't going to be part of that. Killian had changed her mind on that. The whole point of this arrangement was to get out of the arrangement with her dignity in tack. She was a goddamn kinbakushi, and she would not dishonor that by cheating on even a false husband.

"You're serious."

"Deadly." Cece nodded.

Christ, the money she was going to use on batteries.

"All right," Paul agreed. "It'll be motivation for us to stop this before it gets that far."

Cece felt the astonishment on her face. She hadn't even considered the possibility that Paul had someone he'd want to see. She shook her head, heading back neutral. "If you'll agree to it, we'll make the pre-nup a year. I don't much feel like waiting years and years to see if we can get out of this and into the lives we want."

"Agreed. I'll have my lawyer on it tomorrow." He reached into his pocket. "I don't want to sully what should someday be amazing for you, but I know people will wonder if you don't have a ring. I had planned to be more elaborate, but...simplicity seems to be our common ground." The black velvet box sat under his hand and he slid it across the table. Lifting his hand, he pushed it just the last little distance. "I know it's not the romantic gesture that all girls dream of, but I don't want to take that away from your secret paramour."

Cece stared at the box. For some reason, she knew that opening this box was going to make it far more real than signing a piece of paper. She slowly reached for and pulled it over to her. Carefully, and with a huge measure of disbelief, Cece opened the top of the black velvet box.

The ring was gorgeous, a perfect princess solitaire. It sparkled in the dim light of the bistro and was almost too pretty to actually wear.

"I feel like a fraud." The words came barely a whisper, and worse, she wanted someone else to give her this ring. She wanted Killian sitting there across from her, even if it was the unromantic gesture that this was.

"I'm sorry," Paul whispered back, grabbing her hand before she went any further. "But, Cece. We're in this together. And together, I think we can get out."

"You might as well just collar and leash me," she stated and stared at him dead in the eye. It was a double edge sword, that statement. She wanted to see his reaction. If they wound up married, there was no way he wouldn't find out about the Club.

"I'd rather think of this as a pretty manacle," he answered. "One that we both have the key to, and we can both unlock when the time comes."

The diamond sat sparkling in the box. There was no way to avoid this, not if she wanted her sister safe and healthy and able to make her own decisions about life and love. Temporary, Cece reminded herself. Paul didn't want this either. And he wasn't nearly the monster everyone had made him out to be.

She lifted the ring out of the box and slipped it onto her finger. Her brain supplied the sound of a jail door being shut, but she knew she was being overly dramatic. Both of them weren't going to be in this forever. They had a purpose and reason for this, and together they could get their goal accomplished and get out of the marriage without irreparable damage.

Paul slipped his hand into hers, looking at the ring. "It does look good there, Cece."

"It's a beautiful ring, Paul."

"Hardest substance on the planet." He smirked. "Kind of like our will to see this out?"

The grin Cece couldn't contain was completely genuine. "Absolutely."

CHAPTER TEN

CECE WALKED AROUND HER CREATION. Mister Smith was bound up, blindfolded, and trussed in wonderfully magical knots she had been anxious to use after the week she'd had. He was suspended and was breathing slowly, just as he ought to be. He was completely in subspace, and Cece realized he was one of the few clients she had who really sought this place out, sought out his subspace. This John Smith was meant to be dominated by rope.

She stopped near his blindfolded eyes and leaned into him. She spoke soft so she would not pull him out of his subspace. "Mister Smith, thank you for this. It is a rare man who can truly find the ability to let go of everything and let the ropes control the moment."

"Mistress." His answer was quiet, reverential, and the one word carried all the thanks she needed.

There was a drink waiting for her on the sideboard near her Queen Anne chair. She sat down and picked up the glass of white wine, considering the low candlelight through the pale liquid. Only a week and she felt oddly naked without the engagement ring. Sipping the wine, she placed it back down on the sideboard and noticed the envelope there. Address to her, Dusty Rose Milan, in precise, male hand writing. The flap wasn't sealed, so she opened it and unfolded the paper.

Mistress,

Through these last few months I have greatly enjoyed our time together. Your talent for shibari has made me a very satisfied man, pleasant and calm. Many of my friends have commented on how much more agreeable I am.

I would however request a discussion with you about the possibility of meeting you in an arrangement offsite. I find myself more and more drawn to you. I know this is a forward request, but I can't help feel that our mutual pleasure would be better reached alone where we could be unfettered by the contracts that make Club Imperial able to operate.

My time is your time; I would ask that at least you inform me that you received this letter and have decided not to pursue my suggestion.

Humbly and Sincerely Yours,
John Smith

Cece sipped the wine and read the letter again. Her entire body hummed the yes she wanted to shout, but her mind kept her in the chair swirling the wine in the glass. Placing the letter on the sideboard again, she sat back in the chair and looked over at the man she'd intricately woven into the suspended creation. It was hard to keep herself under control as she wound the jute ropes around his more than supple and well-defined body.

It wasn't the right thing to do. But there was a good chance that she was going to have to play the part of the faithful wife. She hadn't thought to ask Paul if they were going to stick to the game *before* they were married.

She didn't even want to ask. This was going to break Everett once the ban went into effect. She shouldn't be considering this either. Still there was something about this man she couldn't get out of her head. He had never spoken except when spoken to, except for the very rare occasional request. She could imagine him writhing beneath her, finally getting to touch that body with abandon.

Cece could also hold out a hope that once they were together, there would be no sexual chemistry and it would be a one-time thing.

You are fooling yourself, sweetheart. The only thing she wanted more than John in her bed, was Killian. And Killian was a whole other category at this point. Since she couldn't have Killian the way she really wanted, maybe taking up an arrangement with John was the right way to go. Even if it was a short term.

The suspended body there breathed evenly, and Cece watched, enjoying the easy rhythm he had fallen into. The ropes didn't swing at all, they merely trembled as he pushed the air in and out. The delightful subspace he was in brought a calm to the room that Cece had hoped for. She needed the peace, the feeling of floating after the week she'd had.

The wine lasted nearly half an hour, without a sound from John. Once she finished it, she pressed a small call button, to alert the bartender on duty that she was going to need the usual water and Gatorade for her client, and another glass of wine for her. She considered John for another moment, then stood and walked to the creation of which he was the centerpiece. Her words were whisper quiet as she spoke next to his ear. "I'm going to start to release you, John. We'll talk about your letter."

It wasn't hard to miss the twitch inside his briefs. Cece smiled to herself. She knew that his cock was usually very hard the whole time he was in the ropes, but it was the first time she'd seen his clearly impressive length stir.

Her body responded in kind, and a long deep breath was needed to center and calm herself. She walked to where she had fastened the last of the rope and unbound it. The jute wasn't as deliciously soft and satiny as the braided silk, but John had asked for the jute. It was stiffer and left stronger marks in the skin. She slowly worked her creation backward, untying and unbinding John. He knew when to put his foot down, when to support himself with his hand. She had seen very few other men with such control and understanding of their body.

It took Cece just over half an hour to release John from the ropes. She hadn't even heard the bartender come in and leave the drinks in the room, she'd been so deep in her own Domspace. Cece removed the blindfold that was part of his mask and John walked, steady as a rock over to the settee in the corner. He lowered himself carefully down and Cece offered him the Gatorade.

As much as she could manage to remain composed, Cece walked to her own chair and sat down. Her body was humming with desire; she had tried to stay detached while binding him, but it wasn't working. She didn't understand what it was about this mystery man that attracted her so much, that made her entire body thrum.

She glanced over to where John reclined on the couch. He had pulled on the usual hoodie, pulled up, hiding even the mask he was wearing. It was still an odd thing, his mask. She wondered why he had to hide, but Cece knew she'd never find out unless he chose to reveal himself and his motivations.

"Do you need anything, Mister Smith?" She tossed the casual question over her shoulder.

"No, Mistress." His answer was quiet in his gravelly, oddly sexy voice.

Cece waited a moment, taking a sip of the wine. She turned in the chair so she could see him on the settee, sipping the Gatorade. His eyes were closed as he sipped slowly. She finally decided the full-headed mask resembled one a ninja would wear.

"I wish to discuss your letter, Mister Smith." She saw his eyes open slowly. He was wearing colored contacts, to make his eyes blue. He didn't say anything, but looked at her with equal parts odd interest and submission—letting her know he was waiting for her to broach the subject.

He was so deliciously obedient.

"I am curious about where you heard of these arrangements."

John didn't race into an answer. "They were mentioned in passing while I was waiting for the Mistress one night."

"Inside these walls." Cece nodded, relieved it wasn't common knowledge. "What makes you interested in something like this with me? Or that I would be interested in such?"

"A feeling," he answered briefly. "I have found

myself fantasizing about your ropes, and I would adore the chance for an occasional encounter to be unfettered by Club rules." He sipped the drink again and let his eyes close. "I feel Mistress's frustration at the end of our sessions."

"That is not of your concern," Cece said, quietly.

"I wish it to be." It was a strong statement. "Mistress is able to deliver such pleasure to me, and I wish to be allowed to give her just as much in return."

Cece felt her heated sex surge at the suggestion. She forced herself to still and took a sip of the wine again. "And what of your mask, Mister Smith?"

"Regretfully, it would have to remain. I cannot yet take that chance."

She studied him, with his eyes now downcast, and hand wrapped around the bottle. She knew what was under the hoodie. She was intrigued by everything about him. But she shouldn't be thinking about this. There was no way she should be entertaining this. There were too many complications and too many aspects of this that could go wrong.

Cece didn't know where Paul stood on the matter of a fling before the wedding. And there was Everett—she knew he wouldn't really care one way or another, but she wasn't going to abandon him until she had no choice.

The strongest of her arguments against this was Killian. She knew Killian was off limits no matter how much she wanted him, or how much he wanted her. She wanted nothing more than to give all of this up and be with him alone. But Cece couldn't deny that she loved sex. She loved being in control and to have so perfect a submissive in her reach was temptation she wasn't sure she wanted to pass up. If Killian came to her tomorrow and said he was hers and hers alone, she would walk away. But that wasn't going to happen.

Despite all of that she found herself wanting to agree to this. At a level she'd never experienced before—she was drawn to this man, sucked in and pulled under. She was a Domme and she shouldn't feel this way. But, here it was.

"And what is your suggestion for an arrangement?" Cece found herself saying.

"Just once a month, Mistress," he said. "I would be there ahead of time to make sure that the room was ready and I was fully prepared. I would make all payment arrange—"

"No," Cece stated. "If this is to happen, I will make all payment arrangements."

"Mistress—"

"That's the way this works with me, Mister Smith." Her words were biting. "I am not going to have you pay so I'm your whore for the night."

His head tipped lower. "I wouldn't imply such, Mistress."

Cece sipped the wine once more. "I agree, Mister Smith. Once a month in a hotel of my choice. You will call the office here for the name of the hotel. The hotel will be holding your keycard for you and you will be ready in the room by eight p.m. I will not spend the night. There is no cuddling. The point of this is a total power exchange outside of the confines of this room. And, Mister Smith, there will be protection."

"I would never presume, Mistress," he answered.

She could hear the delight in his voice that she agreed to his proposal.

"What day would you suggest for this, John?"

He kept his eyes down. "I admit that I am anxious, Mistress, and would like to suggest next Friday."

Cece shook her head. "Not possible, I have a previous engagement. I would offer up Sunday as an alternative."

She watched him as he took a few breaths. Cece figured he was thinking about his calendar and trying to figure out if it was clear. He answered a moment later. "Sunday is agreeable, Mistress."

"Good." She smiled and stood. "Then you will rest here until you are ready to go. You will call the office on Monday and they will give you the name of the hotel. I will be there at eight o'clock. I am not responsible if you're not ready, John. If I walk in and your mask is off, I will not be turned off, turned away or deterred from our charted course."

"Of course, Mistress." He bobbed his head in ascent. "I look forward to it."

She gave him just a hint of her anticipation. "As do I, John. Good night."

"Good night, Mistress," he answered quietly.

Cece walked out of the room and headed to the locker room. She needed to get away. She was more than thrilled he had made the proposition, but she really wished that her mind wasn't so fucked up about everything going on. There was so much to think about and so much to do.

The locker room provided a temporary sanctuary from everything fluttering and flickering around on the top floor. Saturday night was incredibly busy, and looking at her schedule, she didn't have anyone else on the list. Technically, she could go home. But since Tessa had stepped down, it was her job now to make sure that everything with the ladies went well. She shared the duty with Darcy L'amour—Peter, in everyday parlance. He would keep the guys in line and well provided for as she would do for the women. Darcy was the most fiercely tender Dom she'd ever met, and she knew that's why he was the Prime Sir.

Sitting on the bench for a moment, allowing herself to just fall completely out of her club character, she lay back on the bench and stared up at the ceiling. It wasn't getting any easier to juggle life and her secret passions, as well as now a fiancé, a paramour, and a forbidden relationship—and all the while pining for another man entirely.

"Tough night?"

Cece picked up her head. Amaryllis was standing there, smirking at her. She put her head back down. "Ever have so much on your mind that your head feels like it's going to explode?"

"Oh yeah." She nodded and sat down on the bench at Cece's head. "You should come with us on Friday night."

"I have something to do on Friday," she answered.

"We're not leaving until ten," Amaryllis said. "You really should come with us. It's Emmy's Bachelorette."

"They got it together?" Cece was surprised.

"Yes!" Amaryllis said. "We're going to Downbound."

"Oh, *Wisconsin* put it together."

Amaryllis laughed. "No, Ally did. But I think Dee and Luscious had something to do with it. They are all going. Come with us? Please? The whole idea is a vanilla night out."

"That actually sounds like a blast," Cece answered.

"We're all going by our real names and we're not allowed to wear anything suggestive or club-y. No frou-frou drinks, no toys, nothing. Totally vanilla." Amaryllis pushed her shoulder playfully. "Come with us. It's going to be a blast."

Cece smiled. "Yes. If you're not even leaving until ten, I can do that."

"Yeay! That's like ten people by now. Tessa is going to have a blast! Promise to help us get her plastered?"

"It's not a party if the party girl isn't drunk."

"Sweet!" Amaryllis smiled and looked at her watch. "Client. Gotta go." She popped off the bench and headed for the door.

"Ama," Cece called.

"Yeah, Dusty?"

"Everything good?"

"Very good," Amaryllis said. "Thank you for asking, Prima. Talk to you later."

Even if Killian knew about the club, even if he turned out to be into the kink, how was she ever going to give this place up? How was she going to walk away from the camaraderie? These were her friends. This place had gotten under her skin; she didn't want to give it up.

CHAPTER ELEVEN

THE MOST DIFFICULT PLACES TO WATCH were the houses and dungeons. By nature, they were far more secretive than the ostentatious presence of Club Imperial, lording over the Monongahela.

Pittsburgh was home to more than a dozen dungeons—for those who wished to take the risks and needed the harder pleasures Franz Dorn wisely forbade on his property—and just a handful of houses. Houses were not nearly as off-the-grid as the dungeons. They were meant to be found by those who were truly looking.

The best of these was Darien Thompson's "Wanderer's End". A strict, well-run, well-appointed, clean house, Darien welcomed the myriad of men and women who defined sex and love outside the cultural norms. An impeccable Dom himself, he could read his students—Doms and subs—with great aplomb and stop troubles before they started.

The house sat miles outside of the center of the city, safely tucked away on a large plot of land. Darien was the newest House Master, having inherited it from George Franklin, who had trained both him and Franz Dorn in that very house. Dorn opted to go more public, and Thompson to stay more low key.

Dorn's lifestyle was more easily acceptable by

the public. Thompson's was not.

Darien had taken good care of the legacy he was handed. He was the ultimate House Master; his judgment on who should and shouldn't be let in the door was flawless. He could tell in just days who would make it through the house and who wouldn't. He knew that rejecting someone from his house could devastate their whole psyche. His house was a wonderful mélange of pleasure and pain meted out as needed.

Should someone appear who needed a firmer hand, who sought a visceral reaction, he would send them to Bella Donata's Sadique House, south of the city—she was merciless and SM almost exclusively. She catered to the extremes, to the people who craved pain. Vanity, Sabrina Worchester, was one of those.

If someone appeared who needed a softer hand, who was seeking more the pleasure of the flesh, more the gentle and tender ministration with a firm punishment being no greater than a moment of fleeting pain, Darien bundled them off to Luc Pollard's Surrender Estate. He trained the most delicate of submissives and the most genteel of Doms, male and female. Luscious, Lisa Grzynski, had been one of the first he sent to Luc.

Wanderer's End, though, was a combination of both the Surrender and Sadique mentalities. Pleasure and pain combined there, and Darien enjoyed all of it. He had long ago accepted that he was more than bisexual; he was, as the best word he himself could find, pan-sexual. He enjoyed women, men, both, several. He could be alpha, he could also submit. He enjoyed everything and anything that had to do with sex and the BDSM lifestyle.

Darien took greatest pleasure in helping others find their way through the lifestyle. He was always slightly sad when he had to send a promising student to the other houses, but he knew they would reap the most benefit elsewhere.

Killian McInnis appeared at the door one day at seventeen years old. Darien knew who he was and gave him no leeway. He was made to crawl into the house as all other seeking asylum there were made to do. Killian spent two weeks there at first. Then every weekend thereafter for six months, learning to be a submissive. The day he was to be collared, Darien took him aside and explained to him that he wasn't meant to be submissive. He had to do the training to learn what it was. He was meant to be a Dom.

It was another two weeks there, and then six months of weekends. And Darien had every intention of having Killian as his assistant—until Killian announced his intention to be a doctor.

What drove Killian to Wanderer's End was still a mystery. While others who had been there—Franz, Jemma, Amaryllis, Rachelle, Darcy, Lucious—were easy to assess, Killian ultimately didn't have an obvious reason. He simply wanted the lifestyle. Which was the best reason of all to seek out a training house.

For the years of his pre-med degree, Killian

was there two and three nights a week. He had perfect grades, and his clients and trainees adored him. But as he got closer to med school, it became more and more apparent that he couldn't keep up his grades and his position. So the position at the house started to slide. And eventually, Killian decided that he didn't need to be a Dom anymore. He needed to be a doctor.

That would have worked, save for the murder of his father.

It took a horrible tragedy in his life to give someone who was natural at the lifestyle a reason to use the lifestyle for more than it had ever needed to be to him. Not only had he come roaring back as a powerful Dom, but he was again, someone Darien wanted to consider as a new House Master.

Darien knew it was a losing proposition. Once Killian's life started to straighten out, he would once again slide from the house and concentrate on being a part of life.

"You're lost in thought again, love," the Hunk said, curling into the couch.

"How is it that someone your size can manage that?" the Watcher asked.

"It's all you."

"Are you going to be okay with this arrangement?"

"Not even remotely," the Hunk answered honestly. "No one is. No one aside from the Robbes who get to keep their estate and their name."

"You mean…"

"The Wainwrights are risking a lot by agreeing to it, too," the Watcher said. "Risking exposing all that underground money they are raking in. But they want the son married off."

"It disgusts me how all these families trade children like Pokemon cards," the Hunk said.

"The younger generation doesn't really want anything to do with it," the Watcher said. "It will stop soon."

"Not soon enough," the Hunk answered. "Just like—"

"Don't say it," the Watcher cut him off. "Just don't say it. It's not worth mentioning again."

"Someday."

"Someday is not now," the Watcher stated. "Everything is falling apart in order to fall together later. Let's hope that this all works out."

* * *

Pulling his shirt sleeve straight one last time, Killian walked into the room and found his student was already waiting. Her posture was perfect and her clothing correctly lacking. He had read up on this one: Bethany, a young professional who worked in the regional office for a nationwide insurance company. She was there at her request prompted by the revelation that she and her husband wanted a far more than just silk scarves in the bedroom.

Darien had told him that she was nearing the end of her training, and she was just about ready to go back to her husband, who had been training with another Dom in another house. *Wise.* Having them in different houses.

The more varied the experiences they brought back, the more fun they would have in the bedroom.

"Good evening, Bethany." Killian closed the door.

"Good evening, Sir." She was quiet and demure.

"Stand up, go over to the wall," Killian directed. "Put your hand out and brace against it, feet apart." He wasn't going to waste any time getting down to the nitty-gritty. He had limits he wanted to test right away.

Bethany complied easily and glided ethereally to the wall. He watched her as she assumed the correct position immediately. The tiny boyshorts she wore clung to her delicious, firm ass and Killian had to hold in a sigh. He'd glimpsed the gorgeous, full breasts as she had moved over to the wall, and her curves were generous and well defined.

All he could think about was Cece.

The tallboy in the corner was filled with a large collection of instruments and toys, and Killian pulled the doors open. "This evening's pleasure, Bethany, will be the flogger."

"Thank you, Sir." Her answer was breathy and soft. He could hear the desire in her voice and it made him smile. This woman was going to make her Sir very happy when they were reunited. He pulled out the flogger that would have more thud to it, creating a deeper sensation in her.

"What is your safe word, Bethany?" Killian already knew the answer, but he always took the precaution of having his subs repeat the word for safety.

"Edelweiss, Sir," she supplied.

"Good girl," Killian lauded. "You will count for me. I'm going to give you ten light strikes to warm you up.

Then as long as you don't feel the need to give the safeword, we'll go on from there." She thanked him again, and Killian walked over to where she stood with her ass presented to him. He ran a hand softly over the curve of her back and found himself immediately comparing the texture of her skin to Cece's.

Damn.

He stepped back just a little and brought the flogger down on her tender flesh with very little serious force. She called out the number, and Killian set his mind to the task at hand as best he could. The ten light strikes went by in a flash, even with his caresses between to make sure that he was warming her up properly.

"Very good, Bethany," he praised after number ten. He walked back to the tallboy and pulled out two more objects: a solid steel butt plug and a bottle of lube. "Tell me, Bethany, how is your tolerance to anal play?" Again, the question was a formality.

"I very much enjoy it, Sir."

"Good girl," he praised. "We're not done with the flogger yet, but I'm going to take this up a notch for you. Slip the panties down and stand braced against the wall."

"Yes, Sir. Thank you, Sir."

She wriggled the boyshorts down, and her lightly pinked ass was bare to him. It really was a glorious ass. He slid his hand over her and smacked a cheek hard, causing her to draw a hard breath. Killian took a drop of lube and ran it over her puckered entrance. Her reaction was a delighted shiver. She didn't just enjoy it—her pussy was soaked and he could see her wetness on her thighs.

So wonderfully responsive. He slipped a finger inside and he heard her stifle a groan. He slipped back out, and this time entered with two fingers. Bethany couldn't stop her delighted sounds this time. Killian withdrew again and cleaned his fingers with a wipe from the nearby table. He took the plug and coated it liberally with lubricant. "This is steel, dear girl, and I haven't warmed it. You are *not* allowed to come."

"Sir!" she gasped.

"Control has been one of your weaknesses, Bethany. There will be punishment if you come."

"Yes, Sir. Thank you, Sir."

Killian was pleased; her protest had quickly shrunk back. He stepped back to her and placed the plug against her dark entrance. She didn't flinch, and Killian pressed forward. Her body was willing, accepting the plug easily. He moved slowly. She had to learn better control of her orgasms. Bethany's breath rushed out and he heard her quiet, "Sssshit," on the breath. He smiled to himself.

He pressed forward and buried the whole toy inside her. He watched her hands curl into fists and she threw her head back. "Oh *fuck,*" she hissed.

But she didn't come.

"Good girl, Bethany," he praised, petting the firm backside. "Take a moment where you are and let yourself adjust." His request was twofold. He needed her body to adjust, and he needed her to back down from her orgasm. She was dangerously close and he wanted her to finish with the flogger.

He let her rest there, walking to the side board and pouring himself two fingers of scotch over the whiskey cubes. Darien always had the best of everything in his rooms; this drink was no exception. Killian swirled the warm brown liquid to cool it and took a sip. He let the hot fire of the cold alcohol burn down his throat and swirl into his stomach.

Killian wanted this woman to be Cece. He wanted to take that gorgeous, brave creature, tie her up and make her surrender to him, take away her thoughts, free her from all the burdens she carried. He wanted to drive his cock deep in her pussy and listen as she screamed his name, again. Feel her come around him, squeezing and pleading for his seed, and giving her every pleasure she could ever desire.

He grunted. So that was apparently the only way his dick wanted to play tonight. No appreciation for the beautiful, able body right here, right in front of him. Just the thought of Cece's hot core.

Killian took the flogger in hand again and walked back to where Bethany was leaning. "Are you ready, dear girl?"

"Please, Sir," she breathed.

"You will take no less than ten hits before you come," he directed.

"Thank you, Sir."

Killian pulled back and released the leather strands on her, all of them clumping just so as they flew through the air and found their target on her ass. The hit, he knew, impacted the plug as well, moving it inside with erotic purpose. "Oh, *God,* one," she managed to gasp. Killian did like the sounds Bethany made.

With each passing thrash of the flogger, he was a little less sure he should be at Wanderer's End anymore.

Bethany and her husband understood and agreed to the polyamory that this training entailed. They more than understood it, they welcomed it. It seemed to be pulling them closer together. As he helped this woman discover her full sexual range, he started to doubt his own place. Just because he was open to polyamory didn't mean that Cece was. Just because he was willing to flex the rules of traditional relationship didn't mean that she was.

Killian held a deep hope that somehow Cece would let him show her this side of his personality. She knew about his bear in the bed, and judging by the holes in the wall, rather enjoyed the whole mating ritual. But would she be willing to subject herself to his will completely, if only for a few hours?

Cece was fiercely independent, he knew that. Could she surrender just long enough to let him show her all that he was capable of? All that *she* was capable of?

Bethany was panting hard, her hands clenched at the wall. Killian's flogger hit his mark again, and she called out, "Ten! *Fuck.*" He watched her carefully as he brought the flogger down for number eleven, and surprising him, she didn't come. She called out the number. He was impressed; this was what they had been working toward all along. Control. He repeated the motion, and again, she called the number.

She made it twice more before she screamed her climax. He caught her by the waist before she collapsed to the floor, shaking from the stimulation and overwhelming orgasm. He picked her up and laid her on the bed, his hand finding her clit in the soaked folds of her pussy and gentling her down. His feather light touch seemed to help tremendously, and he saw her regaining herself. Killian cupped her softly, trapping her heat against her and waited.

He wasn't sure anymore.

"Sir?" Bethany's voice was quiet.

"Yes, dear girl?"

"Who is she?"

Killian stuttered. "Who is who?"

"Your flogger was not for me tonight, Sir."

Killian smiled at her. "You are perceptive, pet."

Bethany's tiny hand fluttered over his engorged cock tucked inside his pants. "She drives you, Sir."

"This is not about me, Bethany."

"And this is not about me either," she stated, stroking him tenderly. "I know I am nearly done with my training here, Sir. I proved that just now." She looked at him, and the adoration for him was breathtaking. "I want to taste you one more time, Sir. Your thick cock on my tongue. Please. Imagine I am whoever you wish me to be, but let me taste you one more time."

She slid down his body, and he was rendered in two. The Dom who was usually so in control had lost some of that, and the doctor who was so in love—yes, *love*— with Cece had gained a measure. The Dom would never hesitate to take his dear girl up on her offer, she had an extremely talented mouth, but the doctor couldn't stop thinking about Cece, about all she was, each curve on her body, the shape of her lips.

Before his brain could register a real protest, Bethany had pulled his pants out of her way, and had her lips around his straining shaft. She licked and sucked him as though she'd never had anything finer. He put his fingers on his her chin and lifted her face to stare into her eyes. "You are no one but Bethany to me, dear girl. I would not cheapen either of you by imaging you to be my someone else."

She closed her eyes and took as much of him in her mouth as she could. Her black hair floated around her like a dark crown as she worked him up and down. She had come to them exquisitely talented and it was a random bedroom event that brought the couple in. Killian had delightfully trained her, and until this very night, thought that he would miss her mouth desperately when she finally finished her training.

Bethany's little hand traveled from where she held the base of his cock to the heavy purse of his sac, and squeezed him. His mind stuttered, and he smiled. She was so good at this, he did not want to sully her or Cece. This was purely for the satisfaction of having an incredible blow job; Cece was connection on another level.

Bethany's finger trailed back down his thick flesh to the sensitive bridge before the dark entrance. She pressed on him, softly, then harder and his entire body wound up and he grew harder and with perfect timing, Bethany slipped her digit inside him.

"Oh, shit, good girl," he breathed. "Good girl. Do you want me in your mouth, Bethany?"

She wagged her head yes, without ever losing her rhythm over his cock. She drew him deeper and deeper with each plunge, and he felt himself hitting the back of her throat. "Second finger, dear girl. Finish me." She withdrew from him for just a moment and he felt the second finger join the first a moment later, and with a push at the same time she swirled her tongue around him, pulling him into her mouth the deepest yet, Killian came. He spilled the hot ropes of come into her willing mouth, and he felt her swallow each and every drop that his body gave her.

She laved him carefully and smiled at him. "Thank you, Sir. For everything. My husband and I are so much stronger now for yours and Master Owen's tutelage."

"Come, lie down, dear girl," Killian said, rearranging himself and tucking his shirt back in. She obeyed, unquestioningly. He rolled her over and reached for the creams after cleaning her fingers. He took hold of the plug and leaned down. "You may come."

"Thank you, Sir."

And come she did, hard, as he removed the plug. Bethany had proved to be excitingly sexual and responsive to some of the slightest touches. Killian massages the soothing, cooling cream into her backside, but he could see there would be bruising—and he smiled.

"Are you going to let your husband collar you, dear girl?" he asked.

"I've asked him to, yes," she answered. "I want to be his alone."

"You are his, Bethany," Killian said. "The collar is a formality. A beautiful public formality. As are most symbols in our society." He put a little more ointment on. "I was impressed by your control tonight, dear girl. There is no reason for us to continue. I will inform Darien that you are ready to graduate from his house."

Bethany flipped over and grabbed his hand. "Thank you, Killian. Thank you. For everything." She kissed his knuckles carefully. "I hope whoever she is, she knows what she's getting when she finally lets you catch her."

Killian smiled. He knew, that just like him, Cece was already caught. They just had to figure out how to get out of the tangled net they were in.

* * *

Darien chewed on the end of this cigar. "You're sure."

"Very," Killian answered. "She followed direction without question and challenged herself to withhold after I gave her permission."

"Well, then." Darien laid the cigar in the ashtray and walked over to where the now more modestly dressed Bethany was kneeling. He leaned down and unbuckled the collar she had on. "You are no longer required to wear that here, Bethany. You are done with your training, and are hereby free to seek a Dom who will earn your submission." He smiled. "I have a feeling you'll have to go no further than your bedroom at home."

Killian offered a hand, and Bethany took it to stand. "I hope you don't mind, but I took the liberty of calling Edward for you. He'll be here in a few minutes to pick you up."

Bethany leaned in and kissed his cheek. "Thank you." She offered the same to Darien with a similar chaste kiss. "We will not be strangers. I swear."

"Of course you won't," Darien said. "We have the dungeon rooms."

Bethany laughed, and Killian was delighted by the sound. So very different from the timid mouse who had come in so many month ago. One of Darien's pets appeared in the door. "Sir, Miss Bethany's ride is here."

Bethany's face burst into a grin and she walked to the door with an incredible smile. The door opened before she could reach it, and her husband walked in. She gasped and instantly dropped to her knees in submissive position. Edward smiled and reached down to take her elbow, helping her stand. "Hello, love. While I appreciate your submission, what I really want is your mouth."

Killian watched the effect of the words on his dear girl, and the smile that spread across her face was wonderful.

CHAPTER TWELVE

"WILL YOU STOP," EMMY COMMANDED.

Cece hid her laugh behind her hand as Lisa settled instantly at Emmy's word. Nadine let out a breath as did Amaryllis and Lacey—*no you're outside the club,* Cece chided herself—Chantal and Heather. Ally snorted and stuck her tongue out at her sister. "Told'ja." Emmy returned the gesture. It was funny to see the two sisters acting like Cece and Hannah had started to act. A relief, too, to know they were on the right track.

Cece was seated with the group around one of the reserved tables at the back of the club. Allison and Morgan had managed to get the whole thing together, as promised. It was nowhere near the typical bachelorette party. She liked the idea, really: they were at a regular club like regular girls celebrating a regular party. Emmy was having a blast, even if she'd had to call Lisa to heel.

The whole group of women popped with excitement, which was affecting the over hyper Lisa. Emmy was trying to stare her down to keep her under control, but when Morgan had told all of them they were going to go backstage later, that was the end of her.

One of the waiters came over with eight mugs of beer and put them all down. He had two extra mugs, full of root beer, for Nicole and Allison. "Courtesy of the band, ladies."

"Nice!" Chantal grabbed hers right away. "You

always get free beer here?"

"Nick usually has a standing tab." Morgan grabbed her beer. "Oliver takes it right out of the box take, so I try not to abuse it."

"I still cannot believe you are dating Nick D," Rachelle said.

"I am, and I have trouble believing it myself." Morgan chugged a bit of the dark liquid. "But it sure is fun. And he's hot."

"That he is," Lisa agreed.

"How's that whole threatening message thing going?" Emmy asked.

Cece looked at Morgan. It was common knowledge in the club that she and Lisa had been getting ridiculous amounts of threatening messages. Franz had put extra precautions in after Emmy's attack, and it seemed like he had doubled it again when the messages to Morgan and Lisa started. She really didn't blame him; Wisconsin—*tsk! No Club names!*—Morgan had shown her a few of them when she had taken a shift upstairs at the Tribute bar. They were unkind, to say the least.

"Let's see. I've gotten forty-nine threatening messages in the past three days. Lisa?"

"I'm up to fifty-two!" She scrolled through the phone. "Oh, wait! Look! I just got another email. That's fifty-three." She rolled her eyes and put the phone back in her purse.

Cece leaned forward and smiled at Lisa. "How is the new do—uh, boyfriend?" They had all agreed to keep most of the talk about the club and lifestyle to a minimum around Nicole and Allison.

She saw Lisa rub her wrist unconsciously as she

smiled broadly. "I had no idea what I was missing out on with Dominic. It is so wonderful to have someone who knows what they are doing and isn't a macho asshole about it."

"Long term?" Emmy asked.

"Nah," she said. "It's fun, but I don't see him as a forever kind of guy. I'm looking for more of a twenty-four-seven kinda guy. He's more like a fuck buddy."

"Can you have a fuck buddy?" Allison's question was hilariously innocent.

"It's more common in the lifestyle than anywhere else," Cece answered. She blanched and looked at Nicole, who had a hand over her laugh, and Allison, who was just batting her eyelashes at everyone. Cece grimaced and apologized. "Whoops. Sorry."

Emmy squirmed a bit and looked distinctly uncomfortable talking about her lifestyle. That was a first, as Cece had taken over her Prima Domme title from the woman. Emmy rolled her eyes and explained, "She's my little sister. It's bad enough she knows about it, she doesn't really need the details of it."

Allison rolled her eyes. "Em, I'm okay with it."

"Ally, I'm not." Her temper flared a bit.

"This is your bachelorette party." Allison poked her hard. "You need to chill and enjoy the hot dudes on stage and drink beer and just relax. You're like an old biddy at twenty-four. Chill. If I want to learn more about the lifestyle, I'll make sure not to ask you."

"Unless it's about whips." Morgan took a swallow of the beer, hiding the laugh.

"Yeah, I have to agree there." Cece grabbed her beer for the same reason. She was glad she didn't choke between the laugh and the giant gulp of beer.

"I'm gonna put that to a vote." Chantal also went for the beer-swig cover.

"All in favor?" Lisa called.

"Aye!" All nine women raised a hand.

"You all *suck*." Emmy laughed, flicking a peanut shell at Morgan's head.

"Only my boyfriend would know." Morgan stuck her tongue out, then blanched when she remembered her little sister was sitting there. Nicole was shaking with silent laughter.

"Nice!" Allison giggled.

Emmy put another shot in front of her and Morgan. "New rule. Every times someone brings up the club at this party, you have to take a shot. Drink, bitch."

"Fuck you." Morgan laughed, grabbing the shot glass and tossing it back.

Emmy laughed and followed her back. Heather had put a crown on Emmy earlier in the night and it flew right off as they downed the shots. She looked down at it and giggled. "Dropped my halo."

Cece threw her head back and roared with laughter at that one. "You never had a halo!"

"Look who's talking!" Chantal pointed at her.

"Sweetheart, I'm not even pretending," Cece reasoned. This felt so wonderfully normal.

"Don't make me give you both shots." Emmy's threat was met with cheers.

Cece could see Morgan and Emmy were having a blast; Morgan kept "accidentally" mentioning Imperial and she kept taking shots with Emmy. Cece did the same a few times, but not nearly as many as the two of them.

Even the two younger girls snuck in two mentions—and Emmy made them both take shots when no one was looking. Cece ordered the shots for them so they would get a little turned off from the game: Three Wisemen. They were devastatingly potent to anyone not ready or used to the taste of alcohol. Both girls gagged and choke. Nadine leaned into them. "That'll learn yah!"

"Not even." Nicole hiccupped.

So Cece made sure the next shots were grain alcohol. Neither girl mentioned the club again.

Morgan pulled out her phone about eight shots in and smiled at it. She slipped off the barstool, grinning like an idiot, staggering a bit like a drunken sailor and slammed her beer. Nadine and Emmy whooped at her and Nadine mumbled, "Where?" with an accusatory finger.

"Booty call, bitches." Morgan tried to straighten herself, but she was mostly plastered.

"Oh, for God's sake," Nicole groaned.

"Seriously?" Allison laughed.

"Damn skippy." Morgan nodded once hard, and Cece tried to hide the smirk on her own face.

"Don't be long." Lisa waggled her fingers.

They all watched as the clearly inebriated, totally infatuated Morgan staggered to the side stage door that popped open for her. Nicole rolled her eyes. "Those two. Gawd, like rabbits. All the time. Did you know they *fell off the piano* the other night? Middle of the goddamn night, SLAM!" She hit her hand on the table. "Who the hell knows what they were doing! I just know I went in there the next day and disinfected everything."

The group of girls burst out laughing.

"Give her a break." Emmy waved her off. "That girl's been looking for someone who could keep up with her for years. Looks like she found it in rocker god."

"I'm just glad that rocker god has a basement apartment," Nicole stated, rolling her eyes. "They popped the bed."

"What?" Lisa gasped, trying not to choke on her drink.

"Morgan slammed her come-fuck-me pumps into the water bed and popped it."

"GOLD!" Nadine yelled, almost falling off her chair. "Why didn't you tell us that sooner!"

"Kind of forgot about it after the piano bench incident."

Cece laughed. "She's a freak!"

Emmy poked her hard. "One to talk."

Cece leveled her amused gaze at Emmy. "Takes one to know one."

Emmy thought about it for a minute, then nodded in agreement. "True."

"Hey." Chantal leaned forward, pointing at Emmy. "How are your boobs doing?" Nadine and Rachelle choked on their drinks. Chantal looked offended and everyone else was just laughing. "It's an honest question. Girlfriend here has had some major boob surgery."

"Will you stop?" Emmy giggled. "My breasts are fine, thank you for asking. They hurt like a bitch for two solid weeks after the graft, and I was slightly worried it wouldn't take. But now that the bandages are off, they look half spectacular."

"Half?" Heather asked.

"The bottom half," Emmy said, palming her own breasts. "The doctor did the bottoms first and we're working on the top now."

"What was wrong with them?" Nicole asked.

Everyone at the table whipped their head over to her and collectively, violently hushed her. Emmy drunkenly waved everyone down. "No. S'alright, yins." She looked at Nicole. "My stepfather burned my boobs when I was younger. I'm having skin grafts done to correct the mess."

Nicole looked sad. "Poor boobies!"

Emmy burst out laughing as Ally leaned over. "You do not have to feel sorry for those knockers. They are more than well loved. Nathaniel comes out of nowhere, puts his hands on them, and just squishes them gently. Hhhhhhhonk."

Ally's special effects were the end of them. No one could catch their breath from laughing so hard. It took almost twenty minutes for them to finally start calming down enough to start up a casual conversation again. Morgan reappeared at some point, and it took everyone at the table a minute to realize she was there, looking extremely happy and slightly disheveled, and the gales of laughter started again.

Cece loved every minute of this. She wished she had thought to include her own sister; Hannah would have loved this group, and would have had a blast with them. She made a note that these nights out were going to have to happen more often and Hannah was going to join them. It felt wonderful to be surrounded by friends. And even though Downbound was louder than Imperial, she was having just as much fun.

Morgan headed them all backstage, which had Lisa popping again. While Cece was getting a little annoyed with her excitability, she also understood. Silver Soul was a local band with a lot of local clout and local fans. The one guitarist gave them shit at the door, and Morgan handled it with cool aplomb and liberal use of insults and snubbing.

Still, Cece saw the trouble when he followed behind them a moment later with five blonde, buxom bimbos who were giggling and barely dressed. Dave led them through the hall and past the group of them. He nodded at one of them, the one with what had to be a bad boob job enough to rival Diane's, who sidled up to Nick and wrapped her arm around him.

Cece whipped her head around and saw Morgan's face go from calm to crazed in a heartbeat.

"Dave thinks we'd be good for each other," the Boobs oozed.

Morgan actually growled at her. "So help me *God*, if you don't take your hand off my man, I will take it off your body."

Nick stepped in. "Relax, Kitten. Penny here was just moving along, wasn't she?"

"You're no fun, Nick," she purred. "Let me show you how much fun I can be."

Everyone could see Morgan was about to take the bitch to the floor. Cece had her foot in motion to stop her when Emmy stepped up. "Morgan, don't." Full on domme voice, she hissed in her ear. Morgan froze.

"Penny, darling." Nick's tone was completely calm and perfectly condescending. "Every damn time you see me, you do this shit. I have my arms around a beautiful woman *that isn't you*. Take a fucking hint, remove your arm from my person, and move on with those fake titties of yours. I got the real deal right here, and I'm just not buying what you're selling. Maybe Dave will let you suck him off after all of your friends get done with him."

Cece bit her lip to keep from laughing at his jibe. Heather, Rachelle, Chantal, and Lisa were standing with their hands over their mouths. Allison, Nicole, and Morgan were just watching, eyes as wide as saucers. He had completely shut her down, in front of all of them—more so in front of Dave and in front of her friends. Only one of the friends actually got what had just happened. The others were all giggling, clueless. Apparently just being spoken to by Nick D was reason enough to ignore the fact that they had all been called to the carpet.

Dave knew exactly what had just happened. He very much looked like he was going to choke out Nick in the next heartbeat. He walked away from the other girls, straight over to Nick. He shooed The Boobs over to the others.

Nick pulled Morgan closer. "I'm not doing this with you here and now, Dave."

"I don't know. Your little speech just now seemed to say differently."

"She had her hands on me while I'm standing here with my girlfriend." Nick leaned forward a little bit. "You know, the one I wrote a fucking *song* for?"

"You don't seem to get it, no matter how many different ways I try to put this to you." Dave was flat out pissed off. "The fat bitch is bad for our publicity."

All of the women standing with Cece gasped in

disbelief as The Boobs and her friends "ooh'ed" and then giggled. She couldn't believe these women were actually enjoying another woman being berated and yelled at like this.

Nick was turning red from his anger. "The fat bitch is, first, not fat, and second only a bitch to you. Third, she's my girlfriend and my fucking muse. That entire fucking album we're almost ready to record in the space of a month is all songs she inspired. So if you think for an instant this woman I've got tucked in my arm is bad for publicity, you're a bigger asshole than any of us thought."

"I'm going to make sure that Quentin throws her out, and she can't ever come back."

Nick stepped up to him. "I will see your ass in the street and out of my band before you can even take the first step toward Quentin if you think you're going to do that. Quentin thinks you're as much of an asshole as I do." He pointed at the five girls standing there. "If a single one of those things step out of line just once tonight, I will hand you your ass on a silver platter and tell you to tongue-fuck your own asshole and like it. And then I will open the door and spill all of your asses out into the cold and out of the band." Dave opened his mouth to find Nick's finger in his face. "One step, Dave. Just one. They keep their hands off me, and they don't talk to Morgan."

Dave stared at him, then quietly spoke. "You wouldn't dare kick me out of the band. You could never find someone to replace me."

"Try me, dickmitt." Nick stared him down.

"Try me too, fartknocker."

Everyone jumped. Vatori was standing against the wall, arms folded, watching the whole thing go down. No one had realized he was there. Cece saw Lisa sigh and watch him like a hawk as his every muscle rippled, moving closer to Morgan.

"Dave, if you haven't been able to figure it out, you've been skating on thin ice with all of us for the past few months. You're not gaining any points by pulling this doorman shit."

"*Look at her!!*" he yelled, pointing to Morgan.

Vatori turned his head and out ogled Morgan. She was a beautiful woman—hips and curves and generous breasts. Full lips, chocolate brown eyes and hair. Cece knew she was drunk because she had the sudden urge to do naughty things to her, and she didn't normally find that women caught her interest. Surprising everyone, most of all herself, Morgan stepped out of Nick's arms and struck a pose.

Everyone, including Cece, offered up a clap of appreciation.

"What about her?" Vatori asked. "Look at those tits. How Nick isn't latched on right now making himself at home I don't know. They're scrumptious." On cue, Nick grabbed her, pulled her in, stuck his face in her cleavage and started motorboating her. Morgan enjoyed it, laughing loudly.

"You know what's even more sexy than her tits?" Chantal offered. "The way he looks at her. The way he eats her up with his eyes. The way he's not afraid to offer her a public Brunski."

"She is fat!" Dave's anger was consuming. "She can't even shop at a normal store! How is she attractive at all? None of our fans want to see this vat of lard wobbling around with our entourage! She's probably just as stupid as she is fat. She's going to wreck the whole band and our look. You need to lose the fat whore."

"Don't you dare call my sister a fat whore!" Nicole screamed at the top of her lungs. Cece could see the damage was done. Morgan slumped and tried not to cry. She stepped up to Dave and slapped him across the face, hard. The sound echoed in the hall and no one moved until they realized a few seconds later that Morgan was running away, out of the building.

"Morgan!" Nick broke into his own run, trailing after her.

Vatori turned and looked at Dave. "What the fuck is wrong with you?"

"She's *fat*."

"Ript, Van, take care of this shit," he said, waving over the other two members of the band. "I have to go make sure that Nick doesn't let her get away." Vatori turned and headed for the door to follow behind the fleeing couple.

Cece watched as The Boobs and her friends closed in on Dave. She looked over at Emmy and the two of them, in unspoken agreement, stepped up to stand with Van and Ript, staring at Dave. He glowered at the four for them standing there, and finally spoke. "You know she's fat. She's ruining our image."

"The only person ruining our image, Dave, is *you*," Ript explained. "Leave. Get out of here before Nick comes back and removes your balls. He's going to, and you know it."

"I'm the only one who brings women worth a damn back here," he snapped.

"Take the bimbos and leave," Emmy growled.

Cece pulled Emmy back. This was her party; she shouldn't be handling this. She pushed between two of the women. "You're leaving, now."

"Who are you telling me what to do?" He gave her the stink eye.

Cece stepped up into his face. "I am someone you don't want to fuck with. You are taking these women and their bad enhancements, and you are leaving. Now. You are not going to ruin this night any further with your stupid, shortsighted, puerile idiocy on the state of my friend's body. Pack your shit and get out. Get me?"

Dave stared at her, confused by his reaction to her command. Cece didn't do it often—pull out her Domme in the real world—but this ass was not going to ruin their night. This was a hiccup, a bump they could get over and get back to drinking and having fun if she could get him to leave.

He finally broke the stare and looked around at the five women, and Cece could see they were confused by this as well. Dave moved, clearly deciding that getting away from the situation was the best option at that point. "Come on, ladies. I know a better place to party where we don't have to party with all these whale watchers."

Nicole surged forward, and Cece caught her with a flick of the arm. Emmy leaned in, and Cece heard her whisper, "Don't engage him, Nicki. He's not worth it."

Dave shoved through the crowd and the group of hangers-on followed him. He motioned them to wait for him while he ducked into the room. The group of women that Cece was with—nine of them—and two men, stared hard at the women while they waited for him. Cece could tell the women were uncomfortable and it was no less than they deserved. They had stood by while Dave insulted another woman.

"Starfuckers," Rachelle mumbled.

"What?" Ally asked, quietly.

"Starfuckers," Rachelle repeated. "Star collectors? Same thing."

"What does that even mean?" Nicki asked.

"Come on, I'm not that much older than you are." Rachelle laughed. "They are people who hang onto famous people, sleep with them, and move on. Star collector."

"Who thought of that?" Ally asked.

"The Monkees," Ript said.

"Who?"

Rachelle cuffed Ally on the side of the head. "Really? Your sister is a musical genius and you don't know who the Monkees are?"

Nicki and Ally looked at each other, turned back to Rachelle, and answered, "Nope."

"Get the hell out of here." Van laughed. "Go. Get out!"

"She could take the last train to Clarksville," Cece suggested.

The tension in the group flowed out at her suggestion, and everyone started laughing. The other five women standing there couldn't make heads or tails of what was going on, and Dave looked even angrier when he walked out of the dressing room to all the people there laughing. The women followed him and his guitar case down the hall to where the door was hanging open, and headed out of the building. He motioned the women ahead of him, and Heather stepped forward.

"Hey, Dave!" she called.

He turned, and as if they were all of one mind, everyone standing there flipped him the middle finger. Cece laughed with the group as Dave slammed the door behind himself, impotently. It immediately popped back open, but he didn't care. He just kept walking.

"Good riddance to bad rubbish," Emmy said. "Now. Where is Morgan and where are our drinks? In that order!"

CHAPTER THIRTEEN

"**HOW'S THE CASE GOING?**" CECE ASKED. She found herself and a few others outside after Dave and his bimbos left. Nick had caught up with Morgan and had brought her back in, with a smile on her face.

Emmy hiccupped. "What case?"

"Lance and Eric?"

"OH! Jesus, I am drunk," Emmy admitted. "I was so preoccupied all day with Paul and ma here, it didn't even occur to me you were talking about that."

Cece, Morgan, and Emmy were outside of the club, needing a touch of fresh air after all the drinks and drunken chatter. Cece gestured with her bottle. "What's going on with them?"

"I'm putting them on the Montenegro Estate paperwork. Deed. I couldn't fucking believe Uncle Charlie never told me I had a goddamn three million dollar estate in Montenegro. And a fucking trust set up to take care of it. I didn't know Dad had that kind of money. Saya and I are going to go over there in a few weeks and check the place out. I've never been, and she hasn't been in twelve years."

"That's so cool," Morgan said. "You have an estate in Montenegro. That sounds...classy."

"What about the others? Lance, Eric...Jillian?" Cece asked. After seeing what Lance and Eric had been up to *that* day nearly killing Nathaniel, she really wanted to know.

Emmy put her head back after taking a sip of her drink. "Okay let's see. Jillian pled nolo contendere, and she was given two years on the kidnapping, and a bunch of minor stuff. Once again, Lance had sweet talked a woman into thinking he was a great guy even if he was planning a kidnapping and murder. She said—and both Nathaniel and I believed her—she didn't think Lance would kill me."

Emmy continued after another sip. "Eric is in for fraud, extortion, child endangerment, accomplice to attempted murder after the fact, and just a crap ton of other stuff that Hagberg has found against him. He's pleading guilty to enough of it that he won't see the light of day for about fifteen years. And I have a permanent restraining order on him." She shrugged. "Not that the order will actually do much, but it's a legal step that needs to exist."

Emmy paused and ran her finger over the rim of her glass for a moment. "Lance. Fucking Lance. He's up for attempted murder one, extortion, fraud, terrorism, terroristic threats, industrial espionage and, best of all, three counts of murder one. Once he heard all the charges brought against him, and realized everyone at the party saw him try to kill Nathaniel and kidnap Sylvia and me, he gave up Tash's body, and two others he had killed and dumped. He's got life. He's three times life, plus fifty or so when you get all the other stuff added in. He will never see the light of day again. Amen. Rot in hell, you asshole."

Emmy spit on the ground.

Cece was taken a little aback by her virulent curse,

but at the same time, Lance Dayton had almost murdered her fiancé and had wanted to murder her. Cece and Morgan exchanged glances, both taking a* sip of their respective drinks, then Morgan cleared her throat.

"So. Does Nathaniel let you spank him?"

Cece nearly choked on her beer. Emmy laughed hard, and Morgan looked confused and possibly as drunk as Emmy. Cece finally managed to swallow the beer and really laugh. "Morgan. What the hell possessed you to ask that?"

Morgan looked at the glass in her hand. "About four Long Island Iced Teas and six beers." She turned to look at Emmy again. "Come on, it's just the three of us for some fresh air. Spill."

Emmy raised a finger and cleared her throat. "It's only because I like you and I'm asbtolutfely shiffaced that you're getting this out of me." She took a sip of the Cosmo in her hand. "Yes. All the time."

Morgan whooped and tried to high-five Cece. Cece wasn't sober either and when the hand came at her, she moved out of the way, and Morgan managed to slap her shoulder instead. Emmy snorted and that started a whole new round of laughing.

Cece regained herself first. "*Nathaniel Walsh* lets you tie him up."

"Tie him up, tie him down, flip it, smack it, rub it, tease it, withhold it, ride it, and suck it," she listed. "I'm sure I mished one."

"Totally serious?" Morgan asked.

"Why would I lie about tying up my fiancé?" Emmy giggled. "He is fucking aaaaah-mazing in so many different ways. I don't think we've had sex without about four orgasms yet. And let me tell you…teashing him how to spank me and use all the toys? Un. Fucking. Believable. He put a blindfold on me the other night and I'm not going to tell you another thing about that, but holy shizz." She pointed to her breasts. "He worships these puppies, and damn. Damn. I am sho glad I didn't let anyone else near them before him. They wouldn't know how to handle them."

"He's not threatened by you taking over?" Morgan was genuinely curious.

"Psssht." Emmy waved a nonchalant hand. "What's to be threatened about? He likes it. He knows he's going to get his, and I get mine. A real man can take it tied up. A real man knows exactly what he wants in the sack and likes it when his woman does too."

"You're not just in the sack," Cece mumbled.

"You're absolutely correct," Emmy said, like a game show host. "He likes the shower. I like… uh. Yeah. Let's not," she paused to belch politely, "go there." She looked over at Morgan. "And like you've got room to talk. Where did you go before?"

Morgan grinned. "I had to prove my bj prowess to my boyfriend, thank you very much."

"Did you really fall off the piano?" Cece asked.

"Augh! Nicole!" Morgan yelled.

The three of them collapsed in laughter against the wall as the door creaked open and a head popped out and gazed around. A moment later the rest of Donovan appeared from behind the door. "Ladies."

They all started laughing again, and Van seemed very confused. Cece motioned for him to give them a minute. He walked out and let the door close. "What's going on out here?"

"Girl talk." Morgan seemed confused for a moment then nodded, assured she had said the right thing.

Cece was a little star struck still; she was hanging out with local celebrities and had been let into the inner circle. Morgan was already used to it so it was easier for her to recover. "Who are you looking for?"

"Sal, actually," he answered.

"He's probably off macking with Lisa," Emmy stated.

"Macking?" Cece laughed. "We *need* to update your vocabulary."

"Are we back to making out?" Emmy hiccupped. "Because I really do prefer that."

"Yes, I think that's fine," Morgan said, coming off another sip of her Long Island Iced Tea.

"Oh, Emmy!" came a scream from inside. The door flew open again. Ally popped her head out and found the four of them standing there. "Emmy, your lover is here to pick us up."

Emmy hiccupped again. "Don't…don't call him that. I hate that word." She drank the remainder of her Cosmo as a shot and held the glass out for Cece to take. "I have to go home. It's past my curfew. I'm sure hoping there's going to be punishment."

"Gawd!!" Ally cried and banged the door shut. They still heard her. "Insatiable! You two are insatiable!"

Cece caught Van laughing and shaking his head. "You are all bananas with the sex, aren't you?"

"Every last one," Cece answered.

Van looked at Morgan. "By the way, Oliver totally

realized what was going on backstage. He hung around to torture you."

Morgan's mouth dropped open as her face flushed red. Cece found herself trying not to laugh again. "No! Oh my God, why? Why couldn't you just have left that out!"

"Because I like to see you utterly embarrassed," Van answered with a shrug. "You and Nick are out of control for each other and it's fun to watch."

Morgan was hiding her face in her hands. "Why, why did you share?"

"Oh, poor Wisconsin—" Cece started.

The door popped open again, and Nick's head popped out. "Hey, kitten. There you are. I have to steal you for a while. Emmy, Nathaniel is looking for you out front."

"We've been informed." Morgan hiccupped. "Excuse me, ladies, my man wants some attention." Cece and Emmy laughed her off, but Emmy suddenly dove for Morgan and wrapped her around her. "Thank you so much for such an awesome, incredible night of drunken normalcy!"

"You're welcome." Morgan laughed. "We'll do this more oftener."

"You're next so, yeah." Emmy laughed. Morgan cuffed her shoulder, and Emmy staggered back a step, laughing hard. Nick held the door wide, and Morgan walked in—but not before she slammed Nick into the wall, kissing him hard. She continued her walk into the building and Nick's smirk took over his face as he glanced at Cece, Emmy, and Van. He waggled his eyebrows and followed her a moment later.

Cece looked at Emmy and shrugged. "I'm drunk enough to ask. Is your sister gay?"

Emmy nodded a bit. "There's a ninety percent chance of that."

"She hasn't come out yet?"

"Not to me," Emmy said. "I'm not even sure she knows yet. She's just fifteen. It'll happen when it happens." Emmy took a sip off the last of her drink. "The bigger question I think is if Rachelle knows she's gay."

Cece bobbed her head. "You're right about that. She's in a hetero contract, isn't she?"

"Yup." Emmy nodded. "I mean, she could be bi."

"With the way she gravitated straight to your sister?" Cece asked. "She didn't even give this hot ass a second look." She hooked her thumb at Van. "And not looking at the hot asses in this band is just a crime against humanity if you're hetero."

Emmy leaned back and took a solid look at Van's ass. "True." Van gave her the side eye as Emmy and Cece started laughing. "Some days I think it's a sin I'm engaged. Then I tie my husband up, and I remember why I am."

"Ally's right," Van said. "Insatiable."

"You just hope you can find a woman you can't keep up with." Emmy smiled. "Are you—"

Van's hand shot up, silencing them. Almost as if someone had thrown a switch, they were completely quiet and listening. Cece felt her buzz die down a bit as the night's quiet surrounded them.

Then they all heard it.

"…no…"

Faint and quiet, but close by, it was a woman's tone. They could hear a half-assed struggle going on, somewhere near. Van put a finger to his lips and he headed for the corner of the building. Cece followed with Emmy just next to her. She could tell Emmy was a lot more sober than a moment before as well.

As they got to the corner of the building, the struggle became clear, but not louder. The pleas to stop were muddied in an alcoholic haze and the sounds were all muffled. "No, stop, stop. Don't. Please."

"You're so drunk you won't remember in the morning." Distinctly a male voice, gruff and hopped up on emotion of some sort, Cece didn't like it—and saw the realization of what was going on slide over their faces at the same time.

Donovan vaulted out from behind the corner of the building before Cece or Emmy could grab him. The only thing they could do was follow him around into the darkness there. There was a light above the trash bin, which was now over-flowing, and it created hard shadows on the ground. The sound of the struggle came from the other, darker side of the bin, and they followed Van around.

What they found was a total nightmare.

A hulking mass of humanity with a black hoodie was kneeling on the ground between a woman's legs. Her pants had been ripped down. Not off, but down and out of the way. His hands were on his erection as he tugged on it, not even realizing the three of them had come bounding over. The woman had two swollen eyes, a broken nose and split lip. She couldn't see from the swelling, and was just rolling her head back and forth whimpering.

Van drop-kicked the guy in the side of the head while Emmy stepped back and pulled out her cell phone. Cece ran over to the woman and yanked her up and out of the way, against the wall of the building. Van's kick had startled the would-be rapist and he had hit the ground hard, his head echoing. It didn't take him down for good, though, and a moment later the hulking mass of humanity stood and slowly turned to face them.

A car squealed around the building, distracting them, and two men tumbled out of it. "Emmy!" one of them screamed—distinctly Nathaniel's voice—and they ran over to where they were standing.

While Van was distracted, the would-be rapist elbow dropped his shoulder and knocked him back and away. Upon seeing Nathaniel and the large man with him, the hooded figure turned and started running into the dark of the parking lot behind the building. Nathaniel waved his companion after him as he raced for Emmy. Cece held the injured and totally inebriated woman as Van dropped down next to them.

"Are you all right?" Nathaniel asked, grabbing Emmy and pulling her close.

"I'm fine, fine," she managed through her inebriation. "I knew you had Quinn with you, that's why I called you back here."

Van was running his hands over the woman, examining her. She was squirming and crying and trying to get away from his touch. Cece leaned down. "It's okay, it's okay," she soothed. "We're here to help. Donovan is just checking for broken bones. I'm Cece. Relax."

Nathaniel had his phone to his ear and was chatting with what Cece assumed was the 911 operator. She looked at Van, and he had a look of some relief on his face. "Nothing broken," he offered. "But she's been beaten hard. There's probably internal injury."

"How do you know?" Cece asked.

"Volunteer paramedic, once a week," he answered.

Quinn came running back up. "Sorry, Nathaniel. He was way too fast. He ran into the woods and there was no way I could find him. Is everyone okay?"

"Except for the victim here," Nathaniel said. "Do we know who she is?"

Van gasped and Cece looked at him sharply. "You know her?"

"Oh shit, yes," he said. "Don't let Morgan or Nick back out here."

"Who is she?"

"Casey," he said. "Casey Lind. Nick's ex-fiancée." Van looked up at Nathaniel and Quinn. "You can't let them out here. Don't let them know she was here. Just…trust me on this." He looked down at the woman, and he looked genuinely concerned for her. Cece realized the woman had passed out at some point, and a moment later they heard sirens for the ambulance and cops. "I'll go with her to the hospital."

"We're going to have to give statements," Quinn said. "Did you see the guy's face?"

Emmy and Cece looked at each other and shook their heads. Cece inwardly cringed. There was now a would-be rapist on the loose in the city.

CHAPTER FOURTEEN

THE KEYCARD WAS WAITING FOR HER, along with a single rose and a note. Cece raised an eyebrow but accepted everything from the desk clerk and headed for the elevator. She opened the note as she waited for the car to arrive.

Mistress,

A simple thank you for this moment together. I truly hope I can please you in every way.

Yours,

John

The door slid open, and Cece stepped in. As much as she had tried not to get excited about this meeting, she couldn't help it. John was magnetic, and she was being pulled in. The note was short and to the point, much the way everything they'd had together to that point was.

For just a moment, in the elevator car, she hesitated; Killian slipped into her mind. Her forbidden Killian. She couldn't help herself—she wasn't even sure he would be agreeable to her lifestyle. She didn't know if she could give it up. She didn't even know if polyamory was something he would consider if she didn't or couldn't give up the lifestyle.

But she wanted to sample John. Just this once, if that's all she could have. Someone so wonderfully compliant, so willing, so able, was just something she had to sample once. She hoped, and feared, this wouldn't be as wonderful as her sex seemed to think it would be.

The doors slid open on the fourth floor, and she stepped out to the hall.

Her fear peaked for just a moment when she saw a figure disappear down the hall. She was overreacting, but after finding Casey Lind in that mess, and having to give a deposition on what had happened, she just wasn't sure anymore. That had been the most nerve-wracking experience since Tessa had been beaten-up in the room at the club.

Cece abhorred the rapists out there; she was disgusted she had been so close to one and possibly made it onto his hit list—either for an assault or for a literal hit. She truly hoped he didn't remember any of their faces.

The shadow was gone now, and she walked down to the door she had the keycard to. She opened the door carefully, swinging it only as wide as she needed to slip into the room.

What she found was nothing like what she'd expected. It was radically different from anything she and Everett had planned.

The room was warmly lit with glowing blocks of light—instantly recognizable as battery candles in small, opaque vases spaced around the room. The usual hotel furniture was rearranged to be out of the way, giving the room the illusion of more space. All the brand-recognizable bed clothes were gone and in their place were black satin sheets, and more than two hundred feet of white silk rope in four bundles lay in the center. And in the middle of the new space created, knelt John Smith, masked and hooded, wearing a pair of black satin boxers, eyes downcast, hands on knees, perfectly submissive.

Cece's whole body thrummed once again. This was *hers* for the taking tonight.

She stepped in and walked around him once. "Good evening, John."

He didn't answer.

Perfect.

"You may answer my questions for now," Cece amended. "You have leave to speak."

"Thank you, Mistress," he said.

"What is your pleasure this evening, John?"

"A full bind, Mistress, if you please."

Cece walked to the door and placed her bag and coat in the closet. She quickly discarded the clothes she had been wearing all day and left herself dressed in a black corset, thong, and thigh highs. She was already wet with anticipation of this. Walking back, she picked up a bundle of rope. "This will take time. You are prepared for that?"

"Yes, Mistress." His voice was breathy and low, and she imagined it caressing her skin. "I wish myself to be fully at your disposal, Mistress. Take whatever you wish of me. I would consider myself in your favor if my cock would fill you tonight."

Oh, how Cece wanted that. So very much. And tonight, she could have it. She looked at John there, and decided on two binding sessions—one to see if she could get him into subspace, and one for them to play around in.

"Are you ready, Mister Smith?" She walked around him again, making sure he could see her heels and hose.

"Yes, Mistress."

"We're doing two forms, John."

"Mistress?"

She leaned down so he could finally see her. "Two forms. I want you in subspace. I want to enjoy getting you there. I want you to feel each and every strand of this magnificent rope you brought with you as it slides across your skin. I want you to lose yourself in the sensation of my hands guiding it around you. I want you to be so lost in sensation that you come without a single touch to your magnificent cock. And I want you to be hard again a moment later, so I can slide you inside me, and I can join you in that perfect bliss."

His only answer was an exhale of breath, loaded with the soundless touch of lust. Cece stood. "Knees together," she stated. "Hands on the floor in front of you. Press your chest to the tops of your legs."

He complied immediately, and Cece couldn't help running her hand down his smooth, muscle-rippled back. She wanted him to take off his hood so she could see who this was. Nothing would ever turn her away from Killian, but being able to see this man properly would be a wonderful substitute until she could get out of the mess she was in.

The silk rope uncoiled easily and she dropped down behind him. Slipping the rope under his ankles, she started weaving an intricate web of silk around his feet, his toes, his ankles. She wove up his calves a little way, and then lashed the rope over his lower back. Cece pulled it tight and did it again, just a few inches further up.

This time, as she pulled it taut, she heard a sigh escape the stoic figure on the floor with her. She smiled and lashed it around him four more times, binding him to his knees. Each turn around his body brought a deeper and more contented sigh.

Cece paused only to grab the next bundle of rope. She started at his hands this time, weaving and threading it around his fingers, wrists, arms. She slid the ropes through her fingers, winding them around his muscles, up over his back and back down the other arm to be bound neatly together.

She was lost in the sensation and patterns she was creating. She didn't know how long it took for her to finally lash the last pieces of rope together. She forgot who she was, all of the problems that surrounded her. Cece floated along, consumed by the feel of rope and skin, the pressure of winding the silk around the muscle, the occasional soft sigh of satisfaction from either herself or John—she wasn't even sure who it was sometimes.

She was thoroughly in her Domme space. And even after she was done with ropes, the forms, the patterns, she still trailed her hands over his skin, over the ropes, feeling the intricate weavings she had created for him— and for herself.

She knelt in front of him and lifted his chin. She couldn't see his eyes; she wanted to. She could see his lips. They were parted slightly as he breathed through the bindings.

"You've done so well, John. So well."

"What I wouldn't give to have this every night,

Mistress."

"It wouldn't be as amazing if you did." Cece leaned in and kissed him hard. She delved into him, tasting him, dueling with him. Dominating him even in their kisses. He was a perfect submissive. He gave whatever she asked of him. "Where are you, John?"

"Floating, Mistress."

"You can stay there?"

"Forever."

Damn. He really was amazing.

His breath brushed across her lips. "Mistress. A request."

"Yes?"

"I wish to stay like this, but I would like you to take your pleasure. I brought you a gift to accomplish that."

"Did you?" Cece was intrigued.

"On the night stand, if it pleases you."

She turned and her eyes landed on the wrapped box that sat there. Moving fluidly, her whole body relaxed from the rope work, she picked it off the stand and plucked the ribbon off. The paper fell away and she was left with a box in her hand. The box showed the contents inside.

A very sophisticated, very pretty, very *effective* vibrator.

Well.

Cece unboxed the raucous pink object and inspected it. Simple, and elegant, it declared itself to be waterproof with two different vibrators inside. She found the buttons and it did have two vibrators on either end. One was high and fast, one was low and deep.

And John Smith wanted to watch her use this.

Grabbing a pillow, she sat in front of him again. "This is a magnificent vibrator, John. You did your research on these. I'm pleased with this choice." Leaning in, she spoke again softly, "And you want to see me use this on myself. Would you like to watch me come with your gift?"

"Please, Mistress." His breath was a little ragged, and Cece figured that was from his anticipation. She was going to enjoy this. So was he.

Cece removed the mask from over his eyes so he could see, and she was a little disappointed he was wearing colored lenses. She didn't let it deter her—she slipped the tiny little thong, which hid nothing anyway, down her legs, grateful she'd gone with the clipless corset. As she slid it off, she saw his eyes watching her move, watching the little scrap of fabric slip down. Cece ran her hand back up her inner thigh to where she was wet with her own silk, his eyes following her fingers. She ran her hand up over her inner most lips, spreading the wetness over herself, and carefully separated the folds that hid her clit.

Her own finger was an electric jolt through her body; she didn't try to stop the sigh that escaped. The domme space was still there, heady and heavy and sexual. She palmed the toy and turned on the low, deep rhythm to tease herself.

She guided the vibrations around her vulva, not touching the sensitive spot again. She wanted to enjoy this tease as much as he did. "Is that what you want to see, John? My whole pussy quivering for you, because of your little toy?"

"Yes, Mistress." His voice was heavy with lust.

She moved her legs so they were on either side of his body, slightly bent. "Your own private porn, John. Watching your mistress make herself come, just for you." Cece stroked the vibrator over her entrance slowly and the slick gush of her own heat matched the delightful clench of her whole body as the sensation rushed out from her more-than-willing sex.

Reveling in that sensation, it sent wave after wave of desire flowing through her veins. Cece turned on the other vibration and angled the narrower end to press against her clit. She dipped the thick end into herself, the violation feeling sinful and filling. The low thrum against the excited skin pushed her lightheaded desire up again. She leaned back on the pillow and bent her knees even more, pulling her sex open, making it even easier to slide the vibrator deeper into her soaked channel.

"Shit, this feels wonderful, John. I cannot wait to feel your dick inside me, sliding against my clit, stuffing my whole pussy with that magnificent shaft."

And she couldn't. She knew what he looked like—that large cock just dripping with his pre-cum as he sat there bound in her ropes. She wanted him, in the worst way. She let the vibrator have its way with her as she thought about riding that toned, muscled body below her. As Cece lay fantasizing about him, and what she would do once he was inside her, her mind wiped away the hood, and firmly replaced him with Killian's face.

She remembered his hands, his touch. His slick skin as he fucked her—from above, from below, from behind. The vibrator in her hands became his tongue as it danced across her clit, her whole vulva. He delved into her with his tongue while his fingers played with her bundled nerves.

Cece lost herself in the thrust of the vibrator in and out of her tunnel, bucking her hips against the toy as it filled her. She pressed it all the way to the top and pulled it back out, holding against her clit as she imagined it was Killian's face there, licking and sucking—forcing her desire to spark and catch fire in her very blood. With a quick twist of her wrist, the vibrator was in a new position, and Cece pressed it hard against her clit while the rest was deep inside her. It was the perfect storm of sensations, and she found herself passing just the exposed tip over her clitoris, panting and pushing her hips against it.

There was a touch of skin, and Cece looked down to find that John had managed to inch forward, and he was there at the juncture of her thighs. He had placed a kiss on her mound then pulled back and blew a cool stream across her soaked pussy.

It was the end of her. Her hips bucked hard and the vibrator and John's breath ripped the scream of orgasm from her throat. Her mind blanked, the feelings overwhelming every sense. The blood roared through her ears and every part of her contracted in time with her full channel.

John's tongue was there, caressing her, soothing her as she started to drop down from the heights that the toy—and her memories of Killian—had taken her. She allowed John to have his way for a few moments as she let the vibrator slide from her sheathe. Her breath was ragged, but she finally sat up again, wishing she could touch his hair.

Cece pulled him away gently. "Did I give you

permission to lick me, John?"

His head lowered. "I could not resist, Mistress."

"Punishment is in order."

"Yes, Mistress."

Cece gave herself another moment before she stood. She needed a paddle of some sort—and before she could think about violating the Gideon Bible for her purposes, she found that John had laid out a selection of implements for her to choose from on the dresser. He hadn't just brought punishment either. There were all kinds of toys she could use.

"Well. Your thoughtful thoroughness goes to decrease your punishment, John. But there is still punishment to be meted out." Cece considered the two of her favorites that were sitting there. The flogger and the long wooden paddle, and choose the paddle. She wasn't familiar with that flogger and didn't want to injure him.

She knelt next to him, giving her the perfect position for his paddling. Since this was, ostensibly punishment, the only warning she gave was, "Count to six, John."

The paddle came down on his ass hard. Not a yelp, not a flinch, and only the words, "One, Mistress," found their way out of his mouth. She swung again, just as hard and with the same result. His acceptance of his punishment was perfect: no complaints, no calling the safe word, no movement. Simple acceptance.

Christ, she wanted to fuck this man.

Stilling her own drumming heart, she found the soothing cream on the dresser—he had not only thought of everything, but knew his mistress—and carefully, gently applied to bright red hits on his ass. Cece enjoy the moment, smoothing the cool cream over the soft, firm globes, running her fingers teasingly along the seam there.

"I'm going to leave you in this form, John. We took our time getting here, we'll take our time coming back out." She studied the objects on the dresser again, and found that, delightfully, John had offered several different options for anal play. She'd have some fun with that in a moment.

Cece took the time he was wrapped and embraced by the ropes to clean herself and the toys, and then sat on the bed to watch him.

John's breathing was steady, his head bent. The ropes bit lightly into his skin and he remained perfectly still.

Cece didn't know what to do about him. He was a perfect submissive. There was something about him that was familiar, and yet wasn't familiar. As if she were missing a clue. Of course, he was withholding something from her anyway, by wearing the mask all the time.

She wanted to pull off that disguise and put her curiosity to rest. But just as she had rules, so did he and that's the way it worked. The Trust. If there was no trust, there was no agreement, there was no lifestyle. It was the ultimate rule in the lifestyle, especially for those into the hardcore pain and punishment. There had to be trust, in both directions. Dominant and submissive, the other had to be sure the other wouldn't cross that line. Whatever that line was.

Cece knelt in front of him again, this time with a

bottle of water and a few pieces of her favorite chocolate. "John. You need a drink."

"Thank you, Mistress," he answered quietly.

She held the straw up for him and let him sip carefully. "And how are you?"

"Calm, Mistress. Everything is green."

"Good," Cece said. She offered him a few pieces of chocolate. "I'll unbind you in a few minutes and we'll rearrange." She leaned into his ear. "On the bed, John. I plan to fuck you hard."

He exhaled, the words dancing across her cheek. "Thank you, Mistress."

CHAPTER FIFTEEN

"READY?"

"Never," Cece said. "Do we really have to do this?"

"You know we do," Paul answered and didn't give her a chance to back out, yanking the door open. "Just grin and bear it, Cece. We'll get this all done and we won't have to deal with our mothers for a while."

Cece stuck her tongue out and walked into the house. Despite all the rumors, and her own initial misgivings, she'd found herself enjoying Paul's company. He was fun and funny and none of the infamous temper was anywhere to be seen. Truth be told, she chided herself, she had more of a temper than he did. The only saving grace was that as much as they were spending time together, she hadn't felt more than kind camaraderie with him.

She walked through the gorgeous house that was the Wainwright stronghold, and she was quietly impressed. Where her parents were show-offish old money, the Wainwrights were quiet, understated wealth. Probably coming from the necessity of hiding Paul's father's slightly shady side business.

Slightly shady. Cece shook her head at the underwhelming assessment that was. She'd had Albright check into Wainwright's dealing and even he came back with his jaw unhinged. She forced herself to remember that conversation as they walked through the elegant opulence in the front hall.

Marjorie, her mother, and Rinette, Paul's mother, were sitting at the table, sipping coffee, laughing and paging through magazines and catalogs. They had clearly been at it for a while, judging by the amount of discarded material and the mostly empty coffee pot. Cece stopped at the door and Paul put a hand on her back and pushed her forward.

"Don't start," he mumbled.

"Please, let's not. Can't we go skydiving? Bungee jumping? Cliff diving?"

Paul snorted as they approached the table. He pulled out Cece's chair and sat next to her.

"Good morning, you two lovebirds." Rinette giggled. Cece cringed and was going to say something when Paul poked her leg in warning. "So, Marjorie and I have been going over these invitations and we have a few picked out for us."

Cece opened her mouth to snap, but Paul poked her again and spoke over her. "Well, it's good you have an idea of what will work, but I think we should go through them and Cece and I will pick what we like."

"Remember, darling," Rinette said. "There are lots of names that have to go on our invite."

"Who's getting married?" Cece grumbled. There was no stopping that comment.

"What's that, sweetie?" Marjorie asked.

Cece toned her question down. "Just wondering what names you're talking about."

"Yours and Paul's, mine and your father, Rinette and Yuri, grandparents on both sides—"

"I don't think we need to put grandparents," Paul

stated, anticipating Cece's objection. "That's a bit much."

"But how will people know your pedigree?" Rinette asked.

"I'm not a dog, Mother," Paul snapped, beating Cece to the same answer. "I don't need a pedigree on my wedding invitations. Parents and bride and groom. That's it. End of it." Rinette opened her mouth to say something else. "End. Of. Discussion." Paul's angry tone was clear, and Cece was impressed.

Rinette rolled her eyes. "Fine. Then Marjorie and I will work on the flowers."

"I was thinking roses." Marjorie reached for a new catalog.

"Well, you'd be thinking incorrectly," Paul said. "I'm allergic to roses."

"You're allergic to *roses*?" Marjorie gasped. "You're not trying to be difficult, are you?"

"Mom, you'd want to keep in mind that Paul is going to be your son-in-law and probably not someone you want to get off on the wrong foot with." Cece stared at her mother, hard.

"Yes, I'm allergic to roses," Paul confirmed.

"Well, that shot my ideas down." Marjorie sighed.

Rinette patted her hand. "Ranunculus?"

Cece's mother popped her head up with a smile. "Ranunculus!" She grabbed a magazine. "Of course! They look of roses but are not roses! Lots and lots of pink and white ranunculus!"

"No pink," Cece stated.

"Don't be silly—"

Cece closed the catalog she had just opened. "Mom.

When have I ever, *ever* liked anything pink? Honestly. Think about it. I'm not a pink person. Blues, greens, reds. Never pink. No pink."

Marjorie stared at her daughter a long moment. "You really don't want a pink wedding?"

Cece shook her head. "No, Mom, I don't want a pink wedding."

Marjorie blinked a few times. "A black and white wedding! I've always loved those!"

"Who is getting married here?" Cece asked again, the anger rising in her tone.

"You have to consider our guests."

"*My* guests!"

Marjorie clucked at her. "Darling, we're paying for this wedding."

Cece snorted and laughed. "No, you're not!"

Paul grabbed her elbow. "Cece, please take it down a notch."

She whipped her head around to snap at him, but stopped. She took a deep breath and nodded. "Sorry. This whole thing is very stressful."

"That's okay, darling." Marjorie smiled.

Cece bit her tongue. The apology had not been for her mother—only for Paul. She took another deep breath and looked back at the catalogs. Paul gave her the side eye, and she knew she had to give her mother and Rinette a non-offensive, non-intrusive job. "Why don't you work on the linens? They'll have to be white, but there are so many different styles, and I really don't know much about that."

"Of course!" Rinette was gleeful, pulling a different stack of magazines over. "There's so many different styles and we have to figure out the place-settings."

Cece tried not to roll her eyes, instead opening the invitation catalogs. She pushed one at Paul, who was trying not to laugh. He nodded and started paging through it. "So, tell me, my little jitterbug, what colors do you want? Because that's going to make a difference."

Putting a hand to her mouth, Cece tried not to laugh. *Jitterbug*? She paged through a few more samples and sighed. "I love blue and purple. Dark blues, dark purples. Not at the same time. Yellow pops of color with either."

"That eliminates this whole catalog." Paul closed it and tossed it onto a different pile.

"Blue? Purple?" Marjorie was clearly horrified. "Darling, are you going for a colorful wedding? That's not really the kind of wedding I'm envisioning for you. That's why I was thinking about a black and white wedding. It's elegant and—"

"Mom. Stop." Desperately trying to rein in her anger, Cece continued to flip through the catalog. "I like blue or purple with yellow. That's what I like."

"It's not elegant," Marjorie cautioned.

Cece gave up and lost her mind. "I don't even want a wedding! I don't want invitations or dresses or tableside choices for dinner! None of it!"

"You can't elope!" Rinette cried. "You can't!"

Cece swept the magazines off the table. "I am not eloping! I am not having a pink wedding. If we are doing this, it's going to be on *our* goddamn terms!"

"Well, that didn't take long," Paul mumbled.

"*What*?" Cece snapped and turned on him.

"Jitterbug," he said, grabbing her elbow, "why don't you pop out back and take a moment to yourself. You're stressed and acting out."

"You're not fucking kidding I'm acting out!" Cece snapped. She grabbed the magazine on the table and threw it at the wall. "I'm having a goddamn tantrum at this point! I'm having a wedding I don't want with colors I hate and flowers the groom is allergic to! Don't you think I have a little bit of a right to lose my shit?"

Marjorie was horrified. "My *God*, the mouth on you!"

"You have no f—"

Paul slapped his hand over her mouth. "Frances. *Please*. Take a walk outside for just a few minutes. You need to cool off." The look he gave her didn't match the kind tone of words. Cece had to resist the urge to bite his finger. She shoved the stool back and marched out of the back door of the kitchen to the ridiculously expansive grounds the Wainwright home sat on. She walked over to the trash cans and kicked them hard, wishing they were the old metal ones so she could feel the kick do damage. She turned and kicked it again. The urge to inflict damage on something was nearly overwhelming. She wished she could cause some serious destruction.

Someone grabbed her arms.

Without thinking, she stepped back, set her feet, and yanked them up and over and onto their back, winding them instantly.

Paul.

"Fuck! Goddamn it!" she screamed, dropping next to him. Cece slid her hand under his shoulders and he pushed her away. "I'm sorry, Paul. Shit."

The next instant, Paul pulled in a huge breath of air and started coughing. He sat up on his own and looked at her, panting, desperate to catch his breath. "What the living fuck was that? What the hell is wrong with you?"

"Paul, I'm sorry—"

"You have a real temper, honey, and you need to curb that shit." He climbed to his feet, clearly in pain. "You could have really hurt me. What the hell were you thinking?"

"Someone was attacking me," Cece admitted quietly.

"Cece, you need to chill out." He rubbed the small of his back. "You have got to take this intensity down a notch. I don't want this either. You know that. But you can't go and attack your mother and mine because you don't want pink flowers. Christ, have some reason. We both have too much on the line here to piss off the masses. I don't want a wedding with pink flowers either. I don't want the wedding. But we're here, and we have to make the best of this in order for a believably amicable divorce."

Cece turned away for just a moment to collect herself, then turned back to him. "Are you all right? The move I used is supposed to wind and injure."

Paul rubbed his back again. "A little rough, but I think I'll live. Come on. Let's go sit in the garden for a while, so you can relax and I can recover. You need to be away from the house to get your head on straight."

"I'm really sorry, Paul." Cece felt sheepish and mostly a fool. She shouldn't have let her anger get the better of her; she knew how to control herself and the reactions she had—to her mother and to someone laying a hand on her arm—were inexcusable.

She knew why, though.

John.

She hadn't expected the evening to go so perfectly. Certainly, she knew he was a willing sub, but to be so attuned to him so quickly...it wasn't her normal reaction. By his reactions, it wasn't John's either. Just everything between them had been perfect. And she realized she couldn't give it up. Not just John, but Everett and the Club as well. She loved being in charge. She loved everything having to do with the lifestyle.

Paul sat down on the bench, facing the opposite direction that Cece had sat. He stretched his long legs out ahead of him, and she watched him crack his back with a sigh of relief.

"So what the hell is bugging you, jitterbug?" Paul asked.

"Jitterbug?"

"I don't know, it sounds endearing without being typical." He shrugged. "My question stands."

Cece sighed. "What are our sleeping arrangements going to be, Paul?" Plucking at the bench, she avoided eye contact.

"Oh." The answer was small and full of realization.

"People are going to expect a kid."

"Uh..."

Nodding, Cece finally looked up at him. "Yes. Exactly. I like you and all, Paul, and I think we can get through this. But that promise we made to not mock marriage while we were in it is starting to look like a hard promise to keep."

"Well, I..." He paused.

"I don't want to be celibate for eighteen months. I don't. I don't think I can, more importantly." Cece picked at the bench again. "Are you seeing anyone?"

He nodded unhesitantly. "I am."

"Will she wait for you?"

He nodded.

"But can you really ask her to do that? How is that fair to your relationship? Have you stopped seeing each other since this whole farce started?"

"No," he admitted. "I'm there nearly every night. We practically live together."

Cece leaned forward and put her elbows on her knees. "Paul, I'm going to tell you this because I trust you and we have two years that we have to deal with each other on a one-on-one basis." She looked at him. "I cannot be celibate for the length of this marriage. I can't do it. I don't want to. I don't know how you're going to take this, but my second job won't allow me to be. At least, not and remain sane."

Paul turned his head slowly toward her. "Second job?"

She nodded. "Second job. And before you ask me, I'm not a prostitute and I'm not a call girl."

"Oh, well, that's a relief," Paul grumbled. "And a great segway for this conversation."

"I'm trying to be honest," Cece answered.

"I realize that and I appreciate it, but I'm sure you understand how this just took a hard left into bizarro territory," Paul said. "We're talking one instant about getting laid, and the next you're denying you're a prostitute when I never accused you of that." He raised an eyebrow. "What would make you defend yourself before I could accuse you?"

"Most people have assumptions about my second job."

"Most people don't even know you have a second job."

"I like it that way."

"What the hell do you do, Cece?"

"I work at Club Imperial as—"

"The *kink* club?" he gasped.

"The kink club," Cece confirmed, taking a deep breath.

"Jeezus, Cece," he said, leaning up and sitting straight. "What do you do there?"

"I'm Prima Domme," she answered, spitting out the words before she had a chance to be afraid to say them.

"Holy *shit*." Paul almost seemed to choke on the air. "You're a dominatrix?"

"Yes."

Practically jumping off the bench, he paced away from her and ran a hand through his hair. "Jesus shit, Frances. Crap on a stick. Are you serious?"

"Why would I ever kid about something like that?"

"No wonder you started with the working girl opening," he said. "How the hell did you end up there?"

"As Prima Domme?"

"At a kink club."

Cece raised an eyebrow. "I like kink. I like the lifestyle."

He shook his head. "No, how did you get into it in the first place?"

Cece took a deep breath and smirked. "I'm not that interesting, Paul."

"I don't know about that," Paul answered, walking back. "You just confessed you work at a kink club."

"It's not really that exciting," she said.

"Try me."

Cece picked at her nails. "I slept with my high school boyfriend when I was seventeen. And it was the most miserable experience ever. I think seventeen-year-old sex generally does suck, but I kept seeking out someone else who could figure me out. There was always something missing. Something that didn't allow me to really be happy with sex, but I wanted to.

"One of the household help noticed I was acting out, constantly angry. He was one of those men who were actually concerned about me and Hannah, and after I came home one night in utter tears he asked me what was going on. I didn't want to tell him, but I couldn't hold it in anymore. Gordon took a chance that he knew what was going on.

"Right then and there, he dommed me for the first time. Took complete control of me and finally gave me my first...well. You know."

"Orgasm?"

Cece nodded. "I'm terribly blunt when it comes to talking about this, Paul. I don't know how much your delicate ears will stand."

"Be blunt. Please. We have to figure this out, and I need to know what's going on here."

Cece nodded. "He dommed me. Do you know what that means?"

"Tied you up? Took over?"

"Yes, well...close enough. He took me to his quarters and showed me what I was missing from the horrible dalliances I was permitting myself. It was exactly what I had been missing. And we didn't even have sex that first night. He took me under his wing and started to teach me how to be a bedroom submissive, and I loved it. Eventually, I agreed to go to a training house—"

"Training house?" Paul more fell on to the bench than sat down.

Cece nodded. "Gordon was a great Dom, but he was not a good teacher and there was more to the lifestyle than he could show me. So I went to a training house. And I learned to be the perfect bedroom submissive."

"Just a bedroom submissive?"

"I don't have inclination to be a full submissive, in that position all the time. I'm only a bedroom submissive and only when the mood strikes me, which is why I've become a Domme—dominatrix, if you like. The training house saw I was better suited to be in charge. Once I completed the training for both, I was offered a position at the club. I had a unique talent with rope, and Franz wanted me there. So I agreed, and through a series of happenings I've become the Prima Domme. And I have no interest in giving that up. Now or ever."

"Nothing sordid about your past at all?"

Cece laughed. "You seem disappointed."

"Kind of, yes," he responded, laughing with her. "So, you're telling me this because you don't want to give up the domme thing."

"I don't want to give up the lifestyle, correct," Cece said. "If we stay with our promise to not see other people during this marriage, I have to give it up.

Because the sexual aspect is inherent, and I won't make myself suffer with the shibari without the possibility of relief."

"You need to get it on?"

Cece laughed. "Absolutely."

He leaned back on his hands. "I guess that makes sense. I mean, the whole idea is sexual submission or domination, and without the climax, it's all just an exercise in futility."

"Not all of it is sexual, but the part I like is." Cece nodded.

"So how would we work this?"

"Discretion is the better part of valor. I'm not saying we be out and out about the fact we're seeing other people and not sleeping together, but if we can be discreet—and I'm guessing we're both very good at that—I don't see a reason why this would mock marriage any more than we already are with our sham wedding."

"Somehow, right now, I'm very glad that this is sham wedding," Paul said.

"What?"

"I don't think I could keep up with you in the bedroom."

Cece let out a genuine laugh. "Most people can't."

"People?"

"I'm not picky about who I tie up." Cece smiled. "Only who I fuck."

Paul's eyes popped open and he let out an amused blast of air. "You don't beat around the bush."

"Or do I?"

Paul doubled over in laughter. "Shit, Cece!"

She shrugged. "So now you know. And now we have something else to work out before this marriage happens."

Paul wiped a laughter-tear from his eye. "I don't think it's really a problem. Like you said if we're not flaunting our so-called infidelity, I think we'll be fine. Tracey will be thrilled with that." Paul started and jerked his head around to look at her.

Cece smiled and patted his arm. "Your secret is safe. No one is going to hear her name from me."

"Thank you," he said, and relief in his voice was palpable. "Are you calmed down enough to go back in and deal with The Mothers?"

"Is your back still hurting?" Cece tried to distract him; she didn't want to deal with her mother.

"It'll be bruised, but I'll be fine," he answered. He opened his mouth to say something else, but instead they were interrupted rudely by a cell phone ring tone. Paul yanked out the phone and looked at the face of it, and swore. "Work." He looked at up her. "I'm sorry."

"That's okay," she answered. "I can try to deal with them."

They both stood and headed for the back door of the house, but halfway there he pulled her to stop. "Would you like to go with me?"

Cece jerked. "What?"

"I have ride along privileges too," he said. "Come with me. See what it is I do. I *promise* I will not let you in if it's too gross. My fiancée should have the right to see what it is I do."

"A *crime scene*?" Cece was really shocked.

"It'll be secured by now, and I won't make you do

anything you don't want to or go near the scene if you can't handle it."

Cece started at him. "Yes. Yes, all right. I'll go."

Paul nodded and marched them into the house where Rinette and Marjorie were wearing holes in the floor. He stopped and looked at them, then grabbed Cece's hand. "I have a call. I promised my fiancée could go along with me to see what I do. We probably won't be back today. Pick out the place settings and flowers according to the colors that Cece just told you—purple or blue with a yellow pop. End of story, don't argue with us. You can select a few invites that you like, but I make no promise we'll choose any of them."

He turned and headed the two of them for the door, but paused with his hand on the knob. "You'd do well to remember this is our wedding, and we're not pleased that it is. So tread lightly. Or there will be problems ahead."

With that, he pushed the door open and they walked out to the car, the door slamming shut behind them. Cece quickly folded herself into the car—she was getting used to that move—and Paul followed her. She laughed when he closed the door, started the car and dropped into reverse all in one motion. "I'm not the only one who wants to leave, eh?"

"I just want to get out of here before they can try to argue with us again," he said. He glanced over at Cece. "Keep that in mind next time. I don't want this either."

"But it's more socially acceptable for the bride to be a 'zilla, as opposed to a groomzilla."

"Look, if they put squishy strawberries in my cake, shit's gonna get real."

* * *

The car struggled up the steep, winding drive and popped out into an estate that had clearly been the victim of the 70s. The mansion that was the centerpiece was lacking any and all charm, and just looked as though someone had vomited on the architectural plans and drew around it.

"This is the Tiropolous Estate, isn't it?" Cece craned her neck to get a better look at the grounds.

"It is," Paul answered. "When Andros lost his wife, this place went to pot. I'm sure this looks like a hording nightmare inside."

Cece's brain tickled a bit and spit out a memory. "They had a daughter?"

Paul cleared his throat. "They did."

Cece felt her stomach plummet into her feet. "Dina."

"The report is of a deceased female at the residence," Paul supplied.

"Dina was older than us." Cece thought for a moment. "She was in high school when we were in sixth. She was an outcast because her father was so quirky after her mother died. I don't know what happened to her after high school."

Paul pulled the car around to the front of the house where there were ambulances and several police cruisers—and the all too familiar car Detective Garabaldi usually drove. Paul parked next to the detective car and sighed. "You don't have to come in. You can wait here."

"If I'm allowed, I'd like to come with you."

"You're allowed." He nodded and popped his door open. "You may not like it."

"As long as I'm allowed."

They climbed out of the car. "Please don't touch anything and find a corner to stay out of the way. I don't know what this looks like in here, but I'm going to have to do all the field work so they can move the body. Shit."

"Shit?" Cece asked, following his gaze. She landed on the ambulance waiting there. The back doors were open and a frail old man was seated on a wheel chair with a blanket and an oxygen mask. He looked tired and beaten down, and his face was wet with tears as his body shook with sobs.

"Andros Tiropolous." Paul looked at Cece for a moment then seemed to take just two strides over to the officer near the closer of the cruisers. Cece ran after him. "Did Tiropolous find the body?"

The officer nodded. "Yes. He could barely get the address out to the dispatcher."

"Crap," Paul said. "Does he have anyone else?"

"Grandchild, but she's four." The officer pointed to the ambulance again. There was a small child sleeping on a bed inside the truck. "Found her in the closet. Didn't see a thing. She heard what she said were bad noises and hid until her grandfather came home. Had a hell of time trying to get her out of there and keeping her away from the mess."

Cece shivered. The poor thing. Paul was on the move again, his long legs carrying him away from the officer to the front of the house, and again she nearly had to run to catch up. She hadn't seen him grab the backpack he had over his shoulder, but suspected that it was full of his…work tools.

The officer on the door nodded at Paul, but stopped Cece cold. "And you are?"

"Doctor Wainwright's fiancée, Cece Robbe." It felt weird to say it, but Cece was feeling strangely disconnected from reality at that moment.

The officer looked at Paul, who had pulled up short at his full title. He turned and looked at her and nodded. "Yes. She's with me."

"Lieutenant Garabaldi doesn't like ride alongs on—"

"I'll deal with the lieutenant," Paul snapped. He turned and walked away from the officer after motioning Cece to follow.

Paul was all business from that moment. He walked through the house with confidence, following the path of the officers that lined the hall. Cece kept up with him, but it was a trick. He was an imposing figure in the house; seemed to almost push the ceilings away from himself.

Paul stopped dead at a door and looked in. Cece almost slammed into him, his stop was that abrupt. He held out his hand and pushed her back, away from the clear view she would have had from the door. "Let me go in here and deal with this first. It doesn't look gory, but…" He glanced over. "My idea of gory isn't anyone else's."

Cece nodded and pressed herself against the wall, ready to wait the whole night because it was twice as gross as what he thought gross was. She took a deep breath.

"Who the *hell* is that?"

Paul and Cece turned to find Lieutenant Garabaldi standing there, looking really pissed.

"Wainwright? Who is that? Why are they at my crime scene?"

Cece cleared her throat and gave Garabaldi a clear view of her face. "Good evening, Lieutenant." Garabaldi's mouth dropped open. "Good to see you again."

He finally recovered. "Ms...Robbe, isn't it?"

"Yes, sir, it is," she confirmed.

Garabaldi looked at Paul again. "Why the hell is Robbe here?"

"Ride along."

"On a fucking murder, Wainwright?"

"Oh, I'm sorry," Paul said. "Tell me when the coroner doesn't have murder and I'll make sure to bring her back that day."

"Why her?"

"My fiancée," he answered simply.

"I thought that—"

"You thought wrong." Paul was getting upset. "Every minute we sit here and argue, that body gets a little colder. Can we do this after temperature?"

Garabaldi sighed. "Could you clear the ride along with me next time?"

"Sure, Dad," Paul answered.

"Fuck you," Garabaldi said. "Run down?"

Paul dropped the bag on the ground, routed around and came back with a pair of gloves. "Go for it."

"Female, mid-thirties, brown hair, brown eyes. About five foot four, clean cut, well dressed. Clear and obvious signs of trauma. We can't detect the cause of death. Minimal blood loss."

Paul snapped on the gloves and motioned Garabaldi to the door. "Let's. Do you think Cece can handle the scene?"

Garabaldi turned a wicked grin on her. "Oh. Her? Yeah. No problem."

Asshole. Cece smiled at him, and after both he and Paul walked into the room, she was just behind them. She didn't want to get in the way, so she slid against the wall—and watched. If there was one thing she was good at, it was observation.

She recognized the woman in the middle instantly. It was Dina—battered and a bruise that half formed and would never fully bloom on her face. Her hair was frizzy and grayish, and she looked as though she had been working the night shift at a scrubby truck stop. She was naked from the waist down and her shirt and bra torn away.

Cece gasped and put a hand to her mouth. Paul and Garabaldi looked at her, and the shock must have been written on her face. They both walked back to her, and Garabaldi grabbed her elbow. "You're not going to puke, are you, Dusty?"

"No, no." She shook her head violently. "No…" She looked at Garabaldi. "That's the same way Casey Lind was splayed out when we found her. One leg straight out, one leg bent, arms up and over her head. Her skirt was yanked up, but her shirt and bra were ripped open like that as well." She looked at Paul. "I would put money on Dina having ligature marks on her neck."

In sync, both men looked back at the figure on the

floor. Paul looked at Garabaldi, who sighed. "You need a rape kit, Wainwright."

"You need an investigative team, Garabaldi," Paul replied. "We have a serial rapist murderer."

* * *

The murderer had finally gone a full step forward. It wasn't a welcome development. With Casey Lind, he had tried, but was foiled. With Dina Tiropolous, he hadn't failed in his quest to double his prosecutable offenses. In the worst way.

Murder was foul, but the coroner's report reflected the fact that Dina had been raped—vaginally and anally—at least twice. Which meant the murderer had been there a while. Everyone agreed it was fortunate Dina's daughter hid the whole time. It was also clearly why she wouldn't be coaxed out of the closet.

Her father was a mess. His eccentricities were more pronounced as he grew older and with this, it seemed as though he had lost his mind completely. He wasn't allowed to go back into the house he had lived in his whole life, and to add insult to injury, the state decided he wasn't able to care for the granddaughter. She would go to live with a cousin. There was a feeling this was a great injustice to a once great man, but time would tell what really would happen.

Dina was, as was kept on the down-low, a dancer at the worst sort of go-go bar. She was a known prostitute, but had no record. It was easy to keep that information from the press—though from a lawyer it would be more difficult. And certainly no lawyer would pass it up.

The further the police dug, the more apparent the Tiropolous family had fallen on desperately hard times. The house was weeks from a sheriff sale for back taxes. The house was a hoarder's paradise. There was nothing in the bank accounts; though they weren't completely broke. Andros had taken to depositing money in an old mattress. There was enough money in that stash to keep them going for a long time.

There was general belief that the murderer had probably been a john. However the coroner and several of the police weren't convinced of that. They had better information than the general public. With the information from Cece Robbe that the body was in the same position Casey Lind had been rescued from, it was clear they were looking at a serial rapist and murderer.

It was not going to be an easy case. The biggest problem was a lot of the murders were out of district. The police had been coordinating with several other districts—some as far as DC and Cleveland—to try and trace the modus operandi. And they all had at least two murders that fit the modus. It wasn't a good situation. There were far too many murders that were unsolved, all leading to the same suspect—except, no suspect.

Not only was there no suspect, but the DNA was undocumented. There was plenty of DNA too. To a point of being completely disgusting, cluing the police in that this was a sex-motivated crime.

Dina's body was in the same condition as the others that stats had been shared on. Cleveland and DC weren't really interested in taking over the investigation. They had plenty on their plates, and the random crime didn't interest them. But the 'Burgh didn't usually have this kind of spree. Not to this magnitude. Not of this sort.

It all weighed heavily on his mind. The death of Dina, the attack on Casey, the other murders. It was all getting too close, and too frequent for his liking. Casey was barely two weeks ago, and now Dina. It was as though this murderer was circling his wagons to hit his primary target and soon.

"How is he?" the Hunk asked.

"Horrible," the Watcher answered. "They're hospitalizing him. The house is going to be condemned. The granddaughter has a hefty inheritance the cousins are working on keeping for her. Dina will be buried quietly in a week. There's nothing."

"Nothing?"

"Nothing to go on."

"You have the DNA."

The Watcher sighed. "We have the DNA of someone who has never been in the system before. All it's doing is showing us that this suspect is a huge monster. Which isn't a mystery."

"He has to slip up soon."

"Christ, I hope so," the Watcher admitted. "I want this beast put away."

The Hunk handed the Watcher a martini glass. "For you, babe."

"Shaken, like me."

"You are never shaken," the Hunk said.

"I am this time."

The Hunk stopped and turned to him. "This is that bad?"

"This is worse than you think. Worse than I can let on to you."

"As bad as that."

"Yes."

CHAPTER SIXTEEN

CECE SIDLED UP TO THE BAR AGAIN, and the bartender gave her a sidelong look. She threw the look right back at him. It was none of his damn business if she was on Slippery Nipple eight. This was *her* engagement party, and she'd get shitfaced if she wanted to.

Diane's nerve-twisting laugh flared right next to her ear and if Cece had been one drop more drunk, she would have turned around and punched her. Which would have been bad. But when Diane turned and actually addressed her, Cece wished had been just that one drop more drunk.

"So, I need to see this ring!" Diane pushed her glass at the bartender, who looked more disgusted by her than by Cece. Diane grabbed Cece's hand and hauled her around to look at the ring. "Oh, my gawd. It's *gorgeous*!"

Cece nodded. "Thank you. Paul has awesome tastes."

"Oh, I just can't wait until Killian gives me mine!"

Briefly, Cece wondered if Diane was looking to have a fist drilled into her throat. Because she was more than ready to oblige the woman. Just as Cece was getting ready to unleash on the woman, someone slid smoothly between them, and the fog in her mind cleared enough to recognize the new person as Saundra Oetler-

Milhouse. Everett's soon to be ex-wife.

Because this isn't awkward.

She laughed sweetly at Diane. "Oh, now, Di, come on. Leave Cece alone. Chas sent me over here to pry you away from the diamond."

"Why would my brother send you over?" Cece concluded her statement with an unexpected hiccough.

"Because he asked me to," she explained.

Cece gave her the best stink face the alcohol would allow. "That doesn't answer the question."

"Girlfriends and boyfriends help each other," Saundra answered.

"Are you *fucking* with me?" Cece gasped.

Saundra took a step back. "What?"

"You are dating my brother?" Cece stared at her, shocked.

"We've been going out for a month now, yes," Saundra said.

Cece grabbed the drink off the bar and took a solid drink as someone put an arm on her shoulder. She looked before she decided to flip the person on their ass. It was the right move; Killian was standing there.

Even more awkward.

"Your fiancé is looking for you," he said, pleasantly.

Cece swiveled her head to find Paul standing behind the chair at their table. He smiled at her and nodded to the other chair. She looked back at Killian, who smiled and nodded at the chair. Diane moved right into Killian's space and Cece was delighted to see him go from sweet to downright pissed off as she put her arm around him.

"Diane, back off," he snapped.

"Oh, but, babe—"

"Hands. Off."

Cece laughed; she was too drunk to care. Killian pinned her with a deadly stare, and took her arm. "Come on. Paul's waiting." Cece wrapped her hand around her drink and allowed herself to be led away. "Cece, for shit's sake. Could you be discrete?"

"Why?" she asked. "I'm at my own engagement party to a man who doesn't want to marry me, and who I don't want to marry, being escorted over to him by the man who's clothes I want to rip off and fuck right here, and just found out that my brother is seeing—and by seeing I mean fucking—one of my client's ex-wife."

"Client?" Killian asked. "I didn't know librarians had clients."

"It's a good way to describe some of the shit I put her through," came a new voice.

Cece turned her head again and found Everett standing there.

Jesus Christ. The night would only be complete if John Smith and Donnie showed up.

Diane was suddenly in front of the three of them. Cece couldn't believe she'd be able to move that fast. "Why hell are you all fawning over this freak?"

"Diane, back the hell off," Everett said. "This is her party and half the reason she's drunk is because of you and your floozies."

"My floozies?"

"Friends," he offered. "Whatever you want to call them."

"Just as rude as ever, I see, Everett."

Cece's head turned yet again, and found Susan standing there. "Are you following me?"

"Well, it's your party," Susan answered. "You're the main attraction."

"Do you think this is a freak show too?" Cece snapped, her delightful buzz wearing off quickly.

"No, I don't," she said. "I just think that Paul could do better than you."

"Then why don't you talk to your fucking boyfriend about that." Cece took a few dangerous steps toward her.

"There you are!"

Yet another person cut into the group—this time, much to Cece's relief, it was Emmy, who immediately enfolded her in a giant, sisterly hug. "You're being hogged up by all your admirers, Cece. Come on. Let's take a powder and chat."

"Paul—" Cece began lamely.

"Oh, I just talked to him. He'll hold the toast for us." Emmy took her arm and deftly moved the crowd out of their way. She immediately commanded the room and took all the eyes off Cece, for which she was eternally grateful. Emmy led her out of the room and instead of going to the bathroom, she maneuvered them down the hall a few steps further and into a private suite that was unused.

Cece sat in the chair there with a great 'whomp' and Emmy leaned against the door with her arms folded. "Frances, what the fuck is going on out there? I know you're supposed to be the center of attention, but you are acting the ass right now."

"What the hell am I supposed to do?" Cece asked. "I don't want any of this." She took a swig of her drink again. "Do you realize that in the space of three minutes, my fiancée, my lover, his jilted ex-girlfriend, my offsite, his ex-wife, and my brother's *new girlfriend* were all hovering around me at once? Just now. How the fuck do you expect me to act? Christ, one of the guys in this room could be John and then wouldn't that be a fine kettle of fish." She hiccupped.

"Cee, it doesn't matter who was around you," Emmy said. "They don't know the whole picture and you can't show it to them. I know you don't want this wedding. I know Paul doesn't want this wedding. Anyone with half a brain can see there's a reason you're getting married—and it's not for the hot sex. But you can't draw the attention to you like that."

"What the hell does any of it matter at this point?" Cece flopped back in the chair. "I can't do what I want when I want to. There are too many damn obligations and no one will just let Cece be."

"So apparently you're a giant whiny bitch now?"

Cece snapped her head up. "Excuse you?"

"You are acting like a petulant child, Frances. I *know* you don't want to marry Paul, but you're acting like you have no control over your life and what a load that is. You are the new Prima Domme and you have balls bigger than most men I know. So this 'poor me' routine doesn't fly. Nor does this intoxicated idiocy you've drunk yourself into. You need to quit this crap and deal with it." Emmy sat next to her. "I was exposed and I survived. Because Nathaniel did damage control, and because I was attacked by a genuine psychopath. You don't have that luxury, and there's no reason you should need it."

Cece cocked her head at Emmy. "I hate when you make sense."

"It does suck being right all the time."

Cece threw her head back and laughed. "Emmy, why the hell did it take us so long to figure out we could be friends?"

Emmy laughed and confessed. "Because I didn't realize I could have friends in the lifestyle. I thought it was a fuck and flee, and since I don't swing your way…"

"You are too much fun." Cece giggled.

She was about to go on, but there was a knock at the door, and it creaked open. Paul's head peeked in. "Ladies? They are waiting for the toast." He stepped in and closed the door. "I told them I would come and get you. Are you okay?"

Cece shrugged. "As good as it gets with this sham." Paul looked momentarily shocked, but Cece waved him off. "Oh, please. She figured it out. Emmy is the one person I know who knows what a real relationship looks like, and she spotted our fake out a mile away."

"Well, everyone else out there is still fooled." Paul laughed and motioned both of them to the door. "You can come back later and verbally hack the rest of the Gossip Girls to bloody ribbons after everyone fake toasts our fake wedding."

Cece flopped her head to the side to look at Emmy, who was nodding. "He's right. Get it over with. We'll do our best to keep people off you."

"Keep Saundra and Diane the furthest away, please," Cece said. "Those two are going to end up with my stiletto up their ass."

"In Saundra's case, you'd be lucky to get your foot back." Paul tried not to laugh at his statement. It didn't work. The three of them burst into gales of laughter as they headed back to the main dining area. As Paul had promised earlier, he'd held the toast and everyone was seated and waiting for the three of them. Emmy scooted over to where Nathaniel was waiting and sat down, tossing the two of them a wink.

Paul's best man stood, and Cece was momentarily taken back. She'd completely forgotten that Nicholas Dovadsky was also the infamous Nick D. from Silver Soul. She'd disassociated the two because Paul always talked about just Nick. But the very gorgeous lead singer was now standing there in his full rocker get up, and Cece smiled. She wondered if he was in on the ruse only briefly before he confirmed it for her.

Nick tapped his knife on the side of the toasting flute and waited for silence in the room. "So the other day, Paul walks up to me as I'm chemically dissolving some bone and says, 'Dude, you busy in six months?' I was a little confused as I usually don't know what the hell is going on tomorrow. 'I'm getting married to his hot, rich chick, and I need someone to play along as my best man.' Well, I mean what do you say to that? I'm always down for a good prank. Turns out, dude is really getting married to this hot rich chick. Who knew?"

Nick raises the glass. "So, here I am, making a toast to a friend. A good friend. A man who deserves nothing but happiness and joy in his new life. A man who should have nothing less than the perfect partner at his side. I don't know if that's Cece, though, dude."

Cece pitched her dinner roll over at Paul and caught Nick on the side of the head.

Nick turned and winked. "In all honesty, if you

were going to pick anyone, Paul, you got a good one in Cece. She's an honest, caring, straightforward woman who holds no secrets and pulls no punches."

Cheeky fucking bastard, Cece thought, grinning innocently at him. She caught sight of Wisconsin sitting on his far side, laughing her ass off. She realized most people weren't being fooled by this marriage, and it gave her a sense of relief.

Until she realized she was going to have to kiss Paul.

Her heart dropped into her feet. She and Paul had actually become very good friends, but there was still absolutely no spark between them. They were awesome at faking it, they enjoyed being together—but there was no romance. And now she was going to have to kiss him.

Nick held the flute up. "To Paul and Cece. May your marriage be everything you dreamed it could be. May your purses be heavy, your heart be light, and holes in the wall behind the bed deep."

Without a single hesitation, Paul turned and kissed her. It was probably for the best. Cece wasn't in the right frame of mind to handle this well. A small consolation prize was, Paul was a good kisser. A very good kisser, and still there was nothing there for her. After an appropriately long kiss that gave everyone the idea that maybe they liked each other, he pulled back.

Cece smiled. "It's like kissing my brother."

Paul nodded. "Yeah, like kissing mine too."

Cece threw her head back and let her laugh ring out.

* * *

The stress of trying to pretend she cared about all of these people around her drove Cece back to the suite that Emmy had dragged her into earlier. She lay down on the couch for just a moment before the door burst open.

"There you are!" Diane's shrill voice pierced the silence. She flounced into the room and giggled. "All this time, and I still haven't seen that rock!"

Cece flopped her hand out. "Have a look. But, Diane, I'm exhausted. I need a few minutes to just unwind. There are so many people."

Diane grabbed her hand. "You ought to get used to it. I know you avoided all this when you were younger, but as a society hostess, you're going to have to learn to kiss ass. After all, they expect it and if you don't, you get ostracized." She studied the ring quietly a moment. "You wouldn't want to be ostracized, would you?"

"Right now, that sounds delightful," Cece answered.

"Oh, please," Diane said. "You don't hate this stuff. You grew up in it. It's your birthright."

"Diane, darling, I am so not into that birthright stuff. I want to be left alone with my books and my cottage and just go on each day like none of this ever happened, ever existed, or ever darkened my doorstep."

"You're not going to be a very good society wife."

"Stepford wife," Cece mumbled.

"I can't wait for Killian to give me my ring," Diane answered, moving to sit on the chair across from her. "We'll have a grand wedding with all the trimmings and a huge wedding party. I want a big cake, and gorgeous flowers…and I guess that I'll have to get used to the idea of spitting out a few kids."

"You really think Killian is going to propose?"

"His mother and my mother have been talking about it for a long time."

"Don't you want a say in that?" Cece sat up on the couch. "Don't you have any aspirations beyond society trophy wife and mother?"

"Why would I?" Diane seemed really confused by the question. "I marry Killian, I pop out a few kids. Hand the kids over to a nanny, go out and find myself an affair and do what. Ever. I. Want. Why would I need more than that?"

"You're not curious about anything? There's nothing you'd go to school for to learn more about?"

"School is for the bourgeoisie."

"Do you even know what that means?"

"The common folk."

"Um. No. You're the bourgeoisie. If you're trying to find a polite insult for the people who value education and hard work, you're looking for plebes, or the proletariat. I don't even know why I'm telling you this. You don't care."

"Not even remotely," Diane said.

"It's that attitude that's going to cripple you, Diane."

"Look, all I care about is that ring. I mean, why should I go out and better myself when I already am better than ninety percent of the population."

Cece looked at the woman sitting across from her. "Do you even like Killian?"

"I like him enough to fuck him."

"Seriously." Cece thumped her head back. "Do you believe in love at all?"

"Waste of time," Diane answered.

"What about Nick and Morgan?"

Diane shook her head. "New money. Nicholas Dovadsky isn't marriage stuff. He's wild, filthy fling material. You can't marry someone who isn't established."

"What about Emmy and Nathaniel?"

Diane grunted. "Okay, there's real love there, but that whole thing was so damn...weird. The whole thing with the whips and corsets and..." She picked at the arm of the chair. "I see that they really love each other. The whole thing with Lance was bizarre. Lance..."

Cece turned her head to look at Diane again. "Lance what?"

Diane cleared her throat. "He was slimy. Scheming. He always gave me the creeps and the heebee-geebies. There was just always something off about him. I get that people like that kink stuff and hey, what's wrong with a little dirty play and a good fucking? But Lance just took it too far. Or too seriously? Or maybe not seriously enough."

Cece was sure that her shock showed on her face. "Did Lance..."

Diane pursed her lips. "Yes."

"What did he do?"

"Tried to choke me." Her demeanor changed in that second. She seemed to fold in on herself. "When we were in high school. He said he wanted to kill me and fuck my dead body."

Cece just watched her. "I had no idea."

Diane shrugged, her eyes drifting over to the door. "No one ever talked about it. I just made sure I was never alone with him again."

There was a knock on the door, and a moment later it cracked open. Everett's head popped in. "How are you doing, Cece?"

"She's fine." Diane the society whore was back in that moment. "She could come back out and mingle with the party people."

"Don't ever say that again," Cece groaned. "I need another minute alone."

Everett nodded and motioned to Diane. "Come on. Give the lady a minute to recoup herself." Everett motioned Diane out of the chair. She obviously wanted to keep taunting Cece, but Everett made it clear that she needed to go. Diane huffed as she left the room. He watched her go and closed the door after stepping in.

"How are you?"

Cece tossed a dramatic arm over her eyes. "Exhausted. I want to get completely shitfaced and not give a damn about anything."

"I can get behind that." Everett laughed. He sat on the edge of the chair Diane had vacated. "Tonight made me realize something, Cece. We…"

Cece waved him off. "I know. We can't anymore. We have to stop the whole thing. It's the smart and the right thing to do. With everything that's going on, there's no way we can."

Everett nodded. "I don't want to either."

Cece let out a long breath. "I'm sorry."

"I'm not." The smile was in his voice. "I do not regret one thing about any of this. It's been amazing and it's been fun. Now, things are changing too quickly to hold onto something that has to change as well. There's only one thing I would ask."

The word 'mistress' was implied at the end of his sentence. Cece smirked into her arm. It was going to suck not having him around for a good shibari session. She'd learned to read him so well. "What's that?"

"That Dusty and Tessa might help me find a new partner."

Cece turned and peered at him, approving his use of hers and Emmy's club names. Who knew who might be listening outside the door? A moment later, she smiled and nodded. "Of course. You know they'll help you. I'm sure there's a student or new hire who can help you with that." Cece bobbed her head. She actually had someone in mind. "Let's set up a…um…interview this weekend?"

"Sounds good."

"However, I think you shouldn't be too hasty to cancel your Tuesday research."

Everett cocked his head. "It's drawing to a close."

"Mm. It is. But that doesn't mean you can't find what you're looking for one last time at the library. You know I'm happy to help you with that. Just one last time."

Everett coughed and adjusted on the arm of the chair. Cece laughed inwardly; she knew he had a raging hard-on at her suggestion. And she liked the idea that just the thought of what they could and would do together got him hard. "Well, I do think that last article is hiding in the stacks."

"Me, too."

The door flew open this time with no pretense and no warning. Everett came close to tumbling off the chair and managed to grab the edge of the chair at the last moment. Cece whipped her head around to see who was being rude.

Killian stood there. "Ev, Saundra is looking for you. The sitter called and Imogene is really sick."

Everett was out the door almost before Killian could move out of his way. Cece sat up and trotted over to the door. "What's wrong?"

"High fever, vomiting. The nanny took her to the hospital on my order. Saundra was panicking." Killian looked at her. "Apparently, your brother is pissed Saundra wanted Everett to go with her instead of him."

"My brother is an asshole." Cece peered down the hall. "Did the shithead leave?"

"He was going to follow them to the hospital, but Saundra wasn't having it." Killian glanced down at her. "Imogene isn't his kid. And Ev loves that little girl."

"Not even remotely disagreeing with you." Cece stepped back in the room. "I was just kind of hoping my jerk sibling was going to go away for the rest of the night."

The door closed and the feeling in the room changed. Cece didn't know if she liked it or not, but turned to find Killian stalking toward her. His arm slid around her waist, swooping her around to back her against the door. His eyes were burning—but she couldn't name the emotion there.

"Did you like it?"

His voice was a low, angry growl.

"Like what?" Cece was shocked at how mousy her own tone sounded.

"Did you like kissing Paul?" Wordlessly, she shook her head. There seemed to be no air in her lungs around

Killian. His hand was hot against her skin, sparking things in her that weren't supposed to be lit at her own engagement party. "You didn't like one thing about it? Not one?"

She swallowed. "He's a good kisser—but it wasn't right."

"Right how?" Killian's visage grew dark.

"Jealousy doesn't become you, Kay." Cece started to find her voice again.

"This isn't jealousy." His face drew near. "This is possession. I want you. You're mine."

Cece couldn't stop her reaction to him. She stepped into him. "I know I'm yours. But we have to pretend. We have to see this through. I have to remember that Hannah needs this. She and I will come out the other end free of this bullshit."

Killian breathed slowly, his exhale tripping over her skin. "Having Paul near you when I can't touch you in public makes me a monster."

She caught his eyes with hers. "We're not in public."

There was no answer Killian could give to that, save to capture her lips with his in a searing, punishing kiss, sweeping his tongue into her mouth and removing any memory or trace of the kiss with Paul. Cece's entire body reacted to him, leaning closer, wrapping her arms around him. She welcomed him as he licked and sucked on her lips.

"Goddamn it, Cece," he barely managed.

She brushed her words across his lips. "Fuck me, Killian. Right here. Right now."

"It's wrong…"

"I don't give a shit." Cece wound her fingers into his hair. "Nothing that has happened tonight has been right. Make this be the one wrong thing that feels right."

He didn't answer—instead he growled again and owned her mouth with his. Killian's hands found the edge of her skirt as he slid her whole body from the door to against the wall. Cece flipped the lock and her hand very quickly found the zipper on his pants.

"Shit, you're hard," she breathed.

"You're wet." His fingers found home in her folds, telegraphing his intent through her whole body. "No panties."

"My own little rebellion." Cece's hand found his cock, and she dropped the pants off his ass. "Did you get angry when I kissed him?"

"Furious." Killian's free hand worked her blouse free of its confines, and yanked her bra up and over her breast, palming it. "I wanted to rip his balls off." His hand was possessive, plumping and pinching her.

"Did you want to show everyone what you really thought?" Cece asked, cupping his sac in her hand, rolling him, taunting.

"Yes." He found her entrance and drove two rough fingers into her pussy. "I wanted to grab you and throw you on the floor and fuck you senseless. I wanted to fuck you and let everyone know you're mine and no one else's."

"God, yes," Cece managed. She crashed her mouth on his and their heated tongues tangled desperately with each other. "Get your cock in me, Killian. Get it inside me."

His hands moved quickly to her ass, and hoisted her

up against the wall. Cece wrapped her legs around him, locking them at his waist, while her hand that had never let go of his erection guided him to his rightful place inside her.

Killian shoved into her once he was at the entrance, filling her completely. Cece bit her lip to stop the scream she wanted to let out at his intrusion. She knew what they were doing was wrong on so many levels, but she didn't care. This was the man whose ring she should be wearing, the man who should be sharing the toasts and gifts and well-wishes with her. And if she couldn't have him, she could damn well have his dick slamming into her.

"Damn it, Cece, you're so wet." Killian's shaft slid easily in her, and she was impressed with his strength as he held her against the wall.

"Just fuck me," she hissed in his ear. "Make me come. Fill me with yours."

"You're a filthy woman." Killian lowered his mouth to hers. "I fucking love it."

"You have no idea," Cece mumbled just as his mouth and tongue tangled with hers. He drove himself into her at a relentless pace, bracing her against the wall. It was a heartbeat later that she felt his fingers on her clit with no mercy at his punishing rhythm. "Oh, shit, yes."

"Filthy gorgeous woman," he repeated. "Come for me. Come soon."

"Rub my clit," Cece directed. "I'm getting close."

"I want to feel your pussy around me, squeezing me."

"This is wrong." Cece laced her fingers into his hair and breathed the words into him.

"So, so wrong," Killian agreed. "And I don't care. I want to spend the rest of my life doing wrong with you."

"Oh, God, yes," Cece cried, both as a response and as a warning that she was going to hit her climax soon. "Yes, please, yes."

"Coming." Killian pressed her harder into the wall, leaning one hand there, leaving the other on her clit in his own form of torture and trusted that she would hang on to him and the wall could hold her still. His onslaught was animalistic, rough, possessive. Cece understood that feeling. "I'm coming, Cece."

"Come, come," she chanted, pressing her hips into him. "Make me come too."

He knew her body already—just as he thrust into her as hard as he could and released himself into her pussy, he pinched the bundle of nerves at his fingers hard. The rough, demanding pinch shot through her and her whole body erupted in a mind-shattering climax, making her undulate over his hand, around his dick. She arched her back, and her head slammed against the wall. Cece let out a string of incomprehensible noises, unable to form a coherent thought as both of them enjoyed the release they brought each other.

Killian's hands were around her waist again, and he brought her over to the chair. He sat down and cradled her against him, never slipping out of her. "I want to feel you as long as I can." His words were a mere whisper. "How long?"

Cece looked up at him, her eyes tired. "How long what?"

"How long do we have to keep this a secret? How long do we have to steal little desperate fucks with each other?"

Cece blinked, the post-coital haze threatening her with a drop into sleep. "A year. Paul and I discussed it. One year."

"One year." He nodded. "One year and then I can tell the world that I love you."

Cece was overwhelmed by sleep in the next instant. She was simply too drained to keep her eyes open another instant.

When she woke, barely fifteen minutes later, she was alone, fully dressed on the couch. She let herself lay there a long, long few minutes, staring up at the ceiling.

Killian had said he loved her.

She didn't want to go through with any of this. She wanted to find Kay and spend weeks naked in his arms, fucking, having sex, making love and then falling asleep together so they could wake and start all over again.

Instead, she was stuck marrying Paul, hiding Killian, and abandoning both Everett and John.

The only word she could come up with for the way she felt at that moment was loathing.

The door cracked open and Paul's face appeared there. "Hey, jitterbug. How are you?"

Cece burst into tears.

CHAPTER SEVENTEEN

KILLIAN SWIRLED THE SCOTCH IN THE TUMBLER. He knew Darien was watching him with keen interest, but he wasn't sure if he cared enough to call him out on it. This was twice now he'd let what he felt for Cece dictate what he was doing. He let it take over his senses.

Everything that was wrong about what happened yesterday felt so right. Holding her up against the wall, slamming home inside her. Damn it all, he'd even admitted he was in love with her. He was. So desperately. Was there any way the two of them were going to make it through the engagement and marriage without someone figuring out what was going on?

All of the friends he talked to, who knew Cece, knew this whole thing was a sham. It was obvious Paul and Cece weren't a real couple—even the kiss that had pissed him off was perceived as fake. Unconvincing.

Except to the people who felt this was a triumph. To the people who thought this was a victory for old money, and they would see their traditions of misery continue. And in some ways, they were right. Neither Paul or Cece had any intention of consummating the marriage and were already planning their escape in a year—meanwhile "cheating" on each other.

"Killian." Darien interrupted his thoughts.

"I don't want to hear it."

"I was going to suggest that you and Paul, Cece and

whoever Paul is seeing sit down and discuss this. I don't think what's going on here is good for anyone. You're being a miserable prick."

"I can't get it off my mind."

"Then talk to them."

"I can't do that either."

"Oh, for—why the hell not?"

"Because I know why she's doing this. And there's nothing I can do about it. This has to happen."

Darien swirled his drink again. "Then maybe you should apply to be the pool boy."

"Christ, I would if I could."

"You're so smitten."

"I'm consumed."

"You can't touch her again." Darien's words were a warning. "You know you can't. You won't be able to stop if you keep letting this happen."

"I wish it was just me letting this happen, Darien. It's not. It's both of us. We're both letting this happen. We both want this to happen. God, she was so hot and so fuckable last night. She fell asleep in my arms in that room."

Darien sighed. "I can't help you anymore, Killian. I'll listen, but if neither of you can curb your appetites for each other, then I can't help. This is just going to get more and more complicated. End of story." He leaned forward and turned to Killian. "You are just going to have to deal with the fallout when you're found out."

"Who says we're going to be found out?"

Darien snorted. "You fucked her against the wall at her engagement part, Kay. Do you really think you can hide this?"

"What the hell would the fallout be? She's not in love with Paul."

Darien tapped his ring on the glass. "Let's walk through this, step by step. Follow me here. She and Paul get married. No attraction, no consummation. Separate bedrooms. Fine, if you can believe that. She's off screwing you every chance, and he's off screwing someone else. Even with a mutual cheating agreement like that, someone outside of all this is bound to catch wind. Bound to. Even the best kept secrets have a way of getting out. And you aren't trying to keep it secret from each other."

"Fine, whatever."

"No, not fine. Not whatever. These are the elite, the snobs, the old monied families. You know what this is like. You know what your mother is like. Do you know what will happen if either of them get caught? Think about it. Let's say you and Cece get caught and it's made public. Paul's family is going to go after her, hard. Relentlessly. They will strip whatever her family has from her. And I'm quite sure that whatever the reason she has for going along with this idiotic charade will be completely destroyed by the fact that you couldn't keep your dick out of her."

Darien leaned forward. "So. I would suggest that the two of you back the hell off of each other until you can really gauge what is going on here."

"I know what's going on here." Killian stared at the floor. "She's marrying someone she doesn't love."

"*For a reason*!" Darien slammed his hand on the table. "There is a reason why that girl is marrying Paul. There is a reason why she got over the fear every other woman in Pittsburgh has of that man. Whatever her reason is, it's stunningly compelling and you'd better realize women don't do shit like that for the hell of it. Women have motivation for action. Frances Robbe is no fucking exception to that rule." He stared at the scotch again. "Stop fucking her against the wall, Kay. Stop pushing limits and boundaries. If her reason for this marriage is compelling enough to say no to the man she clearly loves, you're just playing with fire."

"She wanted it."

"Tell. Her. No." Darien shook his head violently. "Damn it, man. Tell her no. Say no. It's a powerful word that works both ways. It's a year, Killian. One year. It's not going to destroy you." He pointed a finger at Kay. "And if you say you love her one more time I'm going to punch you in the throat. If you love her, say no. *Help* her with whatever reason she has to not marry you first."

Killian was quiet. Cece's reasons were compelling. Hannah and their safety. He would never want to get between the woman and her sister. He didn't know how to say no to her, though. He'd fantasized all day about taking her against the wall. The woman had him enspelled and he just didn't know what to do about it.

"I know you're thinking about this."

"I hate that you're right."

"I hate that I am too. She makes you happy."

"I don't want to stay away from her."

"This is not about what you want, but what's right for both of you." Darien raised his eyebrows. "You need to look beyond your libido and realize that long term is important. If something goes awry and there's something about this plan that's messed up, there's a very real chance you will never be able to be together. And then you lose everything forever. Not just a year."

"How are you so good with relationships when you refuse to have one?"

"It's human nature. Study it. Be amazed by it. You're a doctor, don't you see patterns and reasons in people all the time?"

"I see people screwing up because they..." Killian stopped and sighed. "Because they don't see the long term repercussions in their actions."

Darien leaned back in the chair. Killian swore.

* * *

"He lurked the whole time."

The Hunk shook his head. "Surely, it couldn't have been the whole time."

"Nearly so. Only left the area when dinner and the toast happened." The Watcher sat on the couch and motioned the Hunk over. "I don't like this. There is something going on and that man is behind it. Or a part of it."

"I thought you were supposed to be impartial."

"I can't be impartial to this. I just can't. I'm going to have to warn them all off. Maybe even send people away from the 'Burgh while we investigate this."

"You know that's not going to work," the Hunk answered. "If you send people away, the exact people who are being targeted, the hand will be tipped. Everyone has to stay where they are."

"Do you think there's any hope for us to get this solved before that bastard strikes again?"

"I can only hope."

The Watcher shook his head. "Not good."

"Not good at all."

CHAPTER EIGHTEEN

CECE DUMPED HERSELF INTO THE CHAIR. It was Tuesday, two full days since the engagement party and she still felt hung over. It wasn't a fun feeling. She wasn't sure what was really bothering her: did she have that much to drink or was it the fact that she'd fucked Killian at her own engagement party?

It had to be the alcohol. She didn't feel an ounce of remorse for their sex against the wall.

The office was quiet, and she was grateful for that. Everything that was going on was too much. With Paul, with Killian, with Everett. Even John.

Cece groaned, dropping her head into her hands. She hoped John wasn't going to take her refusal of arrangement as an insult to his prowess. She found herself daydreaming about tying him up more than once. She had wanted to take him on in a private contract. Now…everything had to hide. She would have to break it to him gently tomorrow night.

Thankfully, yesterday had been orientation and she hadn't had much time to think about all of this. Today, however, it was all front and center. Not only was she worried about whether she and Paul could pull this off, she had Everett on her mind today.

She was going to miss this arrangement, too. No more Tuesday research. It made her sad. She'd helped Everett discover his submissive side and learn to really enjoy it. She liked the bit of sadomasochism they had going, too. He enjoyed the bits of pain she gave him, and she enjoyed his reactions to it.

Cece let out a breath. There was no way she was giving up the club. Not a chance in hell. She was going to have to tell Killian about this side of her. Their wild sex was wonderful, but she wasn't going to always be happy with just tossing each other against the wall and going at it. She was going to want to wind the ropes around him, paddle him, tease him. And she'd have to confess that before it could happen—if he was even willing.

"Good morning, Ms. Robbe."

Cece turned and found Everett standing there, purple tie again. What was going to happen if he actually had to come in for research after this? Was she going to be able to stay away from him? "Good morning, Mister Milhouse. I'll be with you in a few minutes."

He smiled and nodded and Cece had a horrible realization that she wasn't sure she was in the right frame of mind for the session. She wasn't focused, she was tired, and she was upset this was coming to an end. It seemed like the longest walk ever to her office to start preparing for the day—both for Everett and for her job.

Taking a long few minutes to clean her auxiliary desk at the main entrance, she made her way up to her office. Pushing the door open, she found Everett sitting on the couch. He stood as she walked in and smiled at her. "Mistress."

"Everett—"

He held up his hand. "I know. I understand. I could

see it in your eyes."

She smiled at him, the feeling genuine, but the demonstration weak. "You know me so well. I'm sorry. I'm so off my game that it's downright embarrassing."

He walked around to lean on the desk. "We have done this so long and so well. I don't regret an instant of this. I still wish that we were able to work this out. But as I understand it, you've found someone anyway. I'm sure I will too. Now that I know what I need, what I want in a woman—a mistress—and a relationship, I know where to look. I have you to thank for that. Eventually, Saundra will calm down and realize she can't keep me from Imogene, and that having a father who loves her that much is a good thing."

Cece desperately tried not to react to his casual reveal that he knew about her relationship. "Who do you think I've found?"

"Don't know." Everett smiled. "But the rumors say you have. Most of the people who have heard the rumor are divided into two camps. Those who don't know you say it's Paul, as I think you want people to believe. I think there are other, better options. But your friends have tight lips and won't spill to little ol' me. They don't trust Saundra and I'm too close to her."

Cece smiled and shook her head. "Like you said, that will change."

He laughed. "And even you won't tell me."

"Everett…the games we're all playing here are dangerous. Paul and I are going through with this for reasons, and they are very strong personal reasons," Cece said. "Someday, I will tell you. I trust you. You wouldn't be standing here if I didn't. And it's not you

I'm hiding from this. At least, not you alone. There are a dozen or more people I have to hide from."

"You're good at hiding."

"Do I have a choice?"

Everett shook his head. "No. I know you don't. I've lived the reasons why." He shrugged. "Funny how the people I thought would be happy to see me out of their lives are the ones pulling me back in."

"No matter what they say about us, they are the unrepentant sadists," Cece stated. "We might like pain, but they dole it out and take no joy in it. Our bruises are pride, memories of delight. Theirs are nothing but a brand on the skin, a way to show the world they think they are in charge. The truth is oh so different."

Everett nodded. "I'm glad that things with Saundra didn't work out. I couldn't have kept up with that front. It wasn't fair to us. Worse, she never would have agreed to a polyamorous situation, even if I left all the sex for her. But she'd have no trouble cheating on me."

"That is true."

"And apparently, with your brother."

Cece held up a hand. "Yeah. Let's not."

Everett laughed. "I won't. I'm a little grossed out by that one too."

Cece walked around to the chair at her desk. "I talked to Tessa last night for you. She has a few people in mind who might be a good pair with you. You understand, of course, there's no off-site agreement implicit in their taking you as a client."

"Of course, Mistress," Everett answered.

Cece reached into her desk. "Well. I am feeling a bit calmer now. I don't want you to be disappointed in this day. So perhaps we can find a little happy medium."

"Are you still available for this evening, Mistress?"

"I look forward to it." Cece pulled a thinner rope out of her drawer. "Do you know what I use this for, Everett?"

"No, Mistress," he answered.

Cece held it up. It was a coarse jute rope, not refined and polished like the silk and nylon she used most of the time. "This is for a little bit more pain. A little tease. You've told me you want to explore a little more of the masochism. We'll start here." She glanced over his shoulder. "Is the door locked, Everett?"

He quickly walked to check the door. Finding it was unlocked, he turned the tumblers and scooted back to where Cece was waiting. "It is now, Mistress."

His voice had gone quiet and breathy. Cece knew he was waiting to see what she was about to do—and what she was about to do was something she didn't usually partake in. But their conversation had turned to Everett seeking more pain, pushing more limits. She knew this technique from her training and it was a good place to start.

"Pants down, Everett." She snapped the rope between her hands, and he complied readily. She hadn't even explained what she was doing and his cock jutted out proud from the dark patch of hair there. She did love that beast between his legs.

Cece slipped her hand over his erection and stroked it a few times, the last time dragging the rope up his length. She wrapped around him once, twice, and then dropped it down, threading it down behind his heavy sac on one side and up the other. Two more times around the thick length, then up around his waist to cinch it in place. Then around his cock again, pulling it tight. For every loop around his shaft, there was one under his balls, and slowly, surely the erection he had was pulled down, and down. Slowly, Cece bound his hard dick to his sac.

"Do you know what I'm doing?" Her words were soft, enticing.

"CBT, Mistress." Everett was sweating a bit, shaking. He was as hard as when she had started.

"That's right. And you're taking this so very well. You like this, don't you? This little cock and ball torture I'm treating you to."

"Yes, Mistress," he breathed.

Cece pulled the jute a little tighter again. "You're going to be hard all day, aren't you?"

Everett swallowed hard. "Yes, Mistress."

"There's a measure of control in this too, isn't there?" Cece prompted him.

Clearly having trouble controlling himself. "Yes, Mistress."

"What is it, Everett?" Cece nearly had him bound all the way down, his shaft covered in the wound ropes, pulled tight against his sac.

"I'll have to piss sitting down."

"Correct." She leaned in, running her fingers over the tight rope that covered his cock. "Do you like that idea, Everett? Does it make you hard knowing that I've made you sit down to piss? That I can even control you when I'm not near you?"

"Yes, Mistress," he managed.

She ran her finger over the just-uncovered head of

his dick and gathered the pre-cum that had been building there. "You want to come, don't you?"

"Please, Mistress."

"No." The word was a whispered teaser. "Be good, Everett. And maybe tonight, we'll not only do a little CBT, but some anal play too." His whole body shook at her suggestion. He was so responsive, so sexual.

Cece was going to miss this play time so much. She was determined to make sure that whoever took him on next was someone who appreciated just how deliciously sexual and submissive this man was. Every suggestion elicited reactions from him. He was just plain fun.

* * *

Cece watched Everett for the rest of the day out of the corner of her eye. He would have to stop and collect himself once in a while, and a shiver of erotic pleasure ran through him a moment after. She was enjoying this. She knew he was too.

She'd slipped him the room key at lunch, patting the pocket, but not really the pocket. He shuddered again, and Cece couldn't stop herself from winking at him. Everett let out a breath and the want on his face almost made Cece take pity on him.

Almost.

It was more fun to make him wait—for both of them.

Cece stacked the cart with the return books that were going to have to be wheeled out and put back. The student assistant hadn't bothered to show again, and after staring at the car for too many minutes, she decided to put them away herself.

She rolled the rickety cart to the elevator, and just as the door was about to close, someone's hand appeared between the doors and it was shoved open.

Chas.

He stepped in and the car seemed too small for him and whatever emotions he brought with him.

"Hello, sis." His words were a drawl, accompanied by a nasty sneer.

"What the hell are you doing here?" Cece really felt trapped in the elevator as the doors slid closed.

"We need to talk."

Cece shook her head. "You've already trapped me in a marriage I don't want, what the hell else could you possible want from me?"

"Why are you still working?"

Cece's brow wrinkled. "What?"

"You're here. Working. What the hell is going on?"

"I have no idea what you're talking about, Chas."

"You should have quit the moment you got that ring. Don't you think it's a little inappropriate for the fiancée of one of Pittsburgh's wealthiest sons to be working?"

Cece slammed the cart into the door. "That is none of your goddamn business. What Paul and I decided about our careers has nothing to do with you and your input is unwelcome." She reached around him and hit the button for the fourth floor. "I think you've had quite enough to say about marriage. As in creating one that neither of us wanted."

Chas growled. "Your whole family's wealth is riding on you—"

"No, I do believe it was all riding on Black Beauty

in stall five during the second race."

Chas slammed his hand on the wall next to her heard. "Don't you *dare* be flippant about this. This is your family. Blood is thicker than water."

"Why don't you just marry Oetler and have done?" Cece asked.

"Saundra and I have nothing to do with this."

"You are the biggest asshole on the planet, Charles. The biggest. You want me to sacrifice my life and freedom for the bullshit you call this family, but you go off and fuck Saundra and that has nothing to do with the family."

He clearly wanted to hit her. Cece had never felt so threatened in her life, and being in such a small space didn't allow her much defensive space. "Do not ever use such crude language about my love interests, Frances. Don't you ever do that again. Saundra is traumatized from the revelations about her husband."

"Oh, please, she is not," Cece snapped. "She's a nasty cunt rag using Imogene—"

The slap came hard and fast. Cece didn't have time to block or even back up so that it didn't hit square on her cheek. Her mouth fell open with a gasp as her hand jumped to her face that now stung from his hand.

"I told you to watch your mouth—"

Cece jabbed him in the side of the neck, in the tender spot below his ear, a special hit that her jujitsu master had shown her. She watched as the shock and pain ran through her brother, and the temporary paralysis surprised him as he slumped again the side of the elevator. It was only his arm that wouldn't work for about ten minutes, but at least he couldn't hit her again.

She pushed the cart to the side and hit the 'stop' button on the panel. She slammed him against the wall, and saw him wince as his shoulder hit wrong. He might not be able to move it, but he could feel the hit. "You have no place in my discipline, Chas. None. You are trying to assert a power over me that you don't have. The only reason I've agreed to the fucking farce is for my sister. I've already told you that. If you *ever* hit me—or Hannah—again, I will remove your balls and feed them to you. Don't believe me? All I did was a simple move to paralyze you. Imagine what I could do if we weren't standing in a fifteen by fifteen box."

"You are completely out of control, you little bitch."

"You know I am," Cece answered. She hit the resume button. "Watch your ass with Saundra, Chas. She will chew you up and spit you out, like she did with Everett."

"How would you know? Fucking him?"

Cece snorted. "Rumors fly both ways, asshole." The door opened for her floor and she grabbed the cart, wheeling it out into the hallway. She turned to see Chas standing in the middle of the car. She waited until the doors started to slide closed, and flipped him the middle finger.

She heard the elevator start to descend, and let out a sob, leaning against the wall. Gathering herself, she pushed the cart to the bathroom and popped inside. The smack was bright red and hand shaped. *God, he'd hit so hard!* She really hoped it wasn't going to leave a bruise—she didn't need to try and explain that to anyone. It would involve showing too many cards she hid in her hand.

Cece slumped and let herself sob. Chas was not the same kid from when they were younger. She didn't know what was going on. Forcing her into a marriage, slapping her. What else was on his menu?

There was no way out of this. Chas had guessed at hers and Everett's relationship. She wondered if he suspected she was a Domme. Or worse that he had rung the information from Hannah. Cece needed to move Hannah out of that house, as soon as possible. She couldn't bear to think of her fragile little sister under the purview of that…*monster.*

Taking a deep breath, she collected herself and wiped away the tears. This was no way to act. This was not her. Checking the mirror she found her makeup was still relatively acceptable, save the mascara and eyeliner. Wiping it off, Cece patted her face with the damp cloth to help her feel a little cooler and collected.

She had a job to do here, and she'd get it done. Then tonight, she'd have marvelous, unbridled, filthy sex with Everett. And tomorrow, she would work on moving Hannah out of that house into her cottage. She pulled out her phone to make a note about guardianship, and found a text message waiting.

Mistress.

Cece smiled. The sting of the slap was already fading. She was going to have a long night.

She planned to enjoy every moment of it.

CHAPTER NINETEEN

JOHN WAITED, AS PROMISED.

He was just as delicious as she remembered, and even better, he'd brought everything she'd asked for.

JS: Mistress. I would request an off-site with you today. I have missed your touch and your ropes.

***Prima Dusty**: This evening?*

JS: Whatever would be convenient for you, Mistress.

***Prima Dusty**: I have a previous engagement at 9.*

JS: I would be happy to take whatever hours you can spare before that.

***Prima Dusty**: I'm afraid I'm in an awkward situation, as I have nothing I would need.*

JS: I will bring everything.

Cece's eyebrows rose at that, and her body tingled at the memories of his selections and supplies.

***Prima Dusty**: The room will be paid for and under Dusty Rose Milan. I will be at the hotel at 5:15. Be ready.*

JS: Thank you, Mistress.

While Cece knew this was going to have be cut off before it became a habit, John was still that enigma she craved. There wasn't much about him she knew, nor much she didn't like. And to find him there in the room, kneeling, naked and ready was a mark against her giving this up.

"Good evening, Mister Smith." She dropped her purse and briefcase just inside the door.

"Good evening, Mistress."

Cece circled around him, checking the room. He had the hood on again, and while Cece wanted to ask him to take it off, she knew that would get her nowhere. There was a large duffle bag at the foot of the bed, looking like regular traveler's bag. "What do you have in here?"

"Toys, Mistress. Implements and aids."

Taken back, Cece pulled the zipper open to see what he had. She was in no way disappointed by what was inside: ropes, whips, floggers, plugs, beads, chains, ties—both Velcro and zip. There was lube and at least three different kinds of condoms. The best part about the whole bag was that it was organized. There was a custom insert to hold everything in place. Nothing jingled or clanged when Cece pushed it.

John Smith was no amateur.

"This is wonderful," Cece praised, sitting on the bed. "Before we get started, though, I have some bad news, Mister Smith. I'm afraid I'm going to have to decline any future engagements with you outside of the club. A situation has arisen that puts too many people at risk with these trysts. Make no mistake, I very much enjoy our meetings. But I do not wish to risk anyone's life, and that's what will happen if these continue."

"I must admit, Mistress, I am disappointed. I have just discovered your wonderful talents. But I understand. One has to make hard decisions when it comes to our lifestyle."

"Indeed, we do," Cece said, standing and walking around the well-defined torso he presented to her. "Let's begin then, shall we?" She stood behind him and leaned down to his mask. "Will we need the condoms, Mister Smith?"

"Please, Mistress," he breathed.

She hummed in agreement. "Very good. Stay where you are for just a moment. I'll need to choose some items for us to play with." Cece quickly shucked her outer clothes, folding them on the chair. She was quietly glad that she had worn the tiny thong that day; it helped to give her a more typical Domme look that she had. The bra and garters were her Tuesday favorites.

She left the shoes on.

Cece sorted out a few lengths of rope onto the bed and pulled the covers off, stripping the bed down to the bottom sheet. She quickly jury-rigged the bed with a few ropes for a tie down. She pulled the Wartenburg wheel out of his bag and knelt behind him.

"Your body is amazing, John." Cece put the wheel down for just a moment. She ran her hands up his back, over the bunched muscles, drawing her nails down the sinews, peaks and valleys of the canvas he was. She was spellbound by him, once again. She picked up the wheel and ran it gently down his spine, without real pressure. His shiver was accompanied by a small groan of pleasure, and Cece knew he was enjoying it. She traced the same path again with more pressure, knowing that it pricked at the skin. The little pricks from the sharp points did more to stimulate the skin than just about anything else. They awoke the cells that lay just below the surface and were still raw and tender—and yet did not draw any blood.

His sucking breath of delight ignited her. This was her reward. The sounds and sights of pleasure visited up another being. The sensation of sex as they tripped through her and rose and swirled in her partner. She trailed her one hand behind the wheel as she teased him and started to rev up his body. His shivers and sounds were of the utmost importance; they told her where he was in his head space and if she was doing well or poorly with stimulating him.

Cece knelt up and grabbed the rope, while still teasing him with the little needles on the wheel. "How do you feel about breath play?"

He gasped, and it wasn't the good kind of gasp. "The throat is a hard limit, Mistress."

She dropped the rope and the wheel and put her hands on his arms. Pressing gently, she answered, "I understand, John. No breath play that involves the throat." She didn't want him to lose to the space he was in and needed to reassure him she would not push that limit. She ran her hands over the muscles of his arms, to the defined valleys of his back again and then down to his ass.

What a fine ass... "Mmm. I think we'll do a little paddling."

This time, the gasp was the kind she wanted. "Please, Mistress."

Cece stroked the dimple at the top of his ass. "First, we'll get you in some rope. I want to see the tracks in your skin when I take you out of it."

"Yes, Mistress." His voice was heady again.

Cece grabbed the rope again, and reaching around his waist, she pulled it around his body. She tied the only single, true knot that she used—which she always untied when she was done. If there was a true knot, it was not kinbaku.

Cece commanded him now, though. "Stand."

His ass rippled with the motion and she gave into the urge to nibble on one of the firm globes. She felt him shiver at the gentle brush of her teeth on his skin. *Oh, I could do that all night! Just nibble on his body and watch him react.* She still didn't understand what it was about this man that had her wanting to possess him completely.

She trailed the rope up his thigh, between his legs and back around. Cece made sure that her hand brushed against his sac. He tried not to react, but he couldn't hold back and Cece—still kneeling at eye level to those firm cheeks—smacked him hard on each. "Control your reactions, John."

"Yes, Mistress, I just find you so wonderful."

"Flattery will get you spanked, John." Cece smiled to herself.

Making quick work of the ropes, she flowed them through her fingers and twisted them around his body in a sensual dance, pulling and tucking and spinning them into a woven masterpiece. John's legs, waist, chest, and arms were criss-crossed and spun in the black rope he had brought. It was a marvelous contrast to the pale skin he boasted. His arms were bound together in an intricate weave, disallowing him to pull them apart, but allowing him to reach and stretch.

And he was completely in subspace at that point. Cece could see the bliss throughout his whole body, relaxed and pleased, taking in every sensation of her hands over his body. She had moved him back to kneeling halfway through her patterns and now his head was bowed. Slowly, so that she didn't pull him out of his comfortable space, she trailed her hand to his shoulder.

"John."

"Mmm, green, Mistress. So green."

"Good boy." The praise was genuine. She had very few clients who were able to drop into subspace so willingly or easily. "Lean forward on your elbows. I've changed my mind. We're going to use the flogger."

"Thank you, Mistress." He complied with her directions and placed his forearms on the floor. The wonderful ass she'd been caressing and nibbling on for the past hour was presented in a neat package, waiting for her attention.

The flogger was better for this. Not as hard as the paddle, and when wielded correctly, just as effective. John was in too wonderful a place for Cece to want to pull him out of it. She stood and carefully took a few warm up swings on the bed, and then a few very light warm ups on his ass.

"How many would you like John?"

"Just six, Mistress, please. Very hard."

"You'll get ten, four as warm up."

"Yes, Mistress."

The flogger had a lot of thud to it. Cece could feel that on her warm ups. The first of the ten against his skin were hard, though she could go much harder. The intake of breath let her know that she was on the right track and with the next hit, she put more into it. John gasped again and hissed a quiet, "yessss" between his teeth.

The fifth was the real testament to her abilities, and she let the flogger fly hard. He yelped, loudly, and let it turn into a groan of desire.

At the sound of his groan, Cece's own desire fired in her blood, starting to make its way through her. She let the flogger fly again, again, again—relishing each of his gasps, yelps, and groans. They were musical to her and a reassurance that he wanted this as much as she was enjoying it. Just before the last two hits, Cece leaned down and caressed his now bright red and warmed ass. She relished the feel of him and leaned to his ear again.

"You're not allowed to come," she whispered. "I want your come for myself. I want to feel that inside me. Do you understand, John?"

"Yes, Mistress." His voice was strained. He was going to have trouble holding back his climax. She wouldn't tell him, but if he came, she'd forgive him. It would give her the chance to make his cock hard again.

The flogger flew and flew again, and to her great delight John did not let his climax take him, and held on. Cece felt he deserved a reward for that, quickly rolled him to his back, and swallowed his throbbing dick in one motion. He bucked and cried out, not expecting her lips around his shaft, but she wanted to taste him, to tame him. She swirled her tongue around his head, gathering, savoring the pre-cum that leaked out. He twitched and shook, and stated plainly, "I can't stop it."

Cece pulled her lips off him only long enough to answer. "Don't."

He came in the next instant, jetting into her mouth, thick ropes of come she gladly swallowed, memorizing his taste, the feel of his cock in her mouth, the heat of his climax against her tongue. He did his best not to scream or yell, and Cece was pleased.

She released his now semi-flaccid dick and massaged the thigh muscles she knew were exhausted. She glanced to see his face—forgetting for just the moment that he was hooded and she couldn't see his expression. His body language spoke for him: skin flushed red, chest heaving, and his shaft already rising for another round of amazing sex play with her.

This was what she loved. This was where she wanted to be.

* * *

Hurriedly adjusting her skirt as she ran from the car to the hotel, Cece cursed herself. She had spent entirely too much time with John. Nearly four hours of marvelous playtime that was making her late for her last night with Everett.

There was no reason she was so attracted to John. He wouldn't even give her his real name. But he was so damn perfectly submissive. He wanted everything she could give him. And she, clearly, enjoyed giving.

This time, she'd come close to kissing him. That was one of her rules she didn't really like to break. There were three people she'd kissed during play: Don, Everett, and Killian—and Killian didn't really count because they were just straight up fucking each other like wild rabbits.

If she saw John again, she might cross that line.

Untying him had been nearly as much fun as tying him up. She loved to see the impressions of the rope in his skin. It was one of so many things she liked about the lifestyle, about being a nawashi. Watching the skin reveal the impressions the rope made. Tracks made from the binding of silk and jute and nylon.

Cece smiled to herself as the elevator took her to the floor where Everett was waiting. Jute. He'd never been bound like that before, and it was prickly rope. If he liked that, she'd get the sisal, and maybe think about a touch of itching powder. It caused an amazingly small touch of pain when used correctly, and now that they were moving into the masochistic part of his personality, she had a lot of tricks for that.

She stopped. *Damn.* Cece wasn't going to get to enjoy that part of him because this was their last night. This was the last time she'd get to see him, get to tie him up. It pained her. There was no doubt about that. She didn't want to give him up. He was fun. But she had to think of Hannah.

Fine then. She'd let his next mistress know where they'd left off. She'd make sure Everett got to enjoy every part of the person he really was and was discovering himself to be. She resumed the walk down the hall to the room she'd booked, as usual. Her stomach fluttered.

So much sex.

So much fun...

She slipped the card into the door, pushing it open. The room seemed to be painted red, and smelled oddly coppery. Taking a few steps into the room, things only started to feel even worse. Something was wrong...

"Everett?"

She turned the corner of the room to find the bed.

And what was left of Everett.

She started screaming and all hell broke loose.

CHAPTER TWENTY

"WHERE IS SHE?"

Killian realized his voice was doubled, and found Paul running down the hall in the opposite direction to the same destination as his.

Detective Garabaldi looked in both directions and motioned them into the room. Killian shoved his way in and Paul was hot on his tail. Garabaldi slammed the door and locked it. "You both need to calm the fuck down. Immediately. Having half of her harem freaking out around her is not going to help. We had to book her once she got a clean bill from the hospital—"

"I know, that's how I found out," Killian growled. "If I had known what the hell was going on, I would have told them to make something up."

"I wish you had," Paul stated. "She's pretty fucked in the head."

"You saw the scene, Doctor Wainwright." Killian tried to calm himself down. "What are we talking about here?"

Paul put a hand to his head. "Sweet Christ, Kay. You don't even want to know."

"I do," he said. He looked at Paul and then Garabaldi and back to Paul. "I'm in love with her. I need to know what's going on."

"Did you just…did you just admit to Cece's fiancé that you're in love with her?" Garabaldi shook his head in disbelief.

"It's okay, Detective," Paul said. "We knew that we

were going into this marriage for our own reasons. I didn't know who you were, Kay. But this might work to our advantage."

"What was the scene like? Paul, Simon, please. Tell me what's really going on here."

Detective Garabaldi hit a button and a screen rolled up on the left hand side of the room. It revealed a cold, white room with an industrial table, an uncomfortable looking chair, and Cece. Cece looked like hell warmed over—tears just kept flowing down her face and every once in a while, she'd grow completely hysterical and slam her hands on the table and start wailing instead of crying.

Cece looked haggard, her visage was ghostly. Her usually impeccable clothes were askew and coated in blood. Her skirt was ripped and she still had the hospital bracelet on her arm.

"What the fuck happened?" Killian took a few strides to the window.

"We had to arrest her," Garabaldi said. "We don't have a choice. Not only is she the prime suspect, she's the only suspect at the moment."

"Wainwright?" Killian looked at Paul.

Paul heaved a sigh. "As far as I know, from her hysterics when I got there, she opened the door to find Everett dead. He was in one piece, but just barely. There was a fight of some sort, and Everett Milhouse isn't known for his physical prowess. He was overpowered handily and they tied him up. He was shot in the abdomen, and had his veins cut strategically. He bled out, and don't tell her this, but he suffered badly. She found him, dead. Or allegedly she found him dead."

"Why did she find him? What the hell were they doing there?"

"Milhouse was found with his genitals bound, artfully. It didn't have anything to do with how they found him trussed up." Garabaldi tapped the folder on the table. "Apparently, she and Everett were having an affair. He was a kinky motherfucker; and liked being tied up."

"What has that got to do with her sitting in that holding tank?"

Garabaldi sighed. "They found her cradling him, screaming and rocking him. She was yelling that she didn't mean for this to happen."

"They think she murdered Everett Milhouse?"

"Oh, no. Nothing that simple." Garabaldi shook his head. "They think she screwed him, tied him up, shot him, bled him, and nearly dismembered him."

"What the hell…" Killian was dumbfounded.

Paul put a hand to his head. "It gets worse."

"Worse how?"

"They know she works at Imperial." Garabaldi pulled out his phone to check the text message that had just come in. "Oh, shit."

"Oh shit?" Paul asked.

"They not only know she works at Imperial, but that she's a dominatrix with a penchant for fancy ropes." Garabaldi held up the phone so they could see the screen. "And on top of them holding Cece for the murder, Hannah Robbe has gone missing."

...TO BE CONTINUED...

UNTIED
Out now!

SIGN UP FOR
Katherine Rhodes' Newsletter
http://tiny.cc/NLSUkrRR1

JOIN RHODES' ROGUES
Private Facebook Reader Group

About

KATHERINE RHODES

Armed with a pen name, **Katherine Rhodes** has gird her loins and set her mind to writing erotic romances which are kinky, dirty, and fun. As a lackadaisical laundry goddess, and an expert in the profundities of bad music and awful literature-thanks to her husband-Katherine strives to find balance in the universe and time to cook dinner. An East Coast dweller, currently located in the Philadelphia Tristate area, she is the proud servants of three cats and would take a vacation in Prague over a day at the beach any time…

www.katherinerhodes.com

Join Rhodes' Rogues
Private Facebook Reader Group

Sign up for
Rhodes' Rogues Newsletter

Follow me:
BookBub
Booksprout
Twitter
Facebook
Instagram
Pinterest
Amazon

CONTEMPORARY

CLUB IMPERIAL
Consensual
Broken Bonds
Knots
Untied
Lessons
Now. Forever.
Inevitable

SILVER SOUL
Not Quite Juliet

CITY OF STEEL
Innuendo
Double Entendre

THE REALM
Half-Soul

THE CLUB SERIES
The Darkest Corners
Anything for Her
Teach Me To Sin
Come Fly with Me
with Isobelle Cate
Sweet Pain
with Emily Walker and Jenni Moen

THE DA SILVA HEIRS
All the King's Horses

Princess of the Plains
Empire of Dirt

STANDALONES
Captain
Acts of Contrition
Obsidian Escape

PARANORMAL ROMANCE

VAMPIRE CROWN
Queen of Gods
King of Gods
Death of Gods
Blood of Gods

THE JUNEAU PACKS
Taming Alaska
Frozen Alaska
Exploring Alaska
Uncovering Alaska

SAINTS AND SINNERS
Sleeper

THE COMPLEX
Balance Point
One Thousand Wishes, One Thousand Stars

THE NIGHTSHIFT IN NEW YORK
Moonlight Calling

THE DEMON SLAYERS
Passion Flames

THE ELEMENTAL DRAGONS (Pine Valley)
Darkwater
Skydance
Fireborn (coming 2020)

Discover Katherine's Other books under

J. Rose Alexander

Chatter box, compulsive writer, bon vivant, stunt commuter, and a ninja in her dreams, J. Rose enjoys losing herself in the capes and masks of her superheroes, finding new trouble for her witches and werewolves-- and is always on the look-out for a new adventure, on the page or in real life. J. Rose write sweet, clean(ish) stories that are suited to readers 13 and up, unless she warns you otherwise...

www.jrosealexander.com

Facebook
Twitter
Instagram

THE ORIGIN STORIES
Penumbra: Equinox
Penumbra: Solstice
The Art of Dying
The Art of Living

THE FACTION STORIES
Apathetic Avengers
The Natural Order of Things

The Royals of Grand Island
Shadow in Glass
Family Portraits (coming 2020)

SKELETON KEY
Eunica

STANDALONES
Zenko (Woodland Creek)
Slip the Waves (Hotel Paranormal)